Treasure Me

A SAFE Security Novel

Michele Zurlo

www.michelezurloauthor.com

Treasure Me (SAFE Security 1)
Copyright © December 2016 by Michele Zurlo
ISBN: 978-1-942414-22-3

All rights reserved. This copy is intended for the original purchaser of this e-book ONLY. No part of this e-book may be reproduced, stored in or introduced into a retrieval system, or transmitted, in any form, or by any means (electronic, mechanical, photocopying, recording, or otherwise), without the prior written permission from the copyright owner and Lost Goddess Publishing LLC. Please do not participate in or encourage piracy of copyrighted materials in violation of the author's rights. Purchase only authorized editions.

Editor: Nicoline Tiernan
Cover Artist: Anne Kay

Published by Lost Goddess Publishing LLC
www.michelezurloauthor.com

This e-book is a work of fiction. While reference might be made to actual historical events or existing locations, the names, characters, places and incidents are either the product of the author's imagination or are used fictitiously, and any resemblance to actual persons, living or dead, business establishments, events, or locales is entirely coincidental.

Warning: This e-book contains sexually explicit scenes and adult language and may be considered offensive to some readers. It is not meant for underage readers.

————————

DISCLAIMER: Education and training are necessary in order to learn safe BDSM practices. Lost Goddess Publishing LLC is not responsible for any loss, harm, injury or death resulting from use of the information contained in any of its titles. This is a work of fiction, and license has been taken with regard to BDSM practices.

Acknowledgements

This book would not have been possible without several key people. I'd like to thank Wife for endlessly discussing the details with me. I'd like to thank Twin #2 for troubleshooting plot elements with me while we walked the dog. And a huge shout out goes to Wife, Allyson Young, and Sherry Dove for patiently reading through the manuscript and pointing out every little thing and a few big things. Lastly I'd like to thank my readers for giving this new series a chance. It's been a long time since I've launched a new venture.

Autumn Takes a Case

"Are you being good, Sugar?" The seductive timbre of David's low voice came through on a clear cell signal.

I glanced around the lobby of the SAFE Security offices to make sure no one might have overheard the sexual undertones of his question, but the gesture was pointless. Dean and Frankie had left twenty minutes ago to catch a plane to Miami. That had annoyed the hell out of me. Here I was, trying to show them how valuable I could be as an office manager, and there they were, still making their own arrangements for their missions. I hadn't even known that Dean and Frankie had something scheduled. It rankled that they didn't trust me enough to let me know they had client, and that they totally neglected to ask me to arrange the flight, accommodations, and whatever else they'd need.

Still, it was good to hear David's voice. He'd left two days ago with Jesse. The two of them had been charged with retrieving a stolen painting by Cubist artist Marie

Laurencin called *Danseuses Espagnoles*. Their client had a strong suspicion about where it had ended up, but after a three-year investigation by the FBI, no action had been taken. They were tired of waiting for the legal channels to work. At least David trusted me enough to let me sit in with him and Jesse while they processed the contract, and Jesse had set me up with an access account and a company credit card so that I could book the flight to Phoenix and rent a house with sightlines into the property of the thief.

But my Sir waited for a response. I wondered if he'd found some time away from Jesse or if Jesse was throwing David a disgusted look and wishing he was elsewhere. I wrinkled my nose at the idea of 'being good' and rearranged the pens in my drawer. The collective quartet of my bosses had left me with absolutely nothing to do. The *chink* of plastic against metal echoed through the reception room as I reorganized my pens according to colors of the rainbow. Where did black fall in that spectrum? My new desk was the only furniture in the space. As SAFE Security saw people by appointment only, they hadn't felt the need to make a comfortable waiting area.

"Good" was one of those meaningless, relative terms, and I knew what he was really asking. "If you're asking whether I've broken any laws, then—yes. I'm being good. If you're asking whether I've completed any of the items on the list you left me, then—no. I've been naughty. You might need to hurry back and give me a thorough spanking."

On the other end of the line, David chuckled. "Don't worry. You'll get something when I get back. You still have a few days to do the things on that list."

The list consisted of things I really needed to do, like go to the Secretary of State to change the address on my license, but the last item was something I wasn't ready to take on. That's the one he was really asking about. I sighed. "Sir, I'm not ready to call the Zinns. I need more time."

"Sugar, we've been over this." He injected steel into his tone. "Before you left Michigan, you agreed to call them once you got settled in Kansas City. You're settled."

He'd seen to that. Once Summer had been well enough to make the trip, he'd moved us to the city he'd adopted as his home. Summer had a bed at a top-notch rehabilitation facility, and David had pulled some strings to get her under the care of the best medical team in Missouri. Moving had been easy. Our few possessions had fit in the trunk of David's SUV. Physically moving and emotionally moving weren't the same, and that had led to some heated disagreements between us this past month.

This wasn't a topic I wanted to discuss. If I had my way, I'd avoid it altogether. Life could be so much better if I could just pretend certain events in my life had never happened. Back when David was investigating me because he didn't believe I was who I said I was, he'd found my stash of pictures and texted copies to his buddy in the FBI. Finding them had given Keith Rossetti and the FBI the evidence they'd needed to find out that my dad wasn't my dad, and I wasn't who I thought I was. That was information I could have lived happily ever after without knowing. If I could turn back time, I'd hide the photographs of my childhood better.

I closed my eyes and pushed against the strangled feeling in my chest. I needed to change the direction of the conversation, and sex usually worked to divert David's attention. With a pout he couldn't see, I dropped the pitch of my voice. "Sir, I miss you. My pussy misses you. Are you alone? We could video chat." I envisioned a nice bout of phone sex.

"Aren't you at work?"

Where else would I be at one o'clock on a Wednesday afternoon? "I'm alone. Dean and Frankie just left to guard some horse's sperm. Apparently he's a prized stud." I twirled my hair around one finger, full-on flirting even though he couldn't see it. The idea of having phone sex with my Sir had worked to distract me from the topic I wanted to avoid permanently. "Wanna be naughty together, my prized stud?"

David, used to my tactics, didn't bite. "Since they're gone, there's no reason for you to be in the office. Get started on the list I left."

There should have been a reason for me to be in the office. Dean should have left a pile of paperwork on my desk. He should have given me the password to the accounting so that I could take care of the books. I had experience with that end, but he still insisted on paying an outside accountant to handle the finances. It was a waste of money. "There's plenty of time for that later, Sir. Don't you miss me?"

"Of course I miss you, Sugar."

Glancing at the security camera in the corner of the lobby near the door, I realized why he was resisting my charms. "If I go into your office, I won't be on camera. Nobody will see. It'll be just you and me."

He waited a beat. "My office is locked."

Did he honestly think a locked door would stop me? "Are you making a point, Sir?" I slid my lock picking kit from my purse and headed down the hall and around the corner to his office. "Give me thirty seconds."

His uneasy laugh barked through the speaker. "You've already been in there, haven't you?"

"Of course I've been in your office. You were there with me." I knew he was asking whether I'd picked his lock before, but old habits died hard. It wasn't in my nature to come clean right away.

"Autumn." He infused the warning with his Dom Voice, and it sent shivers of desire straight to my core.

"Oh, Sir. I'm already on my knees." Picking a lock. I left that part off because he knew exactly what I was doing. It took a lot of effort, but I concentrated on the soft metallic sounds of the tumblers locking into place.

"If I was there right now, I'd spank you for being a smartass."

Oh, but that man knew exactly what to say to make my pussy wet. As a sometimes-SAM, I needed to run off at the mouth while he put me in my place. When the stress of life got to me, I would call him names and goad him as he spanked or flogged me. He'd send me to a place past all my inhibitions where it was safe for me to break down and let it all out.

"Are you in my office yet?"

The last tumbler set, and I opened his door. "I'm closing your door right now. Do you want me in your chair or on the couch?"

He groaned, and I knew I had successfully distracted him from his original purpose. "Take off all your clothes and bend over my desk with your legs spread. Move my chair out of the way. That's where I want you."

This was even better. I preferred to have him in control, and he was letting me get away with entirely too much right now. I set to work wrestling out of the cute green dress he'd surprised me with last weekend. He liked me to wear colors that matched my green eyes, and

8

I found myself choosing clothing and accessories with his tastes in mind.

As if he read my mind, he cleared his throat. "I'm going to punish you when I get home, Sugar. You know better than to try to manipulate me."

"Sir, I wouldn't be me if I didn't at least try, and then you would fall out of love with me." Yeah, my convoluted logic was one of the things he found attractive. Or so I hoped.

He laughed, the sexy vocal caress washing over my nerves and urging them into submission. "Perish the thought. Are you in position?"

I bent over and rested my bare chest on his cold desk. "Yes, Sir. My nipples are hard, and my pussy is wet. Are you naked also?"

He ignored my question. "Put your hands on the back of your neck and move about two inches to your right."

Due to the car accident that took my father/kidnapper from my life, I had trouble keeping my left arm above my head, so David always had me put my hands on the back of my neck. I put the phone on speaker and did as he ordered. "Yes, Sir."

"I'm looking at your pretty pussy."

I imagined him sitting in his black leather, ergonomic chair and checking out my woman parts. David liked to look at me naked. Sometimes he didn't let me wear clothes at home, and he would order me to sit, stand, or lay in a certain position so that he could look at his naked submissive. Heat suffused my core, and my vagina wept as I imagined him physically there. I whimpered.

"You like that, Sugar? Do you like that I can see you from this far away?"

I wasn't so lost in the fantasy that his question failed to raise alarm bells. Thought I wanted to lift my head and look behind me, I did not. "You can see me, Sir?"

"Yes, Sugar, I can. I installed a camera in my office, and the feed goes directly to my phone. You're being very good right now, though that won't mitigate your punishment." He chuckled, an evil laugh that had me both hot and bothered.

I barely refrained from squirming.

"Use one hand. Touch yourself while I watch, but don't climax."

He wasn't playing fair, but that had never deterred him before. He reveled in making me orgasm without permission and then punishing me for disobeying. The soft cadence of his voice replayed in my mind. *It doesn't mean you're weak, Sugar; it means that I'm stronger.* I circled one finger around my clit. Touching myself always felt good, but masturbating for his pleasure lent it an intensity and an urgency I couldn't achieve on my own. I wanted to please him. I wanted to make him come just from watching me follow his orders.

My whimpers turned to gasps and loud moans. David and I had a reputation for being loud during sex. I was only quiet when gagged, and even then I managed to make a good deal of noise.

"That's it, Sugar. Now finger yourself. I want to see two fingers in that pretty pussy."

I imagined him alone in his hotel room, slouching in a chair with his hand vigorously stroking his cock. I wanted to hear him come, but he was curiously quiet. "Sir?"

"No, Sugar. No coming for you."

"Please? I'll give you a blowjob when you get home."

His evil chuckle sounded through the phone. "Yes, you will. However if you have an orgasm right now, you'll give that blowjob while you're tied to my table with my largest vibrator in that pretty pussy."

David liked to use sex toys on me that had a large circumference. The first time he tried it, I thought he was going to break my pussy, but he knew what he was doing—and he always respected my safeword. "You're evil, Sir."

"And you love it, Sugar. Move your fingers faster and pump your hips."

Fucker was going to be the death of me. I could hold off or avoid an orgasm if I didn't move my hips, and he knew that. I was so close. Squeezing the back of my neck with my left hand, I tried to avoid the inevitable, but I failed. My body went stiff, and with a long cry, I climaxed.

"Beautiful." His voice washed over me, soothing as it invaded my very being. "I love watching you come."

"I love you watching me come. Thank you, Sir." Though he hadn't authorized the orgasm, I still thanked him for it. "Did you come? I didn't hear you."

"No, Sugar. I'm sitting in a car with Jesse. He'd probably punch me, and that would ruin the moment. When he just glares at me, it isn't distracting."

Poor Jesse. I owed him something sweet. He had a weakness for baked goods. David and I hadn't discussed the idea of public sex play. I wasn't sure if I was up for it. "Did he watch too?"

"No. I'm in the backseat, and he's wearing headphones, as am I. If he heard anything, it was only what I said."

Though I knew that Jesse was well aware of what David and I had done, I still breathed easier. "Poor guy. Ask him what kind of cake he wants when you guys get back."

"You're going to make him a cake? I'm the one who gave you an orgasm."

And he was the one who was going to punish/torture me for disobeying him—because I needed it and so did he—but still! "I thought you liked my muffins better?"

That brought him up short. "Banana walnut?"

I'd bake him whatever he wanted, whenever he wanted. He was my Dominant, and I loved making him happy. "And cherry chocolate chip." I'd text Jesse later to see what kind of cake he wanted.

"That sounds delicious. Listen, Sugar, I have to get going, and you've avoided the list for long enough."

The scene was over, and so I stood up and put on my bra. "If I get it all done, can I try to break into the safe in your office?"

David sighed. "I guess so. Is it pointless to tell you not to go through my stuff?"

If he truly didn't want me to look through his things, then he wouldn't leave them locked in a safe. I'd never met a safe that I didn't yearn to crack, and David was well aware of my addiction. I shimmied into my dress. "I respect your privacy, Sir—just as much as you respect mine."

He chortled, and I pictured him shaking his head as he thought about all the ways in which he'd invaded my privacy. Not only had he charged Jesse with following me after we first met, but both he and Jesse had gone through my things without my knowledge or consent. "That's what I thought. I have to go now, Sugar. Be good. I love you."

"I love you too, Sir." I didn't speak to his admonition to be good. We both knew I wasn't the kind of submissive who always did what I was told, and so there was no point in lying to him by telling him that I'd be good or even better than normal. Holy hell, I was already due for two hopefully fun-ish punishments!

The SAFE Security offices occupied the top floor of a building they owned. The rest of the space was leased to various companies that had been checked and vetted before any contract was signed. David, Dean, Frankie, and Jesse each had an office of their own. They also had two conference rooms, a gym, and a single locker room that they all shared.

The locker room issue was a bit of a sticking point for me. I felt that Frankie should have her own, but when I'd brought it up, Frankie had shrugged it off as an unnecessary expense. She'd maintained that the shower stalls had curtains and the toilets had doors. *And besides, if any of us wanted to have sex, we wouldn't need a locker room for that.*

It took me back to when I'd first found out that David was in business with a woman. I had asked if he'd ever been romantically involved with Frankie, and he'd countered by challenging my assumption that he wouldn't have an interest in Dean or Jesse. They were sexy, handsome, virile men. David had caught me checking out Jesse on occasion. After a workout, he liked to come out of the locker room without a shirt and walk around the office to show off his physique. Only a blind woman wouldn't look.

I wasn't completely sure where I stood on the issue, but I wasn't in a position to make demands or strike bargains. When they finally let me be a full-fledged member of their security force, then I'd bring up the locker room issue. Surely David wouldn't want me to be walking around a locker room with a naked Jesse or Dean emerging from the shower, droplets of water still clinging to their bare skin.

I pushed that image aside. Though I thought they were handsome, I wasn't attracted to either Jesse or Dean. As good-looking as they were, they had nothing on David. Clothed or naked, he was the hottest man I'd ever met. I loved everything about him, though I could do without the way he kept prying into my business.

With a sigh, I decided he was right. There was no reason for me to sit in the office. As I shoved my phone into my purse and grabbed my keys, the elevator dinged. A security company with an elevator that opened directly into their offices wouldn't be in business for long. The elevator opened to a small room with reinforced walls and stainless steel paneling. It looked like a metal holding cell.

Jesse had six monitors in his office, one of which was hooked into the security camera feeds. It sucked that they didn't trust me enough to get me a computer, much less let me keep an eye on the security feed. As the first person a client would see when they came into the office, I should have those things. By rights, I should have been able to go to Dean and ask for it, but they all waited for David's permission before letting me do anything. Seeing as how he'd begrudgingly consented to let me be here, I was going to have to be patient. I hated having to be patient. As a woman of action, patience was not my strong suit.

I went to the heavy door separating me from the unknown visitor and peered at the small screen next to it. The woman didn't look like she was here to kidnap and/or kill me, and I didn't get the impression she wanted to sell pyramid-scheme makeup. In fact, she appeared downright terrified. Since nobody was here, I knew this woman didn't have an appointment, but I opened the door anyway. "Can I help you?"

"Yes. I'm sorry I don't have an appointment, but I was hoping that someone could see me anyway." She gnawed on her fingernail, and her eyes darted around, sliding past the "By Appointment Only" sign and searching for signs of danger. "Please."

The plaintive quality of her plea got to me. I'd been desperate before, not desperate enough to ask for help, but desperate enough to wish for it. This petite woman couldn't be more than five feet tall. She had cinnamon and blonde highlights in her dark brown hair, and she gazed up at me with tear-bright, red-rimmed blue eyes. I motioned her inside.

She practically fell into the reception room. "Thank you. I-I didn't know where else to go." Her gaze never stopped roving around the room. She clutched her purse to her chest, and I noticed fingerprint bruises ringing the woman's wrist. I'd sported fingerprint bruises a few times, and most of the time I hadn't come by them in a pleasant manner.

This woman needed someone to take charge. I channeled my inner Domme and herded her toward the nearest meeting room. "You're safe now. What's your name?"

"Chloe. Chloe Dixon. I want to hire a bodyguard. I have money."

"My name is Autumn." I closed and locked the security door, and then I gently put my arm around Chloe's shoulders. "Come into the conference room, Chloe. We can talk there. Can I get you something to drink? Water? Coffee?"

Chloe shook her head, but she allowed me to guide her to the conference room and seat her at the table.

"Where are the bodyguards? I want one who is big, strong, and smart. He'll need to be able to see threats before they happen. If you show me a list, I know what skills they'll need. Ex-military is best. I can pick one out."

It wasn't every day that someone came in asking for Superman, though it happened often enough for SAFE Security to charge a $20,000 retainer for most jobs. However SAFE Security didn't provide bodyguard services without a damn good reason. I grabbed a bottle of chilled water from the mini-fridge and set it on the table in case Chloe changed her mind. "Why don't you fill me in on the situation, and then I'll let you know if we can help you."

Chloe breathed in deeply and tried to compose herself. She seemed like the kind of woman who was used to situations where she needed to keep her composure. "I need to leave my husband before he kills me. If he finds out that I plan to leave, then he'll kill me to prevent me from going. He's a very powerful man with a vicious, cruel streak." She caught me studying the bruises on her wrist, and she tugged her sleeve down to cover them. "He doesn't hit my face. He knows better."

This might sound mean, but I wasn't sure how much of this I was buying. If the whole team was there, one of them would run a background check while she was being interviewed. I didn't have that luxury, but conning a con was a difficult task, and I was a damn talented con artist. As I listened, I pasted on a sympathetic expression and watched the woman's body language. "How long has he been abusive?"

She shook her head and exhaled a shaky breath. "Probably always. I thought he was dominant, you know? An alpha male who would treasure me and take care of me. At first, he did. He called me princess and sweetheart.

He bought me flowers, clothes, and jewelry." Looking away, she swallowed. "My mother called me two days ago. My father is dying, but Brick won't let me go see him. We argued, and he punched me in the stomach." She wrapped her arms around her middle, as if remembering the pain. "He says that my family didn't love me, that they were nothing to me. We haven't spoken in years."

"He cut you off from your family and friends." I was familiar with this kind of story. I'd witnessed some pretty nasty things growing up in some of the places where we'd been forced to live.

"He did." She sniffed and sat up straight. "I'm not going to feel sorry for myself or my situation. I'm going to do something about it. I'm going to leave him. I can't go live with my parents because they can't protect me from Brick. But I need to go see them. I need a bodyguard who can take me to see my father and then stick around to help me through the divorce."

I thought she needed a few cinderblocks, rope, chains, and a short pier. The Mississippi was muddy, and bull sharks were known to swim this far north. Nobody would find the body. Brick would sleep with the fishes. However Chloe didn't seem like she was out for his blood. I put a hand over Chloe's. "Chloe, SAFE Security solves problems. You don't need a bodyguard. You need leverage."

"Leverage?"

"Yes, something that will make Brick back off permanently. Tell me everything you know about your husband." This didn't qualify as blackmail because we didn't have plans to extort him or anything like that.

And so, for the next two hours, she talked. I listened to what she said, but I also listened for the things she didn't say. Every problem had a solution, and the solution wasn't always the obvious course of action. I aimed to find one that would extricate Chloe from this unfortunate situation and free to lead her life unencumbered by the past.

With all my heart, I wished that I could live my life without the past creeping up to rain a crapstorm all over me. That would be lovely.

David and Jesse Prep For a Mission

"Thank you for that." Jesse's unmistakable sarcasm ricocheted from the windshield and hit me between the eyes, not that it hurt.

"No problem." I closed the passenger door and slid my cell phone into my front pocket. At least I'd waited until my erection had subsided before moving from the back to the front seat. "Autumn is going to bake you a cake."

He quirked a brow, and his scowl downgraded to a frown. "She said that?"

"Didn't you hear?" I'd used headphones to hear Autumn, but that wouldn't prevent Jesse from hearing what I said.

"I was trying very hard not to hear. Sharing a hotel suite or a yacht with the two of you was bad enough." He tapped on the steering wheel of the rental car. Phoenix was hot this time of the year, which wasn't surprising, but it did make sitting in a car for purposes of surveillance uncomfortable. We couldn't run the engine for long without drawing attention to ourselves, so that meant long stretches of no air conditioning. We should have booked a room nearer to our target's workplace than his home. "Did you use the video feed I helped you set up?"

I wasn't bad with technology, but Jesse was better. I knew that Autumn would break into my office eventually, and I'd wanted to be prepared. "Yep. It worked out well for us both." She'd needed me. Whenever she got snarky, I knew that was due to the way she buried emotions she couldn't process. If I was home with her right now, I'd scene with her, and then I'd make her call her parents. "She hasn't called her parents."

Jesse made a thoughtful sound and wrote something in our stakeout logbook.

"I'm not pushing her to do anything she can't handle. She needs to do this."

Sliding the logbook into his pocket, Jesse pressed his lips together. He disagreed with me, but he didn't think it was his place to offer his opinion.

"What? Say it."

"She's obviously not ready. She's been here a month, and before that, her parents were in Detroit for three months to see her and Summer. She avoided them as much as she could when they were there. *You* talked to them. *You* developed a relationship with them. She didn't."

Autumn had been kidnapped at the tender age of three, and she'd been raised by her kidnapper. He'd given her a new name, and he'd raised her and Summer as if they were his children. Being so young, Autumn had forgotten her old life, and she only remembered the lies with which she'd been raised. Summer, having been six, retained traces of memory, and she'd been okay with meeting her real parents. Autumn vehemently wanted nothing to do with them.

20

After that first meeting with them, I'd thought she would come around to the idea. But somehow she'd rationalized keeping them at a distance. She'd leave the room, find a chore or errand to do, and then she'd find a reason to stay away. Summer and I had tried our damndest to get Autumn to sit down and talk with Sylvia and Warren Zinn, or their brother Leon, but Autumn had thwarted every effort.

"They're good people." I felt for them. Sylvia, heavily pregnant with her third child, had run into the house for a minute to use the bathroom. She'd left her two little girls playing in the backyard, and when she'd returned, they were gone. It had taken twenty-five years and a twist of fate that led to me sending a photo I'd stumbled upon in Autumn's apartment to my friend in the FBI. Keith Rossetti had run that photo through facial recognition software, and it had come back with a positive hit for the two missing children and the ex-con who'd kidnapped them. I'd dreaded telling Autumn because we were having enough problems at the time, and I knew she wouldn't take the news well.

Jesse chewed an ice cube. "It doesn't matter. Autumn has a few fragile parts to her, and this is one of them. She can't handle facing the fact that the man she called Dad, the man who was always there for her, stole her from someone else."

I knew that, yet I had a duty to do right by her, and if that meant pushing her to an uncomfortable place, then I would do it. She'd have me to lean on. She'd have me to be strong for her, to hold her up and be there for her. "You think I should just let her ignore the existence of her parents and brother?"

Jesse stretched, yawned, and scratched his stomach. I figured he was buying time. Finally he shook his head. "I have no fucking clue what I'd do in your place. That's why I wasn't going to say anything. It's easy for me to sit here and tell you to give her more time. I'm not the one who has to turn her parents away or argue with her when she won't answer their phone calls. She'd cry, and I'd cave."

I snorted in lieu of laughter. Ever since Stephanie Ceichelski had tried to kill Autumn by forcing her to take a bottle of sleeping pills, Jesse had treated her like she was precious and breakable. In Jesse's eyes, my lovely submissive could do no wrong. If I doubted my buddy's loyalty, I'd be worried that he'd make a play for my woman. But I knew Jesse too well to think he had an interest in Autumn. You couldn't love a woman on a pedestal, and Jesse didn't generally stay with a woman long enough to notice whether they were on one or not.

He leaned forward, using the steering wheel to stretch his lower back. Sitting in a car all morning wasn't our favorite part of the job. "There has to be a better way."

"Than making her spend time with them?" I wished there was a better way, but there wasn't. "It's going to be awkward at first. There's no way around it. But after a while, it won't be, and she'll have a mother and father who love her, and a little brother who will probably annoy her. She's very much a youngest child."

The object of our surveillance, a Russian real estate developer named Anton Rybakov, came out of the building that housed his offices. Instead of strolling down the street to the place where he'd eaten lunch yesterday, he headed for the parking garage. We had not yet found the exact location of where he'd hidden the stolen painting. Once we did, we could sneak in and steal it back. However we'd narrowed down the probable location to his office. When we'd "visited" his home yesterday, it looked like a family was living there, and Rybakov wasn't in any of the photos, nor were any of his possessions in the house. Thought it was listed as his official address, we'd deduced that it was not the right one.

The office building had a complex security system that we could circumvent, but we needed to familiarize ourselves with the inside first. With Anton Rybakov gone for a few hours, this was the time to get into his office.

As part one of our operation, Jesse called forth his best Russian accent and phoned Rybakov's secretary. "This is the assistant to Ambassador Kislyak. He would like to speak with Mr. Rybakov." Pretending to work for the Russian ambassador would get a real answer instead of a brush-off from the busy assistant.

Jesse listened for a few seconds. "Thank you. I will try Mr. Rybakov on his cell." Jesse turned to me. "Anton will be out of the office on personal business for the remainder of the afternoon."

"Really?" I got out of the car, brushed the wrinkles from my pants, and put on a jacket to complete my suit. "That's unfortunate. I have a meeting scheduled with Mr. Rybakov fifteen minutes from now. I'm a wealthy developer, and I'd like to work with Anton on my next high-end project right here in Phoenix."

Jesse donned his jacket, but between the way he kept his hair shaved close to his head and his brutish military bearing, he still resembled hired muscle. That's why I got the part of wealthy developer. Though I maintained my physique and military bearing, I'd cultivated a more refined appearance. In another op where we needed to make a different impression, Jesse would take lead. "Let's go, Mr. Calder."

I bristled at the pseudonym he'd chosen. Calder was my father's name, and I wanted nothing to do with that dickhead. I'd left home at eighteen, right after my mother had passed away. I'd changed my name to Eastridge, and I'd never looked back. Not only did I bear ill will because he'd been a shitty father, but when I'd been in the Cayman Islands following a lead that would uncover the person embezzling from my father's company, the old bastard had the FBI arrest Autumn for the crime. My lovely, emotionally scarred girlfriend had spent three nights in jail before Dean had been able to post bail. I'd never forgive him for that.

"I guess if I'm going to be an asshole, I might as well emulate the best."

Jesse motioned to my shirt. "You need a tie."

It was too fucking hot for a tie. I already felt like I was melting. "Female assistant?" At Jesse's nod, I opened a few buttons and went for the playboy look. Hey—if a woman could use her physical appearance as a distraction, why couldn't I? The fairer sex tended to find me attractive.

We entered the building and rode the elevator to the top floor. The air-conditioning was turned to sub-arctic levels, but after spending all morning in the sweltering heat, I wasn't about to complain. Jesse followed a half step behind. We didn't head directly to Anton Rybakov's office. Finding the lay of the land was the whole point of our reconnaissance mission. I counted security guards and noted their locations. Jesse kept an eye out for digital security measures.

The day before, we'd dressed in maintenance uniforms to check out the infrastructure. As the building was relatively new, the layout matched the plans on file with the city. That was a bonus.

I presented myself to Rybakov's receptionist, a young Latina woman with perfect hair and makeup. I flashed a flirty smile, but her gaze was pulled in Jesse's direction. That would affect our strategy. "David Calder. I have a meeting with Anton."

She punched keys on her computer, her eyes scanning the lines on the screen. "I'm sorry, Mr. Calder. Mr. Rybakov doesn't have you on his schedule at all."

Flirting with her wasn't going to get me anywhere. I frowned, a severe expression that worked to strike fear into the hearts of many subs. "My assistant confirmed with him this morning." Though I didn't look at Jesse, I knew he was expertly playing the part of the assistant who'd forgotten to carry out a basic task.

She must not have been a sub. She glanced from me to Jesse and back, but I noticed that her pupils widened when she looked at Jesse. "I'm so sorry. Mr. Rybakov is out on a personal matter. Can I reschedule for you?"

Since my displeasure wasn't working on her, I turned it on Jesse. "Call Tong Li. Tell him we're suddenly free this afternoon." Li was Rybakov's biggest rival. Yeah, we'd done our homework. I turned back to the receptionist. "What is your name?"

"Angela Vazquez." She worried the gold cross pendant on her necklace.

"Ms. Vazquez, I came all the way from Detroit for this meeting. My time is precious. If I can't work this deal with Rybakov, then I'll get it done with Li." With that, I left the office and headed down the hall to the elevator.

Jesse didn't come with me directly. I'd left him behind to see if he could work his magic on Angela. He caught up to me at the elevator.

"It somehow came out that I'd dropped the ball on this one. In the interest of saving my job and scoring points with Rybakov, Ms. Vazquez was gracious enough to call her boss. She has invited us to wait in the lobby."

This was better than I'd hoped. "Does that mean you have a date tonight?"

"I may step out. She's a very nice woman." He paused before opening the office door for me. "And then I won't have to listen to you have phone sex with your girlfriend."

This might work out better than expected. If Autumn completed the tasks I'd left for her, then I could spend some time rewarding her. With Frankie and Dean out on a mission, I might even fly her to Phoenix to stay the night. Some might call me pathetic or whipped, but I disliked sleeping without Autumn beside me. In the five months we'd been together, we'd spent most of our nights apart. Waiting for Summer to get to a point where she could transition her care to a facility in KC had been hell. Autumn had refused to leave her sister for more than two days at a time, and I couldn't effectively move my base of operations to Detroit. Living with Autumn this past month had been an addictive slice of heaven.

"Wipe that lovestruck look off your face, Mr. Calder. You're a powerful, jerk-faced developer about to make a deal with a like-minded asshole." In case I'd forgotten the types of moves assholes made, Jesse sucker-punched me in the back just above my kidney. He knew that it would hurt and that I'd absorb the blow.

"Payback's a bitch."

He opened the door leading to Rybakov's offices. "Yes, Mr. Calder. My apologies."

Ms. Vazquez must have overheard Jesse. She leaped to her feet. "I'm so sorry about this, Mr. Calder. Mr. Rybakov is on his way right now. He should be here in about fifteen minutes. Can I get you anything? Coffee?

Water?" Ms. Vazquez folded her hands, but she was unable to fully hide her nerves.

I shook my head, but Jesse whispered something to her. She smiled before disappearing down the hall.

"I asked Angela to make some coffee." Jesse parked himself at her computer, plugged a thumb drive into a port, and began tapping on the keys. "I'm in big trouble, and since her boss is most likely also a douchebag, this is going to score me major sympathy points."

I didn't comment on Jesse's love-em-and-leave-em philosophy. Right now it was buying us time to hack Rybakov's network. We were after access to their security feed.

While Jesse did his thing, I did mine. Rybakov's office couldn't be far. He wasn't the kind of man who would isolate himself from the action. The suite had one hallway that branched after ten feet, and I went down it. Careful not to let Ms. Vasquez hear me, I turned in the opposite direction from where she'd gone, and I found Rybakov's office. It was locked, but Autumn had jokingly gifted me with a bump key—a kind of skeleton key that fit many different locks and "bumped" the tumblers into place. Picking a lock the old-fashioned way was not a point of pride with me, and I didn't care that the key was illegal. It got the job done.

His office was massive. Floor-to-ceiling glass lined two walls, and a spiral staircase led to a loft-style second floor that covered half the square footage. Sculptures and paintings were tastefully displayed in every open space. Two massive, square columns, together with the spiral stairs, separated the space and provided even more surfaces to display art. His eclectic taste ran the gamut from tribal to Post-Modern. Somehow he made it work.

With my cell phone, I filmed the layout, moving through the huge space to get closer shots of anything I could.

If I was going to hide that painting, I'd do it here. My guess was that he lived here, in his office. The lower level, with a high-end kitchen and comfortable sitting area, resembled a living room more than an office. The bathroom featured a marble shower and countertops. A chandelier dangled from the ceiling. Upstairs I found a massive bed, a huge television mounted on the wall, and a walk-in closet that Autumn would love.

Jesse's signal sounded in my earpiece, so I beat a hasty retreat. On my way back, I bumped into Ms. Vazquez coming from the staff room with two steaming cups of coffee.

I spread my hands in apology. "I came looking for you. Something has come up, and I must leave. I'll have my assistant call to reschedule. Try to have something for me in the morning, preferably around ten." Without waiting for her to respond, I turned away and headed toward the exit. I passed Jesse in the reception area. "Let's go."

He opened the door for me, and we beat a hasty retreat. Ms. Vazquez stared after us, and I saw him glance over his shoulder, probably to wink or make sure she was enjoying the view. We didn't need to continue our surveillance now that we had what we needed. Back in the hotel room, I played the video I'd taken for Jesse, and we formulated a plan of attack.

"There are three elevators total—two in the lobby and a service elevator in the rear." Jesse spread a diagram of the building plans on the bed. "Several of the offices have a terrace, and the emergency stairs are interior."

Whenever we broke into a place, we preferred to use the stairs. Security cameras rarely carried feed from them,

28

and we could navigate them faster than most elevators traveled. The building was only eight stories tall, so it wasn't a hardship.

"I installed spyware on their system. We have real-time feeds." He clicked through several screens. "Rybakov doesn't have a camera in his office."

"That's because it's his apartment. He lives there. But you have the hallway. We can see him come and go." We spent the next few hours combing the footage I'd taken, watching the security feed, and erasing any trace of us. In the end, we came up with a solid plan. I clapped Jesse on the back—hard, to pay him back for sucker punching me. "It looks like you're going to need to get copies of Ms. Vazquez's keys and her keycard."

Jesse snorted. "Once again, I'm the honeypot."

"I didn't say you had to sleep with her." I rolled the blueprints into a neat tube, which I flattened and folded in half. This would have driven Dean off the deep end, but Jesse wouldn't have cared if I'd folded it into a one-inch square.

He ran his hand over his hair to make sure it wasn't too long. Jesse preferred his hair to meet very exact specifications. In the middle of this ritual, his phone rang. I didn't recognize the ring tone, but he did. He fumbled for it. "Hey—is everything okay?"

I'll admit to curiosity. I wasn't aware of anyone that would make that note of concern creep into his voice. I continued to tidy our workspace/my bed as I listened to his half of the conversation.

"That's okay. I can set it remotely. Have you left yet?" He leaned his shoulder against the frame of the bathroom door as the person on the other end squawked. "Frankie and Dean are due back tomorrow afternoon. You won't need to go back until then." As he listened, the line between his eyebrows deepened, and he stuck his hand in his pocket.

Jesse rarely looked or felt guilty about anything, but I knew my friend well enough to recognize the signs.

"I know. Sugar, I'm sorry, but there's nothing I can do about that." He sighed. "Yes, he can, but—"

Now that I knew who was on the other end of that call, I snatched the phone from him. "Autumn, why are you calling Jesse?"

"David?"

"You sound surprised." If she had questions, she should have been calling me, not Jesse. "What's going on?"

"I don't have the access code to set or disengage the alarm at the office." Exasperation edged her tone. "You'd think the office manager would be allowed to open and close the office, especially when all the workers are out on assignment."

I hadn't wanted to hire her as our office manager, and everybody knew it. She'd manipulated Dean and Jesse into agreeing that it would be good to have her around to pick up the slack on the business end of things, and I'd eventually caved as well. That didn't mean I wanted her working at SAFE Security. On one hand, I could keep an eye on her and know she was staying out of trouble. On the other hand, we'd never given anyone access to our company. It was a tough transition for all of us, and I knew it was mainly my fault. Nobody was going to give her any real responsibility unless I approved it first.

Borrowing a leaf from her book, I tried to change the subject. "I bet Summer would love to stay the night at our place. You could watch a movie, stay up late, sleep in, and do some baking." Autumn had once confided to me that

30

she and Summer had dreamed of opening a bakery. I would have loved to support that venture, but she'd abandoned that dream for something yet-to-be-determined.

"Sir, I invented that move."

I loved her intelligence and sharp wit. I perched on the ledge under the window and looked out at our expansive view of the freeway. "You're good at it—I'll give you that—but credit for inventing it? No way."

Jesse rolled his eyes and disappeared into the bathroom to get ready for his date.

"I think it's bullshit that I don't have the codes to turn the alarm system on and off."

I saw that flirting and misdirection weren't going to work on her the way she got them to work on me, but I had one more trick up my sleeve. "Sugar, have you done the things I left for you to do?"

"I haven't had a chance."

Her avoidance behavior exasperated me as much as my reticence to let her assume all the duties of an office manager frustrated her. "Why not? What have you been doing all day?"

"I met someone. We talked all afternoon."

If she hadn't left the office, that meant she'd spent the afternoon with someone in the building. We'd rented out the first floor to several different retail businesses and the second floor housed an ophthalmologist and a pair of doctors who did laser eye surgery. It looked like Autumn was putting down roots. My heart soared. "That's great, Sugar. You made a friend."

"Yeah. We made plans to break into a car dealership and go joyriding."

I chalked her sarcasm up to her continued displeasure with me. A slow smile stretched my mouth as

I thought about all the ways in which I'd coax her inner SAM into submission. "Don't get caught. But if you need me, I'll be all alone, stuck sitting in a car on surveillance duty while Jesse lives it up with a receptionist who couldn't take her eyes off him."

"Don't do that."

Glancing up, I found Jesse standing next to his open suitcase. He'd shaved and showered, and he wore jeans, so he was most likely digging for a shirt. I frowned. "Don't do what?"

"Don't say it like I'm going on a date. It's just a distraction so that I can copy her keys and clone her phone. It's not like I'm interested in her or anything."

His vehement denial disturbed me on several levels. I couldn't investigate that and hold my own against Autumn in her perturbed state. "Sugar, I have to get going now. I love you."

"I love you too, Sir."

Finally she'd used my title. That meant she was getting over her pique. I knew I had to deal with it eventually, but this was a bit of a reprieve. I handed Jesse's phone back. "Why don't you want Autumn to know you're going out with someone tonight?"

Jesse shrugged. "You don't need to share every detail, you know. This is supposed to be a covert operation. There used to be a time when you understood what that meant."

I didn't know how to respond to that. Even if we'd been overheard, nothing I'd said would compromise the mission. Did he think I was letting Autumn too far into what we were doing? It wasn't like she had a history of shooting her mouth off. Well, not to anybody but me. "You want me to fire Autumn?"

32

He pulled a shirt over his head, but his movements were jerky. "I didn't say that, though if you keep treating her like she's a useless nitwit, then she'll probably quit."

I had mixed feelings about that. I'd offered to send her back to school or to help her open a baking business, but she'd turned me down flat. It would be wonderful if she changed her mind. I shoved that line of thought aside and gave Jesse my full attention. "What's really bothering you?"

"She only called me because she's supposed to take over doing all the extra stuff that I used to do—that I still do because I've only trained her to do the few things you'll let her do."

I'd crossed a line. She'd called him because he was her boss, not because she'd been trying to go around me. Autumn would never tell me that I was being obtuse because she'd interpret my interference as my right as her Dominant. Jesse wasn't bound by the rules of that dynamic. "Sorry. I shouldn't have taken the phone from you." It still didn't explain why he was bothered by me telling Autumn about his date.

He knelt down to tie his shoes. "Angela wants me to take her to the batting cages. That's not what I would have chosen for a first date, but it'll give me some great openings to distract her while I get what we need."

I loved visiting the batting cages. "Maybe I should go too. You can pass her keys and phone to me, and I can copy them."

He waved me away. "This is a one-man job, and if she sees you, it's going to raise questions. I'd rather just tell her that you gave me the night off and leave it at that."

Damn. I missed playing baseball. Maybe I'd get together a softball team with the people in our building. I bet Autumn would like to learn to play. "Fair enough. I'll be tailing Rybakov if you need me."

Destiny and Crepuscular Rays

Joyriding wasn't on my agenda for tonight, but I hadn't been kidding about breaking into a dealership. I knew it was wrong for me to deliberately mislead David, but he would have forbidden me from helping Chloe. How could I prove myself a worthy member of their organization if I never got to take a case? After all, my career as an office manager was going nowhere.

There was no doubt that David was going to be pissed at me when he returned home. Now it was a matter of the number of things he'd be upset about and the degree to which each one contributed to the punishment I was steadily earning. Though I might not sit for a week, the prospect of a spanking didn't deter me. More than anything else, I wanted him to accept and be proud of me. Like me, he was mulish in his beliefs, and he was of the mindset that I should spend my time engaged in safe, mundane pursuits. I had faith that he'd see reason eventually, but I'd have to repeatedly shove it in his face for that to happen. This was my version of being patient.

Chloe had spent a couple hours pouring out her sob story to me. Her husband was physically and emotionally abusive, and she wanted out. Though I sympathized with her, I could not empathize. Nobody had ever been abusive toward me. My father had been supportive and encouraging, and my sister was my best friend. David and I were still building the foundation of our relationship, but so far it was built upon mutual respect and lots of carnal attraction. He was a great listener, and he was driven to take care of me. He genuinely liked me, and I liked him back.

After crying through a box of tissue, Chloe had gone home to get ready for a dinner party she was throwing for several of her husband's business cronies. I wasted no time getting to work. Research was always the first step in anything, so I looked up Brick Dixon. I wanted to verify as much as I could about Chloe's story and double check the facts. He owned a string of successful, high-end car dealerships. Images of him with prominent local and state politicians flashed across my screen. Yep—if this guy was the douchebag Chloe had described, then leaving him would only be accomplished on his terms. As I clicked through the images a second and third time, I realized that he was too well connected not to have a skeleton or two in his closet. There was no way he wasn't doing illegal favors for some of these politicians, though even the appearance of impropriety could cause problems. Many of these political figures wanted to graduate to higher-profile offices, and that wasn't going to happen if scandal was attached to their names. With that in mind, I knew I was on track to find the leverage I needed.

Now that I'd decided on blackmail, I had to dig up something. I noticed that in most of the photo ops, some kind of expensive car was in the shot. There was one of the mayor in a Porsche Panamera, various City Council members were in pictures with Bentleys and a Rolls-

Royce Drophead Coupe. I saw a state senator in an Aston Martin One-77 and the governor sitting comfortably behind the wheel of a Lamborghini Reventon.

One of my dad's friends had owned a chop shop, and he'd refused to take cars like this. They were tough to recondition and resell. That hadn't stopped him from dreaming about owning one. The walls of his office had been papered with posters of these exorbitantly expensive cars. I'd once asked him why he didn't get one for himself. I remember the expression on his face as if the conversation had taken place yesterday. Full of regret and yearning, he'd shaken his head. *Those cars were for people who either had nothing to hide or had confidence their secrets would stay hidden.*

Well, I was confident that Brick Dixon had secrets, and I wasn't going to let them remain hidden. I gathered the tools of my trade, and then I broke into Jesse's office to gather some of the higher tech tools he'd left behind. He'd bragged about a scanner that could clone a phone, and he had another gadget that could bypass the password protection on a computer to allow someone into the files. The scanner was gone, but I found the password bypass gadget in his desk drawer.

This was a lot to carry, but a woman could get away with having a big, stylish bag slung over her shoulder. I sent Jesse a text telling him that I was on my way home so that he could engage the security system. It rankled that I didn't have the passwords. Seriously—if I wanted to get in, no security system was going to keep me out.

I went home first, but only to get a change of clothes. I needed something that wouldn't show up if a security camera happened to come across me. Dark clothing was my friend, but in the oppressive heat, I needed something stylish that didn't scream, "I'm all dressed up and ready for a little B-and-E." Chloe had disclosed that Dixons of KC employed two night security guards, ex-cops who were armed.

Surveillance was my next objective. The dealership had branches all over the Kansas City metro area. Dixon had an office and showroom downtown, but most of his cars were on lots in the suburbs. I parked my car (really it belonged to David, but he insisted it was mine) on the street, fed quarters to a meter, and strolled the vicinity. Kansas City was a gorgeous place to live. I loved the fountains and the fact that I could sit on a bench beside a bronze statue of Mark Twain. That reminded me—I'd never finished reading Huck Finn to Summer, but I guess since she was no longer in a coma, she could finish it on her own.

The city cameras were positioned to have very few blind spots. It made the area safer, but two of them made my job difficult because they covered both doors that led to Dixon's offices. Though the damn city made it unnecessary for Dixon to need additional camera security, that didn't stop him from plastering his own cameras everywhere. Every entry point of the building was covered by angled security cameras. Someone with that much security was definitely hiding something.

The heat eased as the sun trekked west. I sat on a bench and posed like I was looking at my phone, though I was studying angles and trajectories—which I mapped out on my phone using this cool app that Jesse had showed me. It was for architects, I think, but it came in very handy when considering a breaking-and-entering strategy. Every system had a weakness, and I was going to find it. Ideally I'd case this place for several days before making a move, but I didn't have that luxury. Though a mission like this had minimal risk, there was enough to freak out David. At this point, he might not make me drop the mission, but he'd take it over. I couldn't let that happen, though I'm not sure if I merely needed to prove myself or I seriously missed breaking and entering.

Brick Dixon was inside the showroom. I watched him through the large picture windows that allowed the general population to ogle cars no regular person could ever afford. He was a big guy, and his name fit. It was like his mother looked down at his newborn body and realized that he was going to always be a red-faced, rectangular dude. He had broad shoulders, a barrel chest, thick legs, and a square head that swallowed his neck. I assumed he had one because that's how humans are built, but I had no visual evidence to support the existence of Brick's neck. He'd been a third-string defensive linebacker for the Chiefs for one season, and he proudly displayed his old jersey and lots of other football memorabilia.

The daytime crowd was thinning as employees closed up offices and went home, and there would be a temporary lull before the nighttime crowd replaced them. A well-dressed man entered the showroom, and Dixon crossed the sales floor to greet him. The two exchanged a hearty handshake, and then they probably exchanged pleasantries. I mentally supplied the dialogue.

Guest Douchebag: How is the little woman?

Dixon: Great! I keep her in her place by belittling her, and when that doesn't work, I just knock her around.

Guest DB: Ha-ha. You have to keep them in line. I do the same with my wife.

Dixon: We're the same kind of sleaze. Let's talk in my office about other crap, probably illegal stuff.

Guest DB: Sounds great. Let's go!

My sightline included a view of a backlit keypad that allowed access, I was sure, to Dixon's private office, which is where he led his visitor. As I watched, he punched a sequence into the keypad. Oh, now that was a design flaw over which I'd fire my security team. Lady luck was on my side, and I might have giggled. The guy who'd parked himself next to me glanced over and smiled. I ignored him.

An hour later the staff had left and locked up for the night. I casually made my way to the other side of the building and watched as the staff exited from a lone door in the back. It was one of those steel security doors with the edging around them to prevent thieves from being able to cut the lock, and it also lacked a handle. This door was exit only, which made it a perfect point of entry. The ubiquitous cameras weren't pointed at it, though there was probably one on the inside filming the hallway.

Okay—if I wanted to be ballsy and brazen, I could do this. I wouldn't be able to evade the cameras completely, but I could keep my features hidden. I stood near the door, face glued to my phone screen, and waited for Dixon to come out. I had patience when I really needed it, and I knew that Chloe's dinner party started in a half hour. Brick might be a dick to his wife, but he—hopefully—wasn't going to be late to dine with his friends.

Thankfully I only had to stay in position for ten minutes. The door opened suddenly, banging into my right side. I yelped and stumbled, throwing myself toward Dixon's associate, who had come out first.

Halfway out the door, he caught me. Fast reflexes and a strong grip meant he was either former military or a trapeze artist. "Sorry, miss. Are you okay?" Concern wrinkled his eyes, and I noted they were an unusual shade of gray.

I touched the back of my head, drawing his attention there and making him think that's where I had been hit. This would keep him from looking to closely at my face. "Yeah. I didn't notice the door."

Dixon came around on my other side. The heavy door slammed shut, but I didn't care. I'd put strong tape over the latch when I'd fallen into Dixon's associate. Dixon gave me the once-over before dismissing me. "You're not hurt."

"Just surprised." I lifted my phone. "Texting while walking." It buzzed with a message from David, and I used that distraction to get out of the situation. I smiled and started away as if continuing on my path. "Have a good night."

I ducked inside a coffee bar and waited for Dixon's car to pull out of his private parking spot. He was gone before I could pull on my gloves. Thirty seconds later, I pried open the door. The lack of a handle and the edging were easily overcome with a pocket-sized pry bar. My top had a lightweight hood that was large enough to cover my head and shade my face. I kept my face away from the cameras and beelined for Dixon's office where any secrets would be kept.

The exhilaration of sneaking into a place raced through my veins. All my senses were on high alert, and I was hyperaware of my surroundings. I'd been destined for this kind of life. My father had taught me these skills so that I could steal things, but I much preferred using them to help people, though it was the same rush either way. The two guards wouldn't be expecting an intruder right after closing and in broad daylight, and I didn't run into them on my way in.

41

I copied the sequence I'd seen Dixon use earlier. The light on the keypad turned green, and I went inside. His office had high-end finishes. It had been professionally decorated, but the cleaning staff hadn't touched it in a while. Though he kept his desk neat, a layer of dust coated nearly every surface. I sighed because it meant I was going to have to be careful not to leave fingerprints or smudges in the dust. Even so, I pulled the blinds between the office and the showroom so that security wouldn't be able to see inside on their rounds. The blinds on the single window that overlooked the street were already down.

Starting at his desk, I booted up his computer while looking through the file he'd left in the middle of his desk. Item one on the next day's agenda was a printout of the specs for a Bentley. Someone had printed it out twice, but I'd been to a dealership before. Their practices almost never made sense, like taking a potential buyer hostage under the guise of negotiating a deal or waiting for paperwork. There was probably a copy for the salesperson and one for the customer, but it seemed to me that a good salesperson would know their product without a cheat sheet. My dad's friend may have only run a chop shop, but every one of his employees was knowledgeable about all kinds of cars and was prepared to talk about them ad nauseum.

The monitor flashed, and the logon screen came up. Dixon's username automatically populated the top bar, so I just needed the password. Jesse had said the password finder needed to be plugged into the USB port, but he'd also said the thing could take hours to find the correct combination. If Dixon had set it up to put his username in there when it booted up, then he was probably equally lazy about his password. I checked inside and under drawers for where he might put his password, but I came up empty. He either used the same one for everything or he kept it in his phone. Too bad Jesse had taken his phone cloning device with him.

So I plugged in the magic device and set about searching the office. Chloe had mentioned that anything worthwhile would be in the safe. She'd suggested that I take everything and run, and she'd sort the wheat from the chaff later. Of course I found the safe hiding behind a framed painting, and a shiver of anticipation washed through me. It was a Temberley 307-E. My father used to wrap my presents in a safe every year, and part of the gift included cracking the safe. Once he'd given me one that had taken me seven months to open. That safe had been a Temberley 207-C. I would never say this to David, but stumbling upon a locked safe made me feel even more excited than when he tied me up and blindfolded me before a scene. If my life were a movie, David would be my partner in crime, and we'd pause right now to have sex. That's the level of exhilaration I was feeling.

I breathed deeply to bring my mood back to a manageable level, and then I pulled a notebook and pencil from my bag. This Temberley model had six numbers in the combination and two-level security. My 207-C had four numbers, and it had been my first experience with two-level security. Adding a sixth number would complicate things, mostly because the second level of security reset the combination every time the dial landed on a wrong number. And I'd recently read an article that they had changed the number of "passes" between the last four digits, meaning I'd have to pass up the correct number two or three times before it would engage. If I passed it the wrong number of times, it either wouldn't engage or it would completely reset.

This safe would be tough to open even if I knew the combination.

I challenged myself to see if I could get into the safe before Jesse's electronic device got into the desktop. I put my stethoscope in place, and I set to work finding the best place to listen for the quiet *snicks* and *clicks* that would tell me what to graph. Breaking into a safe required a deep understanding of Cartesian geometry. Rene Descartes, the guy who said, "I think therefore I am," was one of my idols. He'd rejected Euclidean geometry— saying he couldn't assume truths, he had to know them to be true—and insisted on learning the world on his own terms. Like Descartes, I blazed my own trail, "testing myself in the situations which fortunes offered me."

My destiny belonged to me.

Forty-three minutes. Suck it, Dixon. I cracked your safe, though I'll never brag about the time it took me to get into it. I was out of practice, and I needed to change that. Jesse's program was still running, so at least I'd won that contest.

Inside the safe, I found cash and jewelry, which I left alone. If I was going to find the dirt on Dixon, it would be in the paperwork. He had about two inches of papers in there, so I took them out and started reading. The ambient lighting had faded from the cream-colored blind blocking the window to the street. I grabbed a penlight from my bag and read.

Mostly I found descriptions of cars, two copies of each one. The other papers included stock certificates for shares of Techola, lists of customer contact information, and paychecks. Tomorrow must be payday, and some of the salespeople had enjoyed a good month. Lastly I found a paper covered with lines and squiggles. It kind of resembled a map of a cave, which I'd always found hard to decipher. This one had writing all over it, notes and such, and some locations were crossed out.

The computer screen flashed, and then it began startup protocols. Jesse's magic password program had worked. I left it in the drive while I poked through the electronic files, just in case I came across a password-protected program or file. I was finding a whole lot of nothing. Life would be so much easier if bad guys kept a file titled "Stuff that could be used to blackmail me."

I'd been in the office for two hours when I heard the security patrol come by. I darkened the screen, closed the safe, and put the painting back, but all they did was jiggle the door handle to make sure it was locked. I waited for a while before I moved from my hiding spot under Dixon's desk. It's the quiet moments when pieces of a puzzle come together. Following my intuition, I looked again at the duplicate car descriptions, and I found one difference between each printout—the cars were from different states.

Turning the screen on, I searched using the VIN. Half the files showed sales to people, some of whom were names of prominent people around the state. The other half returned nothing in a file search, but yielded a hit on the missing car registry. Dixon was stealing luxury cars from other states, changing the VIN, and reselling them at deep discounts. Holy shit—I had him on grand theft auto. My heart danced with joy as I copied his electronic files to a thumb drive.

Polaroid cameras might be out of style, but they were still around, and they were useful. I grabbed mine from my bag and took a picture of the printed files before I tucked them into my bag. I put this into his safe with a note telling him that the files would be held in a secure location—as long as he signed the divorce papers his wife sent to him. He was to let her move out, and he was to leave her alone. The moment he bothered her, this evidence would be leaked to the national press. And, because I didn't know the importance of the other papers in the safe, I took pictures of those items with my cell phone, but I left them behind.

I slept so well that night.

―――――――

The next morning, I woke up in an exceptionally good mood. My lone, unsanctioned mission had been successful. I'd spent the morning with Chloe Dixon, who had cried tears of relief at the news I'd delivered. She'd been on the phone with a divorce lawyer when I left with five thousand dollars in cash—my fee for a good night's work. I longed to share my news with Summer, the only person right now who would be proud of me. David would be proud once he got over the fact that I'd taken a case without backup or his approval.

Shafts of light penetrated the clouds, otherworldly spotlights shining from the sky. In the parking lot outside Summer's rehab center, I paused to admire and wonder at the beauty of this phenomenon.

"Crepuscular rays. They just take my breath away."

I knew that voice, and I froze. It wasn't a self-preservation move where I mentally listed all the escape routes and selected the best one. Nope, it couldn't be that easy. I had no idea why my body ceased to move and my mind went blank. The woman who'd spoken, who'd stopped to stand next to me and look at the clouds, wasn't a stranger. Well, she wasn't supposed to be a stranger. She was supposed to be my mother.

"It's good to see you, Breanna."

46

She didn't say it, but I heard the censure in her tone. She'd been calling me for weeks, and I hadn't picked up once. A few times, David had. I'd sit there, unable to move, while he apologized and told her I wasn't ready to talk.

At her use of my name—my real name, not the one Brian Sullivan had given me—my heart seemed to stutter. She pronounced it Bre-on-uh, not Bre-ann-uh as I'd assumed. Some of my faculties returned, and I remembered to breathe. "They're pretty." I blamed my inane reply on the recent bout of oxygen deprivation.

"I'm glad you're here." Her voice caught. I knew this was hard for her, and I felt like the lowest jerk in the world for being caught up in my own emotional mess.

"I am too." Unlike Sylvia, Warren Zinn came around to stand in front of me, forcing me to look at him. He smiled gently, as if he understood that I'd run away if he pushed too hard. "We've been missing each other."

Part of me appreciated the out he was giving me, and it helped me to feel less guilty about my avoidance behavior. If David was here, he'd shake his head because he didn't believe in reinforcing that particular fault. I glanced away, feeling lame as I accepted the untruth. "Yeah."

"Jessica didn't tell us you were coming today. What a nice surprise." He inclined his head, indicating that the three of us should head toward the building. I was glad he didn't wait for me to reply. I wasn't a fan of surprises. I preferred to plan every detail, and I didn't like monkey wrenches thrown into my plans.

Jessica was Summer's real name. When we were little, sometimes we'd change our names when we played, and Summer had been fond of being called Jessica. She had a few memories of our real parents, where I had nothing concrete, though David liked to argue that I had subconscious memories because I'd chosen the name "Mistress Bree" when I'd been a Domme-for-hire.

Flanked by strangers who shouldn't be alien to me, I entered the front door of Breckenridge Rehabilitation Center. This was Summer's home until she could transition to living with David and me. His apartment wasn't very large, but he had a spare room, and he'd said that if we needed more space, he'd be open to moving. With all my heart, I wished he was with me right now. On the three occasions I'd spent time with the Zinns, Sir had been by my side. I needed him very badly right now.

"I used to be a science teacher." Sylvia tossed that tidbit into the chasm of uncomfortable silence yawning between us. "I also taught math."

Math was my favorite subject. I said nothing. She already knew that we had been homeschooled, just as I knew that she had been a teacher and Warren had been a supervisor for an automotive company.

Summer's room was on the second floor, but we found her waiting in the lobby. Being in a coma for three years was hell on the body. Even though I'd bent over backward to pay for extra physical therapy, it had still taken months of additional therapy for Summer to be able to stand up. That meant she could help transfer herself from her wheelchair to a bed or the toilet. No more bedpans for her. She leaned on a walker as she waited for us to approach, and though her smile beamed ten thousand watts, I recognized the scheming glimmer behind it. She'd set me up.

Sylvia and Warren each kissed her on the cheek. Normally I would have hugged her, but right now I wanted to punch her. Punching a woman who was using all her energy to remain standing probably wasn't a very sisterly thing to do, so I communicated my displeasure with a brief glare.

Her grin only grew. "Hi, little sister. Check this out." Slowly, and with supreme effort, she scooted the walker forward and took a shuffling step. Then she repeated the action with her other foot, but it took some time.

"Wow." I couldn't keep the sarcasm at bay. Punching her would have helped relieve this pent-up aggression. "You've mastered slow motion."

She ignored my tone. "Mark your calendar. One year from now, I'm going to run a 5K."

Before the accident, Summer had been a pretty fast runner. She'd been training for a marathon. I swallowed any more snarky comments.

"That's great, sweetheart." Warren's eyes shone brightly. "I'll run it with you."

She shot him a grateful smile. I'd never been a runner, though I used to be an okay sprinter—out of necessity. Running fast and disappearing lessened my chances of being caught. I wished I could run right now.

"I bet Leon will too." Sylvia rubbed Summer's shoulder. "I'll be there to cheer you on."

Leon Zinn was our younger brother. Sylvia had been pregnant with him when we'd been kidnapped. Now he was an FBI agent that specialized in kidnappings, and he worked out of Kansas City. He'd been instrumental in expediting the genetic testing to confirm that Summer and I were, in fact, the missing Jessica and Breanna Zinn. Moving here to be with David meant that I'd put us in the same city. That had been a selling point in getting Summer to agree to the move, though David's presence had been all the motivation I required.

They all looked at me, and I realized they were waiting for a statement of support from me. The shock of

49

seeing the Zinns was wearing off, but now I was battling a rising sense of panic. "I'll be the one throwing paint-filled balloons at you."

Summer laughed. "What if it's not a color run?"

"I don't see why that matters."

This time Sylvia laughed, a joyful noise that sparked a weird feeling buried deep inside me. In a perfect world I'd face that feeling, embracing or conquering it as the situation warranted. But this wasn't a perfect world.

"Let's go to the garden." Summer shifted her walker to face the atrium. "I like to sit outside as much as I can."

Though the entrance was only fifteen feet away, this walk was going to take forever. Normally I wouldn't care. I'd be chattering away to Summer, telling her every detail of the last twenty-four hours. However with the Zinns here, I couldn't say a word. It wasn't that I was nervous about how they'd handle the news of me breaking into a dealership, uncovering criminal behavior, and using it as leverage to help a woman escape an abusive marriage. I honestly didn't care what kind of opinion they had of me. No, it was the years and years of training to zip my lips and to shut people out who weren't family. That's what held me back.

"Listen, I can't stay long. I'm meeting a client for lunch. I just stopped by to see how you were doing."

Summer leveled a look at me that screamed, "Bullshit," at full volume.

"I'm glad to see you're up and walking." I continued as if she weren't silently yelling at me. "That's great improvement. You'll be able to leave here even sooner. I'll have to talk to your medical team about what kind of modifications we'll need to make in the apartment."

She stopped walking, not that she'd been powering full speed ahead. She turned to me and put her hands on

50

my shoulders. "Bree, you've done so much for me. You've given up years of your life to take care of me."

Oh, shit. She was going to make me cry. I swallowed the lump in my throat that represented all the things I'd done in my desperation to keep her alive. As always, my response was to change the subject. "I wish you'd call me Autumn."

She shook her head. "That's not your name. I'm finished with changing identities and moving around. I thought you were as well."

I was. That's why we'd taken a stand when our father wanted us to pull another job with him. It's how we'd ended up in Michigan, and it's ultimately how I'd met David. But it didn't mean I wanted one last name change.

"Your name is Breanna Zinn, and I'm Jessica Zinn. Those are the names we'll be using from now on. Got it?"

This wasn't as easy for me as it was for her, and I didn't want to have this argument in front of Sylvia and Warren. They might be strangers, but they'd been through twenty-five years of hell, not knowing if their daughters were alive or dead. I clamped my mouth shut.

Summer—Jessica—recognized my defiance, and she knew better than to pursue the issue right now. "I'm not moving in with you and David. It's a new relationship. The last thing you need is the stress of having to take care of me. It's going to take some time before I'm fully self-sufficient."

I knew all these things. "David is fine with you moving in with us. He even said he'd move if we can't make the apartment work for you." If David had a problem with my dedication to Summer, then I wouldn't have moved here in the first place.

She squeezed my shoulders, but there was no power in her hands. "I know. He's a great guy. I'm happy for you both. But I'm still not moving in with you. I'm going to live with Sylvia and Warren."

At least she hadn't fallen into the habit of referring to them as Mom and Dad. If she'd done that, then I'd be wondering if she was playing an angle. But my relief was short-lived. The Zinns lived in a Minneapolis suburb. I freaked out about the idea of her moving so far away. Summer was the only constant in my life. She'd always been there for me, and I wanted to always be there for her. I shook my head, a vehement refusal to let her go. "You can't move to Minnesota."

"She's not." Sylvia crossed her arms. I'm sure she wasn't happy about this entire conversation. "We're moving here. All of our children are in Kansas City, so we retired from our jobs and put our house up for sale. We only stayed there in case you ever came back. Well, now you're back."

I blinked. This was the harshest tone she'd used with me, and I didn't know how to take it. The news that the Zinns were moving here also sent my brain spiraling into dark and unsecure places.

I left. My feet seemed to be in control, and I was in no state to argue with them. In a minute, I found myself in the parking lot. In fifteen minutes, I found myself sliding into David's spot at SAFE Security. Parking downtown was limited, and nobody there would give me the security codes, so I wasn't holding my breath for a designated parking space of my own.

My cell phone rang, chiming Summer's—Jessica's—ringtone, and so I shut it off. I sat in the car and gathered my scattered wits. That's when I noticed Frankie's Jeep in her parking slot. It looked like she and Dean were back. I went upstairs and rang the bell. It hurt that I had to be let in like I didn't belong there. The optimism with which I awoken had completely vanished, and I forced my mindset to focus on the job at hand. I needed to prove myself useful.

The door opened to reveal Frankie. Dressed in cargo pants and a tank top that looked a lot like fatigues, and with her dark hair pulled back in a sleek ponytail, she looked totally badass. The wide, welcoming smile that lit her face was genuine, but it didn't make her appear any less formidable. "Autumn! I wondered where you were."

I let her hug me. The first time I'd met Frankie, I'd been surprised at her effusive and outgoing nature. From the way David had described her, I had pictured a female version of him—methodical, shrewd, and all kinds of serious. Frankie could be those things, but mostly she was friendly. She'd welcomed me with open arms—every time I saw her.

"I don't have an access code to open the door."

She hissed, the kind of sound that communicated displeasure and a reluctance to delve deeper. "Well, you're here now, and I have some things for you to do."

"Oh, good." I meant it. The more responsibilities they gave me, the more opportunities I had to prove myself invaluable.

She pointed to a pile of folders and papers on my desk. "Jesse trained you on how to take care of the post-mission paperwork?"

"Some of it." I set my bag down next to the stack and started sorting through what she'd left. "I don't have access to the accounting software, so I can't do the receipts." I set those in one pile as I came to them. "And I don't have access to the shared files to input the mission reports." I put their handwritten notes in a second pile. "The best I can do is to borrow a computer to type up what you have here, organize and scan the receipts, and

53

send them to you so that you can upload and input everything."

"What are we paying you for?" Dean's voice came from behind me. His office, like David's, was on the front of the building. Jesse and Frankie's offices overlooked the side of the building. The interior rooms were set aside for meetings and storage.

I flashed my best smile, though under the circumstances, it probably sucked. "At this point, I'm not sure, but you'd better not tell me to go home and bake muffins." The four of them loved my baking. While I didn't mind bringing treats every so often, I didn't want that to be my only function.

A crease formed between his perfectly manscaped eyebrows. He looked at my desk, and then he fixed the green laser beams of his gaze on me. "You don't have a computer."

"David keeps saying he'll get me one."

Dean and Frankie exchanged a long look. I'm sure they had a whole telepathic conversation in sixty seconds that I found awkward. Frankie put her hand on my shoulder. "Want to be my workout partner?"

David had been teaching me some basic moves. Perhaps because he'd taken me to their private workout space several times, the rest of them felt like it was okay to teach me things. Jesse, Dean, and Frankie regularly took me to the third floor to show me a move or two. Frankie, especially, liked to have me along for workouts. I think she was lonely for female companionship. Her three male partners all treated her as if she was, in fact, a guy. While it boded well for the equality of their working relationship, it probably didn't help her feel like she could let her feminine flag fly free.

I had nothing else to do right then. "Sure."

Dean grabbed the stacks I'd made. "I guess I'll do this."

I wanted to apologize, but it wasn't my fault that I couldn't fulfill responsibilities that should have been mine.

Today she showed me how to wrap my hands so that I didn't cut or bruise my knuckles. I thought she'd show me some moves, but she put me through a workout. We stretched, ran on the treadmill, and worked out on the elliptical. She made me do squats and lift weights. Then she showed me a bump-and-roll move that would dislodge someone who was sitting on my chest and pinning me down, possibly even choking me. This was not an easy move, especially after she'd made me work out more in one day than I had in the past month.

In the locker room, she talked to me from the next shower stall. "We're going to work out together three times a week."

My thighs screamed threats and recriminations. My brain shouted with joy. If I wanted to join this team, I needed to show David that I could handle the physical demands. "Okay."

"In between our workouts, you're going to do your own. They should have a cardio and a weight lifting component. And I want you to practice that move because in two weeks, I'm going to pin you down, and if you can't break my choke, you're going to pass out and wake up with a hellacious headache."

I could warn her that David might not like that, but I didn't want to take the easy out. Frankie was offering to teach me—really teach me—how to be a badass. Perhaps I'd never be as good a fighter as she was, but I'd learn to get myself out of jam when I didn't have a big stick to whack someone over the head. "Sounds like fun."

She laughed. "Listen, I don't mean to intrude."

This always meant she was about to intrude. Frankie was one of the nosiest people I'd ever met, which I didn't mind. "But?"

"But when you came in, you looked like you're stuck at the dog end of a day gone by. I know that things aren't going exactly the way you want as far as you being our office manager, but you've never looked so upset before. Is everything okay?"

No, everything was not okay. I'd cleared a case, and there was nobody with whom I could celebrate. If I told Frankie, she'd be obligated to tell David, Dean, and Jesse. While I didn't think Dean or Jesse would be too mad, I knew that David would be livid. On top of that, Summer had set me up. I shut off the water, grabbed a towel, and dried myself off inside the shower. A set of clean clothes were also within arm's reach. With this being a unisex locker room, I had no way of knowing if Dean would come wandering in to change for his workout, so I was going to get dressed behind the curtain.

"Autumn?"

I decided to confide in Frankie. "Summer changed her name. She's going by Jessica, and she wants me to go by Breanna." I made sure to pronounce it *on* instead of *ann*. "And she said that she won't come live with me when she gets out of rehab. She's moving in with Sylvia and Warren, and they're moving to Kansas City."

I emerged from the shower fully dressed to find Frankie similarly attired. She regarded me sympathetically. "You've been through a lot of changes in the past month—moving to a new city, changing jobs, trying to figure out your relationship with David, your parents, and your brother."

56

"I'm taking it day by day." It was all I could do. I think the fact that I was also having to reconfigure my relationship with Summer—Jessica—that made it all seem insurmountable. When she'd been in a coma, she hadn't opposed me in anything. We'd never been closer, and we'd never been farther apart. I might have been harboring a little resentment at Sylvia and Warren for coming between us.

"That doesn't make it easy, just manageable." Frankie hooked her arm through mine and led me out of the locker room. "I know how aggravating David is being right now. I don't want to get your hopes up, but you need to know that I'm working on him. In the meantime, feel free to make use of the gym. It's a great place to work out your frustrations. Besides, if you're down here all the time, it might irritate David enough to get him to accept you as office manager."

At that moment I decided that I liked Frankie a lot. Perhaps one day we could be as close as I was with my friend Julianne back in Michigan.

Dean greeted us at the top of the private staircase that connected the third and fourth floors. After our workout, I really wanted to take the elevator, but Frankie did not present that as an option, and I was afraid I'd lose any street cred I'd gained if I asked.

"Good workout?"

Frankie laughed. She had a husky, deep-throated laugh that always sounded genuine. "Not bad. I can still kick your ass later if you want."

By sheer willpower, I made it up the last step. "She taught me how to get out from under someone who is sitting on my torso and choking me."

Dean scratched his chin, and I saw a cut I hadn't noticed before. "Did you know she's trained in six different fighting disciplines? If she ever decides to become an MMA fighter, I'm betting on her."

"I'd run the bets because the house always cleans up." I grabbed his hand, halting the damage he was doing to his cut. "Let me put some antibiotic on that."

Frankie rolled her eyes. "You should see the other guys."

I didn't know they'd been in a fight. I looked Frankie up and down, but I didn't see a sign of injury. "What happened?"

"As our client feared, thieves attempted to steal the item while we were in transit. They were highly organized and skilled fighters. Six of them hit us while we were loading. Five of them are in the hospital." With her trademark smile, she glided down the hall and disappeared around the corner.

I led Dean to his office where I knew he kept first-aid supplies. "What happened to the sixth person?"

"He gave up fighting after Frankie introduced his balls to his spine. I've never heard a human being make a sound that high in pitch." He chuckled and sat on the guest chair facing the other side of his desk while I retrieved the first-aid kit from a shelf.

That's when I noticed his new safe. It was beautiful, a plain, metallic gray strongbox that sat next to another safe. That one, which always sat out on his shelf, was a work of hand-crafted art. However, the new one caught my interest, and I breathed an exclamation. "Oh, Dean."

"You're sympathizing with the bad guys?" A note of incredulity crept into his voice, though he mostly sounded like he was teasing.

Though I'd grown up being one of the bad guys, I knew he didn't honestly believe that I'd sympathize with his adversary. No, I was enthralled with his new safe. It was a Vault, a special edition safe from Vault and Security. They made between ten and fifty of a single design, each with a continuous weld and 6-gauge steel. I'd heard rumors that the locking bolts extended four inches into the frame, and that it contained a secondary set of locking bolts in the body of the safe that extended and twisted to form an even stronger bond. In order to get into that safe without knowing the combination, a thief would have to be a fucking awesome safe cracker, which I was, or they'd have to use an explosive to open it. A pry bar, ax, or sledgehammer wouldn't work. The idea of getting into that thing made me wet. "I think I'm in love."

His head whipped around so quickly I was surprised he didn't break his neck. "You *think*?"

Crossing back to his desk, I set the kit down and tilted his face up so that I had a clear view of the cut. His scratching had cracked it open, and blood beaded along the jagged line. "What hit you?"

"Pavement. Lucky bastard got in a good hit, and I went down." He peered at me curiously. "But not for long. I subdued him without getting back up."

"I'll bet you did." My first meeting with Dean had been with him in the badass role. Since he'd saved me from being arrested, I didn't hold it against him. Still I knew how scary he could be in action. Hell, he could be intimidating just sitting there. I cleaned the cut and put antiseptic on it, but when I tried to put a bandage on it, he stopped me.

"I'm not wearing a Band-Aid for a little scrape like this. Now, who do you think you're in love with?"

I pointed to his acquisition. "That. Here I am, thinking you're one of those guys who goes for the flashy safes that a child could break into, and then you bring out that bad boy. Dean, you've been holding out on me."

His other safe, the one he displayed on his shelf like a statue, was a 60-inch piece of art. The casing was gold, with parts of it shaped to make it look like actual nuggets of gold. The door had gears made from Black Hills gold, so each one was a different hue. Some of the gears were made from titanium. The color palette and the design made it look kind of like the inside of a clock. It opened via digital lock and a dial that looked like a ship's wheel. Inside it had an open section about 16 inches high for storing larger objects and various size drawers, each that needed an additional key to open them.

He pointed to the flashy one. "I thought you'd like this one. It's a Boca Do Lobo."

I shrugged, dismissing it entirely. "It's pretty, but not functional. Only an idiot would think a showpiece like that would keep your stuff safe. I mean, no safe is secure if you display it, and that one was made to be displayed. Plus you can open a digital safe pretty easily by bouncing it. It'll keep nosey people out of your stuff, but a determined thief isn't going to find it a challenge. They won't even need a pry bar. That other one is a limited edition from Vault and Security. I've never seen one in person before." My volume lowered to a husky whisper. "Can I touch it?"

"Sure."

Wasting no time, I closed the distance between us. This edition of Vault sold for around ten grand. It was roughly the same size as the showpiece, but beneath its plain exterior lay the stubborn heart of a warrior. I'd either have to finesse it or destroy it to get inside. I traced my fingertips over the cool surface, a shiver of appreciation running through me as I studied the single-weld design. A single line of welding meant fewer weak spots, and it was the hallmark of a high-quality safe. This one also had a wheel that needed to be spun in order to pull back the pins, but the plain exterior hid such sexiness. I pressed my cheek to it and caressed the seam where the door met the frame.

"Should I leave you two alone?"

I glanced back to find Dean perched on the edge of his desk with his arms folded over his chest. "Can I open it?"

"I'm guessing that you're not asking me for the combination."

"That would be anticlimactic."

Frankie came in. She didn't comment on the fact that I was pretty much hugging Dean's safe. "It's after six. Do you guys want to grab some dinner?"

"I could eat." Dean jerked his thumb toward the door. "Why don't you two wait for me by the elevator?"

He wanted to hide the safe. Anybody in security knew that putting something in a safe wasn't enough to keep it safe. The safe needed to be hidden. Though I wondered where he kept it, I didn't ask. Just as I didn't give away my hidey-holes, I didn't go asking other people to reveal their secrets. Besides, now that I knew he had a safe, I could look for where he might keep it.

Dean joined us at the elevator. Frankie and I were chatting about purses. She'd started carrying a stylish backpack, and I had one with an extra long strap that could cross my body to keep it from slipping off my shoulder. He didn't say a word until we were on the elevator. "Come in at ten tomorrow morning. I'll let you try to get inside."

I couldn't help it. I squealed and gave him a hug. "Okay, but don't take it out of its hiding place. I want to see if I can find where you hid it."

He looked a little worried, but he didn't turn me down.

Indulging a Brat

"The offices are accessible by two elevators, a terrace, and indoor stairs." Jesse rubbed a hand over his head.

I could tell he didn't like any of those routes, and I knew what bothered him about them. "We can't avoid surveillance cameras if we take the elevators or stairs."

"If we can override their security feed, then I can loop images to hide our presence." Now he rubbed both hands over the short stubble of his light brown hair. "It's going to take some time, though. If we want to get this done tonight, I think our best bet is to rappel from the roof onto the terrace and break in that way. The silent alarm on that door is easy to override. It'll take me, like, twenty seconds."

His outing with Angela Vazquez had been fruitful. He'd successfully copied her keys and her phone only to find out that her access was determined by genetic components. Logging onto her computer required a fingerprint scan, and in order to get into the office suite, she had to submit a retinal scan. Or, as she had giggled into her drink the night before, "I have to look into the camera, and the door opens like magic."

Jesse had plied her with beer, and she'd spilled secrets without being asked. She thought he was a bodyguard, and she'd asked him many questions about security. A master at controlling conversation, Jesse had managed to share next to nothing while encouraging her to talk. Women tended to like a man who was a good listener, and the night might have climaxed in her bed, but Jesse didn't have sex with intoxicated women. He'd kissed her goodnight at her door and promised to call her later if he was still in town.

All of this information had been dumped on me just past midnight when Jesse returned to the room. His recounting had been unemotional, lacking even a glimmer of that spark of pride Jesse usually had when he talked about how smooth he was with the ladies.

"We don't know that the painting is there." I wanted to be sure of our target before I went in, but I suspected that I was being too cautious. Our intel had come from reliable contacts in the fencing underworld.

"Rybakov will be at a benefit for cystic fibrosis tonight. It's our only real shot this week, so unless you want to go home and come back next weekend, we need to do this tonight." Jesse handed me a red tie that had light blue stripes running diagonally across it. "You need to get ready for your meeting. Are you good on the background?"

I'd done my homework, reading up on the Phoenix real estate market. The bubble burst had been pretty bloody here, and right now it was a prime place for a developer with an imagination to swoop in and make a long-term investment. Rybakov, having ridden high when the market was high, wasn't in a position to make large purchases by himself. He needed help, and my cover identity was crafted to pique his short-term interest.

When I was at home, Autumn liked to tie my ties. While I could fend for myself, I preferred having her do it. Doing this tonight had the added benefit of getting me home to her that much sooner. "Yeah. Phoenix isn't a safe investment just yet, and I'm also scoping out deals in Detroit and Cleveland."

Jesse raised a brow. "Detroit and Cleveland?"

"They're both up-and-coming cities with great revitalization plans and tons of Federal dollars flowing to them for improvement zones." Looking in the mirror, I straightened my tie.

Jesse and I grabbed our jackets. This would be our last chance for recon.

Hours later, Jesse and I sat in the car, patiently watching for our person of interest to exit. We hadn't found out anything new, but our recon had confirmed our plan. The benefit started at eight, but Rybakov didn't leave the building until almost nine, his date dangling from his arm. I frowned at the woman in the knee-length red dress. "I didn't see her go in."

"That's Angela. She told me that he likes to take her to these functions because he's having an affair with his best friend's wife, and she provides cover." Jesse double checked his gear, making sure his belt was secure. "Hopefully he doesn't let her drink. She has loose lips."

At eleven-thirty, the two of us entered the building through the service entrance. Jesse had cloned the magnetic strip on Vazquez's ID, making getting into the building easy. Sneaking past the security guards was another story. We'd sent the crew a basket of goodies and a box of coffee from a local shop, and we'd laced the coffee with laxatives. A dirty trick, I know, but it worked. I crouched behind a cleaning cart and swiped a man's ID

65

as he hurried past me to the restroom. We'd need that later.

The first security camera pointed at the service stairs was going to be a problem. We came up behind it, and I stood on Jesse's back to loosen the bolt keeping it in place. Then it was simply a matter of nudging it so that we could get where we needed without our presence being recorded.

If we emerged from the stairwell anywhere else in the building, our images would show up on the cameras, but this one was safe. For this mission, we'd dressed in jeans and button-down shirts that could be untucked for a casual look. We didn't care about the casual look, but the shirts would hide the thick belts we wore to rappel from the roof. We'd be able to walk away from this and blend in with the general population. Recovering a painting in a big city presented challenges, but it provided a ton of exit routes.

Accessing the roof from the stairs meant we had to override a keypad where Vazquez's ID wouldn't work. This is where I used the badge I'd borrowed from the security guard. Two more flights of stairs, and we faced the steel-reinforced access to the roof, a place where nobody had thought to place security cameras.

Jesse nudged it open and poked his head out. After he conducted a visual sweep, he motioned for me to follow. Wordlessly we secured our lines and rappelled to Rybakov's dark terrace. I had a reasonably good guess for where Rybakov had hidden the painting. Once Jesse spliced the wire to fool the system, I jimmied the sliding glass door open. We squeezed through the ten-inch opening, which is all the distance the stretched out wire would give us without disconnecting and setting off the alarm. Typically we didn't like to leave evidence that we'd been inside, and while there would be no fingerprints or surveillance photos, we couldn't install a new wire. After this any reasonable person would upgrade their security. Or stop buying stolen paintings.

Jesse and I headed up the spiral staircase to the loft. He held my flashlight while I felt around the edges of the first of three decorative panels from along the interior wall. It took a few minutes, but I found a hidden button that opened a latch, and the panel swung open. A painting was mounted inside, the frame flush with the panel. Jesse shined the light over it.

This wasn't *Danseuses Espagnoles*, though it was from the Cubist era and probably also stolen. Jesse snapped a picture, and I closed the panel. Now that I knew the trick, the second panel was easy to open, and it revealed our prize. It was larger than I'd anticipated, but luckily we weren't charged with also taking the frame. I took it down and set it face-down on the floor so that Jesse and I could carefully remove it from the frame. That done, we rolled it up and stowed it safely in the cardboard tube he'd brought.

I replaced the frame, and Jesse went to investigate the third panel. He snapped a picture of that as well, and he waited for me to finish my task. One glance, and I recognized the style. It was another Laurencin. I couldn't remember the name, but I'd come across it while researching the history of *Danseuses Espagnoles*. I couldn't fault Rybakov's taste. The artist managed to capture such complexity in a seemingly simplistic painting.

We left the way we came, patching up the alarm on the sliding door after we exited. We hurried down the stairs and emerged using the door with the camera pointed in the wrong direction. We managed to evade the roaming security patrol, and I dropped the borrowed ID on the floor near the bathroom.

Safely back in the car, I grinned at Jesse. Completing a mission was always a rush, but most of my joy came from the fact that I was going home to Autumn two days earlier than planned. "This time tomorrow, I'll have Autumn tied up and moaning."

He rolled his eyes. "Too bad she can't book our flight."

The hot September heat pressed down on Kansas City like a wool blanket on a Newfoundland. A series of rainbows formed in the fountain as I passed the sprayers. Jesse lived a few blocks away from the SAFE Security building, and he'd insisted on parking there instead of at work.

"Did you tell Autumn that you were home early?" Jesse bit into one of his two pears. He'd offered one to me, but I didn't care for them when they looked like they should have been tossed out a few days ago.

"I'm going to surprise her."

"Put tassels on your nipples and a bow in your hair. That'll surprise her."

That wasn't quite the kind of surprise I had in mind. "I'll let you have that one, though your hair is too short. You'll have to hot glue the bow." I adjusted my tie. Damn, it was hot out.

"We should get matching shirts and shorts, like a uniform, that says SAFE Security." Jesse finished one pear and tossed the core in a public trash container. "There's no fucking reason to wear suits."

Personally I liked the way I looked in a suit. "We need to distinguish ourselves from the thugs out there."

"Frankie and I are planning a coup. We'd like your support." With three big bites, Jesse finished off the second pear. "I've already ordered shirts for everyone. Frankie found a place that'll do ladies' tees, so we ordered a couple for her and Autumn."

I'd known this was coming. Dean had waged a passive-aggressive war with Frankie and Jesse from the time we founded our company. "I sincerely don't care what you wear. I'll stick with my suits, though, and so will Dean."

He frowned. "I'll remember this the next time you want backup."

Since I rarely disagreed with Dean or Frankie, I wasn't worried. The elevator to the fourth floor took forever. It seemed the closer I got to Autumn, the more impatient I was to see her. I couldn't deny the pang of disappointment when I saw her empty desk.

Jesse clapped me on the shoulder before heading down the hall toward his office. "She's around somewhere."

My office was in the other direction, and so I went there first. Autumn had asked for permission to get into my safe, and she hadn't texted me photos of her success. Perhaps she'd been spending time with her new friend instead. My door was closed, and when I tried the knob, I found it locked. As I fished the key from my pocket, I noticed that Dean's door was open, so I poked my head inside to let him know we were back. What I found stopped my heart.

Autumn sat cross-legged on the floor next to Dean's safe—the one he kept behind a false panel in the bookcase. She had her graphing pad in one hand and the bell of her stethoscope in the other. Her eyes were

69

closed, and she wore a serene expression as she slowly spun the dial.

"What are you doing?" My question came out harsh because I couldn't believe she would break into Dean's office, search it, and try to get into his private safe.

Her eyes flew open, jubilation replacing serenity, and she shed the stethoscope. Arms wide, she flew across Dean's office.

Due to shock, my arms hadn't been open and waiting. However my body responded reflexively to greet my sub. I held her soft body against mine, taking a moment to indulge in the feel of her.

"You're back. I can't believe you're back." She wrapped her legs around my waist and lavished kisses on my face. "I've missed you so much." She paused in her kissing to lean back, concern wrinkling her chin. "Is everything okay?"

This wasn't the reunion I'd envisioned, but she had to know that this behavior was a violation of Dean's trust. Hell, it was a violation of everybody's trust. I was about to lay into her for breaking into Dean's office when he came sailing in.

He threw a file folder on his desk and sat down. "You're back early. Great. We'll debrief in thirty minutes. Do not have sex in my office."

Autumn giggled and wiggled against me. "I vote that we go to your office."

Dean hadn't chastised her. Since I was her Dom, it was reasonable that he expected me to do it. If our positions were reversed, I'd do the same thing. Disengaging the leg lock she had on me, I set her down gently. "Sugar, what the hell is going on in here?"

She waved an arm toward the safe. "Dean, do you mind if I leave my stuff there for now? I'm so close."

He glanced at the mess and shrugged. "Sure. Can I look at your notes?"

She slipped her hand into mine. "Absolutely." With a tug, she urged me out of his office and down the hall. "Oh, Sir. Dean has the sexiest safe I've ever seen. Just looking at it gets me all hot and bothered."

"You had his permission?" I had to make sure. Autumn had a different relationship with the concept of property ownership than most people.

She leaned against my closed door, arms crossed and a perturbed slant to her mouth. "Sir, you're kind of being an asshole right now. I missed the hell out of you, and you didn't even kiss me back. Did it look like Dean didn't know about and approve my activities?"

It didn't, and she had a point. However I'd asked her a question, and she'd failed to answer. "Sugar, I don't have the patience to deal with a SAM right now. Whether you like the question or not, I expect an answer."

Her eyes narrowed to slits. "Yes, Sir. I had permission. What's wrong? Are you jealous that I like his safe better?"

Rather than answer, I unlocked the door to my office and pushed her inside. "You're not going to sit comfortably for a week." My sub was an occasional SAM, a smart-assed masochist. She enjoyed goading me, mouthing off, and being a brat in order to push my sadist buttons. As mouthy as she was, she only got SAM-nasty when something weighed heavily on her heart or mind. I closed and locked the door.

Standing in the middle of my office, she crossed her arms and cocked one hip, daring me to take action even though she knew I had a meeting in a half hour. I'd planned to be balls deep in her by now, but my sub needed more from me. I met her dare with a firm, emotionless stare and stony silence. I didn't think she was to the point where she couldn't back down from being upset without physical discipline, so I controlled her with gentle dominance.

By incremental degrees, her gaze dropped and her arms uncrossed. "I'm sorry, Sir. I'm upset with Summer, and I took it out on you."

I was her safe harbor, one of the few people with whom she felt comfortable letting out her deepest, darkest feelings. Summer was supposed to be her other refuge. "Why are you upset with Summer?"

Her lower lip trembled until she pressed them together. I let her have this moment to compose herself. "She said I have to call her Jessica, and that I have to go by Breanna. Yesterday I went there, and she can walk. She needs a walker, and she's slower than a snail, but she's walking. When I told her that I'd talk to her doctor to see what we need to do to have her move in with us, she said she was moving in with Warren and Sylvia."

My heart went out to her. After Summer's accident, Autumn had dedicated her life to taking care of her comatose sister. In Autumn's mind, that commitment extended until Summer was able to live on her own and fend for herself. Add the complications posed by her birth parents into the mix, and I couldn't imagine how much she was hurting right now.

I took her in my arms and pressed her cheek to my shoulder. She snaked her arms around my neck and held me tightly. Though she didn't cry, I held her, giving her as much of my strength as she needed. I stroked her hair away from her face. "Sugar, you don't have to change your name unless you want to. Nobody gets to tell you what to be called."

"When I went to change my license, they made me put Breanna Zinn on the paperwork. They wouldn't let me

72

have Autumn Sullivan." She looked up at me, an unspoken appeal glimmering in her bright, green eyes. "I didn't change it, Sir."

I was not going to punish her for not following through right now, but eventually she needed to come to terms with her past and how it affected her present. "Another time."

"Thank you."

I pressed a kiss to her forehead. "You can't force Summer to live with us. Right now she's in a place where she wants to reconnect with your parents. That doesn't mean she loves you less. It's not a rejection."

Jerking back, she tried to loosen my hold, but I didn't let her go. "You knew they were moving closer?"

"You saw your parents?"

"They were at Breckenridge yesterday."

"I've been telling you to call them for three weeks. They wanted to tell you, and I respected their right to do so." I'd hoped they would wait until I was there to do it. They knew she coped better when I was with her. I'd thought the phone call would simply lead to them setting up a face-to-face, and I knew Autumn wouldn't meet until I was home.

She heaved a breathy sigh on my neck, and then she grazed her teeth on my bare skin. "I finished all the other items on the list."

This meant she was over her emotional crisis for now. I let her change the subject back to the one I'd originally wanted to pursue. "That makes three rewards and two punishments for getting mouthy."

This time she eased back to look up at me, and I gave her the necessary slack. She frowned. "One for being a smartass when we had phone sex and one for being upset with Summer and taking it out on you?"

"Being manipulative with your phrasing doesn't change the fact that there was a transgression, Sugar." I squeezed one of her ass cheeks. "Tonight. I'll leave the gag off. Right now, I want to show you how much I missed you." With that, I captured her lips for a searing kiss.

Softening, she yielded to my dominance. I teased the seam of her lips with my tongue, and she opened to me. She slid a hand into my hair while the other one trailed down my chest. I ran my hands from her ass, up her back, to her hair, and back down again. I wanted all of her soft curves pressed against me. She moaned loudly, and with a vicious yank of her hair, I broke the kiss to trail sucking bites down the side of her neck.

She loosened my tie and worked the buttons on my shirt. "If I get your shirt off, it counts as second base."

That was a challenge I couldn't ignore. Her shirt didn't have buttons. I lifted it over her head and unlatched her bra with expert precision. "Too late. I stole the base."

She grasped my dick through the fabric of my pants. I felt the heat of her palm and the gentle pressure of her fingers. "I think I'll take third."

I finished removing my tie, and I used it to bind her wrists. "I'm holding out for a home run."

Wearing only dress slacks and heels, she faced me with her breasts bared and her wrists bound. This travesty couldn't continue. I undid her pants and eased them down her long legs, kissing her flesh as I went down. She rested her palms on my shoulder to step out of each pant leg.

Now she wore heels, plain cotton panties, and my tie—still too much fabric. Through her panties, which were soaked through, I kissed her mons. "You're very turned on."

"I know, Sir. Getting my hands on a new safe does that to me."

I chuckled at her joke before blowing hot air through the cotton, and then I slowly eased her panties down those luscious legs. Without being told, she widened her stance so that she stood the way I liked. Using my thumbs, I spread her pussy lips apart and circled my tongue around her clit. I'd missed drinking this sweet nectar. I felt her hands in my hair, her fingers spreading to let the strands run between them. My hair wasn't long, but I had enough for her to grab.

She moaned, a soft sound, and I added a finger to the mix. I swirled it through her juices, massaging her entire labia until she twisted her fists in my hair and hissed. This quiet lover wasn't my sweet Sugar. I slid two fingers into her vagina, on the hunt for her sweet spot. Fingering her as I flicked my tongue over and around her clit, I drove her to the edge. When she cried out, a prelude to a climax, I stopped.

I sucked my fingers clean, and then I led her to the lone sofa in my office. "Lay down, Sugar. Put your hands above your head, your left leg on the back of the sofa, and your right foot on the floor."

With this beautiful tableau before me, I undressed. First I finished unbuttoning my shirt. She watched, her appreciative gaze following my hands as I revealed my chest. Her breathing quickened, and so I teased her by slowly stripping out of my pants and boxers.

"You're smoking hot, Sir. Any chance you'll turn around and let me ogle your fantastic ass?"

What the hell—I loved to indulge my bratty sub.

She hissed when my back was to her. "Who did that to you, Sir? Whose ass do I need to kick?"

I had no idea what she was talking about, so I twisted around to see a long bruise above my hip. Thinking back to my recent activities, I figured it was from the belt I'd used to rappel to Rybakov's terrace. Since it was for short distances, we didn't have the kind that went around the legs to spread the weight load. "Jesse. The rappelling belts he brought kind of suck."

She nodded, a fierce glint to her emerald eyes that did not match the soft, submissiveness of her pose. "I can show you which ones will work better."

I settled between her legs. "Later. Right now, you're pleasing your Dominant." I lined my cock up with her opening.

As I sank into her soft, hot body, she gasped. "I hope so. My Dominant sure is pleasing me right now."

I went slowly, drawing it out to tease sighs and gasps from her. I caressed her skin, reacquainting myself with the smooth texture of her thighs and hips before traveling upward. She submitted to my kisses and arched into my touch when I closed my hands around her breasts. She clawed at the leather of the sofa, and her thighs trembled against my hips. I reveled in the power she gave me with her surrender and her increasingly loud moans.

"Oh, God. Sugar, you feel like heaven."

"Welcome to the pearly gates, Sir."

We were close, and I wanted to feel her cling to me. "Wrap your legs around me, Sugar, and you can move your arms."

She encircled my hips with those long legs, locking her ankles together to keep me close, and then she brought her arms down, doing her best to hold onto me even though her wrists were still bound. "Harder, Sir. Don't hold back. I can take it."

I knew she could, but I liked what I was doing, and I knew it would deliver an orgasm that would leave her a trembling mess. Altering the angle of my thrust, I luxuriated in her silky heat until I couldn't stand it anymore. My balls drew up as her pussy convulsed and she screamed, and with one last thrust, I buried my cock deep. Wave after wave of climax washed over me, and I rested my full weight on my beautiful, quick-witted sub.

She held me close and stroked my hair even though her hands still shook from her orgasm. When Dean knocked on the door to tell me the meeting was starting, she tightened her hold. With all the love and tenderness in my heart, I kissed her again, and the next time I tried to pull away, she let me go.

We dressed quickly, and she tied my tie.

"I *am* sorry, about earlier. I shouldn't have been so snarky to you."

I kissed her nose. "You're forgiven. We'll talk more about Summer and your parents later, okay?"

"It's done. I've said everything."

"You're still angry and upset. We'll talk tonight, and I'll take you to see her tomorrow morning."

Her gaze darted away, and for the first time, she looked unexcited at the prospect of seeing her sister. "Or we could just stay home and have sex all day. I have about twenty minutes left on that safe, and I don't have anywhere else to be."

Until we discussed exactly what had happened, I wouldn't know how to help her, so I didn't consent one way or the other. I had to go, so I pressed a kiss to her forehead. "Don't leave without me. You're my ride home."

After every case, the four of us got together and debriefed. We reported out where we'd been and what we'd done. We talked about problems that had cropped up and how we'd solved them. We brainstormed different ways we could have responded in a scenario or approached a problem. It was half therapeutic and half business. The next time we found ourselves in a similar situation, we'd have more solutions in our arsenals.

Since we'd both had relatively routine cases, we talked for about an hour. That worked for me. Autumn would be finished with Dean's safe and waiting for me to take her home so that we could make up for being away from each other for five days.

As I rose to leave, Frankie lifted a finger. "Not so fast. We have one more item on our agenda."

We never had written agendas. This was a formal conversation, a model we'd found helpful to hone our skills, but nobody ever wrote down anything. Frankie regarded me with somber, dark brown eyes, so I sat back down. "Okay. What is it?"

"It's Autumn." Frankie pressed her lips together as if she didn't quite know how to proceed.

This couldn't be good. I felt a little blindsided. "What did she do?"

Dean folded his hands on the table. "Nothing."

I gestured for Frankie or him to continue. She said she'd been good, and I believed her. Autumn might be manipulative, and she might like to see how far she could bend rules, but she wasn't a liar.

"That's the problem." Frankie changed chairs. She'd been sitting across from me and next to Jesse, and now she parked herself next to me. She set her hand over mine. "We have an office manager who doesn't have access to reports or accounting. She can't do her job. I

78

know I wasn't around when you hired her, but I was genuinely happy that you guys got us an office manager. We need one."

Dean's expression wavered between guilt and resolve before settling on the latter. "We've been going slow, letting you decide what she can and can't be allowed to do, but it's been a month. She's frustrated that she can't do much except make coffee, and we're frustrated because we can't give her things to do like we should be able to."

I looked around the table, studying the faces of my three closest friends. Even Jesse seemed to be on board with this ambush, and he'd been with me for the past week. Then I remembered that he'd brought this up while we were staking out Rybakov. Had Autumn vented her frustration on them instead of just me? "Did Autumn put you up to this?"

"No." Frankie squeezed my hand and let it drop. "She has no idea that we're talking about this. Far as I can tell, she has faith that she can wait you out. Having spent some time with her over the last month, I've realized that she's a stubborn optimist about most things. Either that, or she's really good at keeping her head in the sand. I don't think she realizes the depth of your obstinacy."

She knew that I went thirteen years without speaking to my father and that I planned to never talk to him again. She knew very well how stubborn I could be. But she hadn't wronged me the way my father had, and so she had no reason to think I wouldn't eventually let her assume the full weight of her responsibilities as office manager.

I appealed to Dean and Jesse. "She said she wanted to open a bakery. You've tasted her baked goods. She has a real shot at being successful."

Dean nailed me with a steady look. "Correct me if I'm wrong, but didn't she say that was her goal before Summer's accident?"

It had been. Dreams didn't die—or so I hoped. "And?"

He barely lifted a brow in response to my challenge. "If she really loved baking, she would have found a way to continue that over the last three years. I think that's one possibility she entertained after they broke away from their father. It's probably the one farthest, ideologically speaking, from the activities they'd previously pursued."

"She wants to be here," Jesse added. "She's been very clear about that. Not a day goes by that she doesn't ask me to train her on something, and I'm getting tired of finding reasons not to. I've seen her in action, David. Her ability to argue for what she wants is a grifter's gift. She knows you're at the root of my refusal, and it's sad when she just meekly gives in. Autumn isn't meek."

"Jesse's right. I'm afraid that you're strangling her spirit, and that's what you like about her." Dean's cheeks reddened. "Yesterday when she saw my Vault, I thought she was going to have a spontaneous orgasm. She stroked it. I felt like a voyeur."

I'd seen Autumn eye a safe with an appreciative gleam, and so I had no trouble picturing her lusting after his Vault. "Is that why you let her take a crack at it?"

He shrugged. "She's good at finessing safes open. That's a handy skill for those times we need to get in and out without leaving a trace. We can't always pry open a safe or a vault and leave behind the remains, and sometimes they're too heavy or big to sneak out."

80

As none of us ever had an issue with a locked door, I didn't think much of this. "That's not an office manager skill."

Frankie patted my arm. "David, if I'm on a mission, and I have something in my safe that I need, it would be nice to know that my office manager can get it out and send it to me. We've run across this problem before."

She was right. I looked Frankie in the eye. "You really think she can handle it?"

Frankie snorted. "I think she could handle being in a mission control position. Think about the times when we've had one of us to coordinate the different parts of a mission. They run smoother."

With Autumn's experience, she'd know exactly what to look for and how to direct us. It was more than an office manager should do, but it was right up her alley. With a graceless nod, I gave in. "Let me tell her, though. I was going to take tomorrow off."

Dean drummed his fingers on the table three times. "You can take a few days, but Autumn can't. She needs to learn the system and get all the paperwork done for the missions we all just went on."

I glared. "That's bullshit."

Frankie got up and fired her parting shot over her shoulder. "If she'd been trained before now, she'd probably just be finishing up now, so this is really your fault. That's what obstinacy gets you."

No Good Deed Goes Unpunished

Today rocked in inverse proportionality to yesterday sucking. I don't know what happened in their meeting, but afterward I found myself in a new office. Dean and David cleared out the smaller conference room and moved my desk in there. Jesse and Frankie installed a computer with two monitors. Frankie even had to remove some drywall to access the private network. This excited me on two fronts: not only was I finally going to be able to prove my value, but now I had another place where I could hide things.

In my search of Dean's office, I'd come across his hidden panel fairly easily, and I'd found two more places where things could be hidden. He'd asked me not to pry up the floorboards, or else I probably could have found a couple more. As they worked, I scoped the room for more hiding spots. Call me crazy, but it seemed that a security firm would have more reason to need these kinds of spots than most other kinds of businesses.

Plus I still had five thousand in cash and copies of Brick Dixon's illegal title papers in my purse from helping

Chloe Dixon, and I planned to hide that money until I could gather the courage to tell David what I'd done.

Jesse spent some time going over the communications software, and he promised to train me fully in the coming weeks. Frankie walked me through the accounting program, which didn't take long because it was similar to what I'd used when I'd been in accounting at CalderCo. Dean set up a meeting time for the next day so that he could go over the client and mission reporting protocols. He also gave me a skeleton key to all the interior doors and the access code to arm and disarm the security alarm.

David was the only one who didn't have training to contribute, and I think that was due to the fact that he was most likely struggling with accepting my expanded role at SAFE Security. At the end of the day, I found him in the gym. He and Dean were on the mats, grappling for the upper hand. Both wore tight, black cotton shirts emblazoned with the SAFE Security logo and black cargo pants that said SAFE Security down the leg. I hadn't seen those clothes before, and I wondered if they'd been in that big box that had been delivered for Jesse three days ago. I'd put it in his office with the rest of his mail. It would be nice not to have to pick a lock every time I needed to get into one of their offices.

Dean slashed his fist at David's side, but David hopped out of the way. Then he pivoted, dropped to the ground, and swept Dean's legs out from under him. Though David was built—a lean and muscular, formidable opponent in his own right—Dean was larger. His shoulders were broader, and he had bulky chest muscles and thicker thighs. Still the two of them were evenly matched. Dean controlled his fall so that he came down on David. Though David tried to roll out of reach, Dean still caught him in a choke hold.

I gasped because I didn't see a way out of that hold, but David did. With an elbow jab and a twist, he was free. I sat on a weightlifting bench and watched them grapple. Their moves were awe-inspiring, honed by years of practice. They were as graceful as dancers, which made me wonder if David would want to take me dancing. We'd never been. Actually I couldn't remember the last time I'd been out dancing. Julianne had never been able to convince me to go, so it had to be before the accident.

"Sugar? Are you okay?"

Startled, I glanced up to find David standing over me, wiping his face down with a towel. "Fine."

"You were frowning quite severely."

"I was thinking that I couldn't remember the last time I'd been dancing." I looked around and found that we were alone. "Did Dean leave?"

"A few minutes ago." He sat on the bench next to mine and draped the towel around his neck. "Look, I want you to be sure about this."

I stared blankly. It didn't seem like he was talking about where I might want to go on a date. "About what?"

"Working here. Being the office manager. I don't want you to choose a path in life unless it's your heart's desire. What I do shouldn't figure into your life choices." He dabbed the end of the towel on his forehead.

"You think I'm here because of you?"

"I know you're here because of me, and I know you had other dreams and aspirations before you met me." He regarded me with a steady gaze, his rich brown eyes heavy with meaning.

"Is that why you've been dragging your feet for the past month?"

"Maybe." His gaze roamed my face. "I love you, but I don't love when you're in danger. I want to protect and take care of you, and if you're here, that brings a whole new set of risks. Our potential clients aren't always above board. It's dangerous work, and that danger sometimes comes here."

I took his hands in mine, but he reversed the possessiveness of the action so that he held mine. "Is this about me following my dreams or your need to squirrel me away in an ivory tower?"

He laughed, accepting the fact that I'd caught him. "Both. I'm dealing with the one, though. You're not an ivory tower kind of woman. You'd find a way out faster than your prince could rescue you. Sugar, I want you to be sure about working here."

I'd always been sure. This was a version of the kind of work I'd been training for since I was a child. "Sir, I want to work here. If I'm going to be totally honest, I want to eventually do what you do. However I know you're not ready for that. Until then, I think I'd be a good resource to help plan missions."

He stood and pulled me up with him. "That's what Frankie said." Still holding my hand, he led me to the locker room.

"She's teaching me self-defense. She put me on a workout plan."

"Awesome. That's all I need—a SAM who knows what she's doing when she fights back." David was always able to subdue me fairly easily.

I lifted his hand and kissed his sweaty palm. "You're due for a challenge, Sir, though if you choke me, I'm more likely to safeword than fight you off."

Dean was finishing up when we came in. He'd showered and changed back into his suit. He shoved his dirty clothes into a bag. "I like these shirts and pants that Jesse got, but we are not adopting them as our uniform."

I liked them, mostly because they looked hot on David. "When you're breaking and entering, you don't want to advertise where you're from. Choose easily forgettable clothing with no labels that can blend into your surroundings. These are good if you're hanging around the office or doing service work in the community. They're sharp, and they're good advertising."

He pointed to a folded stack on a bench. "Those are yours. I'd prefer if you used them in the gym and continued to dress professionally when you're upstairs. Welcome to the team, Sugar." With that parting shot, he kissed my cheek and left.

"I hate when he does that." David pulled his shirt over his head, revealing every ripped inch of his magnificent torso, which was pumped up and glistening from his recent workout.

"I like when you do that."

David fought a smile. "All you think about is sex."

"When you start stripping, it's hard to think about anything else."

"I meant that I hate when he calls you Sugar." He peeled out of his sweatpants and underwear.

"He knows, and so does Jesse. It's a passive-aggressive thing they do because it gets under your skin and facilitates bonding." I followed him to the shower and frowned when he pulled the curtain.

"How does pissing me off facilitate bonding?"

"It lets me know that they care about me, and it lets you know that you can count on them to look out for me when you can't. I'm important to them because I'm important to you. That's how you guys operate." I opened the curtain to see him soaping his chest and arms. "Don't

86

let it bother you. I disliked when you first started calling me that, but I got over it."

At the time, he'd insisted that I was lying about my name, and so he'd decided to call me Sugar in honor of my "sweet ass."

He finished washing and rinsed. Then he emerged, dripping water, and pulled me to him. Warm water soaked through my clothes, and I was going to have a watermark in the shape of his hand on my butt. "I love your sweet ass, Sugar. It's mine. You are mine."

I cupped his face between my hands. "It's not the same when Jesse and Dean say it. I'm yours, Sir. I belong to you and only you."

His kiss was full of sweetness and yearning. "Let's go home. We'll pick up some takeout for dinner. When we get home, you'll have sixty seconds to get naked, and you'll stay that way until you have to go to work tomorrow."

"You're such a romantic caveman, Sir."

He grunted, imitating a Neanderthal, and smacked my ass. "Get your things, brat. I want to be out the door in ten minutes."

An hour later, I found myself seated across from David at the walnut dining table that occupied the space next to the living room and across from the kitchen. He called it a dining room, but it seemed to me that we could use this space for anything at all, which was probably the point of the open concept. A hallway separated the common area from the two bedrooms and bathrooms that made up the other half of the apartment. It was far nicer than anywhere I'd ever lived, and though I had no problem living here, I wasn't attached to the space. David, though—I was firmly attached to him.

Thai food takeout containers littered the surface. Most of them were empty because we'd been hungry. Due to his order to be naked, I sat on a towel and speared a piece of chicken in peanut sauce. "I love this place. They make good food. That reminds me—I owe Jesse a cake."

"And banana walnut muffins for me." David's brows wrinkled with worry. "Chocolate cherry as well."

I wouldn't have time to do all this baking tonight. He had every intention of scening with me tonight, and I was very much in favor of that activity over baking. "Are you worried that I'd forget about you, Sir?"

His attention snapped to me. "You're going to think of me every time you sit down tomorrow."

I had two punishments and at least one "fun-ishment" coming my way. In all likelihood, I wouldn't be sitting tomorrow. David wasn't a pushover, and he took his duties as my Sir very seriously. I smiled sweetly. "I think of you all the time, Sir. I live to serve you."

At this he snorted a laugh, a response to my attempt at manipulation and not a disagreement at the validity of my statement. "Tell me what happened yesterday when you saw your parents and Jessica."

His use of that name for Summer made me stiffen my spine. I didn't want to talk about it. I wanted to have a mind-numbing scene with my Sir. "I have nothing more to say about that."

His irises darkened to a fathomless deep brown, and his lips thinned with displeasure. Sir wasn't going to let me get away with my usual tricks tonight. A firm disciplinarian occupied the head of this table. "That's not an acceptable response."

Of course, I wasn't going to fall in line easily. My stiff smile turned flippant. "That's all you're going to get. We had a conversation. I didn't like some things that were said, and I left. End of story."

He threw his paper napkin onto his plate and leaned against the back of his chair. Though his pose appeared relaxed and casual, I knew he was poised for a violent start to the scene. "Sugar, you're not going to win this."

That was reassuring. If I won, then we would both lose. Still I huffed and rolled my eyes, two things that had worked to set him off in the past. "If I have nothing more to say about it, then you can't make me talk."

He slid his chair away from the table and crooked a finger at me.

I wiped my mouth and slammed my napkin onto the table. When I got up, the chair scraped on the floor, which hadn't been my intention, but it did the job. I stopped next to him with both hands on my hips. "You rang, Sir?"

"Did you get enough to eat?"

Though I'd had plenty, I shrugged.

David took that as an affirmative response. If I was still hungry, I'd call yellow and ask him to delay the start of the scene. He reached up, grabbed me by the back of my neck, and forced me over his lap. The move was swift, and I didn't have time to protest. I barely had time to fling my hands out to brace them on the floor to keep my head from hitting.

He rubbed his palm over my ass. "Let's get your punishment out of the way first, Sugar. There's five for verbal fouls." He smacked my bare ass five times, walloping my flesh so hard that the sound echoed through the kitchen. "Then there are five for coming without permission."

These five didn't hurt as much because my ass was already smarting from the first five.

He kept one hand on my nape, pressing down to keep me in place, and he rubbed his palm over my tender ass. "Ready to talk?"

"You have a naked woman over your lap, and you want to talk? I'm beginning to doubt your masculinity." This was the portion of the evening when my mouth went on autopilot. All my anxiety and anger would come out in the form of name-calling and goading. The nastier I got, the more punishment Sir would dish out. Only when I reached my limit and stopped being a smartass would he take me in his arms and hold me tenderly.

"Go stand in front of the ottoman."

A bank of windows ran the entire width of his apartment, lining the living room and the master bedroom. The moment we'd walked through the door, he'd hit the button to bring down the curtains and ordered me to undress. The ottoman, a padded footstool as long as the sofa, was in the living room, and this order was one he gave quite frequently. I centered myself and stood in a pose that could only be described as half defiant and half submissive.

Noises came from the dining room, the sounds of him clearing the table and from the periphery of my vision, I watched him dump the dirty dishes into the sink without scraping them. He set the food containers on the counter, and then he disappeared in the direction of the bedroom.

He didn't have a dungeon. Though the second bedroom would be a logical place for that kind of setup, he actually had it decorated as a guest room. All his BDSM gear was kept in drawers and closets in the master bedroom.

Soon I felt him behind me. He set out a crop, two floggers, a paddle, and a particularly vicious set of nipple clamps on the ottoman. I eyeballed the selection until he distracted me by gathering my hair in his hand. He smoothed it back from my face, twisted it into a knot, and secured it with rubber bands. I scoffed at this. "Now you're fixing my hair? What's next? Are we going to paint each other's nails?"

He chuckled, and I knew why. That was a lame line. I could do better. He pressed his bare chest to my back, and I resisted the urge to lean against his strong body and give in. His hands closed over my breasts, kneading and lifting them, and then he focused his attention on my nipples, teasing them to aroused peaks. Once I was breathing hard, he spun me to face him. Before I could think of anything to say, he locked his lips around one pebbled nipple. With his teeth and tongue, he coaxed it to a softly swollen state, and then he treated the other in a similar manner. Once he had them exactly how he wanted them, he fitted the first clamp onto the right one and tightened it down until I flinched and whimpered. Only then did he ease it the slightest bit. Then he treated my left nipple to a similar torture.

It hurt. My nipples were fairly sensitive, and he knew that these clamps would cause some serious pain. He also knew what I could handle, and that's why he backed it off a quarter turn of the screw. I tried to distract myself by checking out his half naked body, but that only worked for so long.

Once he had those in place, he attached small, weighted rings to each one. I hissed. "Son of a bitch. One day I'm going to tie you down and do this to you."

"You're not tied down." He turned me back to face the ottoman, and then he bit into the meat of my right shoulder.

I cried out and elbowed him sharply in the stomach. He grunted, and he stopped biting.

He added another weight to each of the rings on my nipple clamps. "Every time you attack me, you're asking for another weight." The wet heat of his mouth closed over my shoulder again, and he bit harder.

Between the pain in my shoulder and the sharp burn of my nipples, I whimpered in protest. The shoulder pain morphed first, becoming a pleasurable sensation that softened my whimper. Then his mouth was gone, leaving behind the sting of desire.

"Tell me about yesterday morning." His low baritone vibrated against my bare neck. "You're upset with Jessica and with your parents."

I sincerely didn't want to think about them right now. "I'm upset with you because you know I hate these clamps. They do not get me off."

He chuckled. "No orgasms for you tonight, Sugar, not until you tell me what I want to hear."

This wasn't the kind of game where he would forbid me from climaxing and drive me to do it anyway just so he could punish me. Nope, this was the kind of game where he was going to get his sadistic way and I wasn't going to enjoy the process. "You're a bastard." I pressed my lips together because I was mad, and I exhaled heavily through my nose to try to mitigate the pain.

"It's a preferable way to look at my parentage. Bend over and brace yourself."

Calling him a bastard may not seem nice, but he'd rather that his father wasn't related to him. In retrospect, I needed to think of better things to call him. I bent over and spread my palms on the ottoman. The weights on my nipple clamps swayed, bringing a fresh wave of pain and a groan from me. Sir kicked my feet farther apart, and from the edge of my vision, I watched the crop slide away.

The leather flap traced a pattern down the back of my thigh. "Why am I doing this, Sugar?"

"Because you're a sadistic, retro Val Kilmer look-alike who resents the comparison and gets off on the suffering of others, Sir."

"Wrong answer." He brought the crop down across my upper thigh. "Care to try again?" This time he didn't wait for me to respond. He lit into my backside with the crop, peppering the stinging blows over my ass and thighs.

I was not quiet. I shouted cries of protest and pain, but I neither moved nor safeworded. I needed this, and we both knew it. By the time he paused, I'd lost count of how many blows I'd endured. My legs trembled with the effort it took to stay on my feet, and I was furious to a depth I hadn't been when we'd started.

He slid his palm over my heated flesh. "How are you doing, Sugar?"

"I think you're the biggest jerk on the face of the Earth, Sir."

"You worship the ground I walk on." He exchanged the crop for the paddle and smacked it against my abused backside. "You're mad at Jessica because you feel like she's abandoning you and choosing your parents over her relationship with you, and you refuse to accept your parents in your life." Spanks punctuated his explanation.

My ass was on fire, and tears smarted at the corners of my eyes. I couldn't believe that he had taken to calling her by that name. "I might hate you."

"You couldn't hate a wasp that stung you."

"Yes, I can." Tears streamed down my cheeks. I was crying in earnest now.

"You don't even hate the woman who tried to frame you for embezzlement and kill you."

Truthfully I didn't. She'd been captured, and now she was in prison serving consecutive life sentences for the many people she'd confessed to killing. Justice had been served. He released the nipple clamps, and fire raced through my system. My arms and legs gave way, and Sir caught me as I fell. He held me as I sobbed.

"I don't want to call her Jessica. I don't want her to want to be called Jessica. I don't want to be mad at her." I buried my face in his neck and grasped at his chest. "I don't want to be mad at anybody."

He pressed a wad of tissues into my fist. "It's okay to be mad. It's an emotion, and you have every right to feel it, Sugar."

I wiped my face and blew my nose. "It hurts my heart to be mad at...Jessica." I forced myself to call her by that name because it's what she'd asked me to do.

He stroked my hair, some of which had come loose from the knot he'd made at the start of our scene, and kissed my forehead. "The only way to get past it is to go through it. I wish I could make it all better for you, but I can't. I can, however, be here to help you through it." He rocked me in his arms until my last hiccup subsided.

I feathered little kisses along the line of his jaw, letting the short stubble there scratch my lips. "Thank you, Sir. I don't feel so achingly furious anymore."

"Good." He stayed still and let me lavish kisses on his face and neck. "You really think I look like Val Kilmer?"

"Mmm." I answered him dreamily. "From Top Gun." At one of the houses we'd rented growing up, we'd found a cache of VHS tapes, and that had been one of our favorites. We'd watched it until the machine ate the tape. "The volleyball scene."

He nodded thoughtfully. "A military man. I'm okay with that."

"But sexier. Your eyes are so much more expressive."

"Even better. Listen, Sugar, you were very stubborn this time, and your backside needs aftercare." He stood, lifting me in his arms.

"But the flogger—you haven't used the flogger yet." I leaned my head against his shoulder and snuggled into his warmth. Sir was very good with floggers, and the idea that I wouldn't feel the sting of his lash made me a little sad.

"We're not going to get to it tonight. I only brought it out in case you broke quickly. If that happened, I planned to flog you into subspace." He took me down the hall and into the bedroom as he explained

I made a pathetic, whiney sound. "I can handle more."

He chuckled and changed direction, heading into the bathroom. "You'll be singing a different puppy song when the endorphins wear off. Look."

He'd paused in front of the mirror over the sink, and I lifted my face from his neck to see that he'd done a number on me. A maze of welts peppered my thighs and ass. Those were from the crop. On top of that, he'd paddled me because he knew I could barely stand that thick leather implement.

My face hadn't fared that well either. My eyes were red and puffy, swollen from crying, as were my lips and nose. Crying didn't give me the haunted or luminous appearance I wished it would. I sniffled and studied my beautiful welts. "This is a great time to get one of those stand-up desks."

"If you'd like." He took me back into the bedroom and set me on the bed. "Lay face down, Sugar."

Aftercare was a time we both cherished. He rubbed ointment over my welts and arnica into my muscles to help with the soreness and bruising. Then he expanded his ministrations and massaged the soreness from my back and neck. Once I was as limp as overcooked spaghetti, he stretched out next to me, and we snuggled.

"I know this is hard for you, Sugar."

I stretched, arching my hips against his pelvis—he still wore pants—and I dragged my teeth along a sensitive point of his neck. "Mmmm. Snuggling with you is a strenuous activity." I knew where he was going with this, and I sought to divert his attention.

He rolled to pin me in place, immobilizing my hands so I couldn't distract him with carnal touching. "Respecting her wish to be called Jessica is great progress. I'm proud of you for accepting it. This means you're moving past denial and into anger. Embrace the anger, Sugar. You're facing a devastating change and loss. Like I said, if you're ever going to get past it, you have to move through it."

I studied the face of the man I loved, noting the sharpness of his cheekbones and the fullness of his lips. More than that, I drowned in the depth of the love radiating from his soft eyes and heavy expression. As much as I wanted to avoid Jessica, our parents, and all the issues associated with them, I knew I couldn't, not without losing them all. Only I wasn't sure if I was willing to do what it took to keep them in my life. Wordlessly, I nodded.

He must have known how much I needed him, how much I needed physical evidence of his love, because he kissed me tenderly. His grip on my wrists eased, and his hands moved over my body. He made love to me slowly, showing me how much I meant to him—and I did my best to make sure he knew that he was the center of my world.

The next morning I meant to wake up early to make muffins for David. Instead I woke to the scrumptious aroma of bacon and coffee. Fighting gravity, I struggled to peel my eyelids upward, and I was shocked to find light streaming into the bedroom. I shifted and stretched, and my backside protested. I groaned.

"You're up." David came in and sat on the bed next to me. "This is quite a milestone for you."

Moving slowly, I sat up. "I know. It's my first day of actual work. What are you doing up so early?" He'd foiled my plan to surprise him with baked goods.

He chuckled, the low timbre vibrating pleasantly along my psyche. "It's not early, Sugar. You slept in."

I never slept in, but not from lack of trying. It always took me at least a month to acclimate to sleeping in a new place, and even then I was an early riser. I looked at the digital clock on his nightstand and found that it was almost ten. Scrambling out of bed, I almost tripped over his feet. "Shit. I'm late for work. Why didn't you wake me?"

"I called Frankie and told her that you'd be in this afternoon." He followed me to the bathroom.

Thankfully I was still naked. I turned the water on in the shower and grabbed my toothbrush. "I don't want special treatment."

Grabbing my wrist, he pulled me to him. "Sugar, in case you haven't noticed, we don't keep regular hours."

"But I'm not a mercenary yet. I'm the office manager."

He sighed, probably at my use of a qualifier and not at the fact that I'd called them all mercenaries. "You'll take an active part in missions over my cold, dead, rotting corpse."

While I accepted that he had a dangerous job, I had faith that he was smarter and stronger than any adversary he'd encounter. "Sir, don't be melodramatic. If you died, I'd have you embalmed or cremated. There would be no rotting involved."

Being such an intelligent guy, he probably figured abandoning that topic was the best course of action. Though I didn't intend to press my agenda right now, I would eventually, and David was going to like it even less than he liked letting me actually manage the office. "You didn't comment on your milestone."

I didn't want to think about Jessica or our parents, but David wasn't going to let me get away with avoidance. "I'd call it a breakthrough more than a milestone."

"I meant the fact that you slept for ten hours. This is the first time you haven't been up at dawn. You're finally settling into your new home." The shower curtain slid back, and he looked me up and down. Appreciation marked his features. "Maybe now you'll start calling this *our* apartment instead of referring to it as just mine."

I turned off the water, and he snagged my towel from the rack. I held still as he patted me dry, and I cooperated when he wanted to rub more arnica into my sore muscles.

"The welts are mostly gone, but there's some bruising."

I turned so that I could see the reflection, and I saw that most of the marks had vanished. "All those pretty welts. I guess that means you'll need to flog me tonight."

He lifted his brows. "Maybe. If you get home early enough. I have other plans for this luscious body."

That meant tonight's scene would be about pleasure. I glanced toward the bedroom. Last night I'd experienced the single best night of sleep in years, and I ached to do it again. Still I wanted to put in a full day at work, and I was already late. David caged me against the edge of the sink and captured my lips in a searing kiss. Molten fire raced to my private spots, and his knowing caress moved over my skin.

I broke the kiss, but he just moved his lips to explore along my neck and collarbone. "Sir, you don't play fair."

He ground his hardness against my stomach. "Fairs are full of clowns, and I'd just as soon avoid clowns."

I slid my hands over his shoulders and let my head fall back. "You're thinking of the circus."

"Actually I was thinking of taking you back to bed and showing you how unfair I can be." One hand moved to my pussy, and he rubbed it over my slit.

"You need a bed for that?"

"Yes. I want to tie you up and do things to you. Naughty and kinky things." He undid his pants, lifted me onto the counter, and entered me swiftly. "But I know how much this job means to you, so I'll make do with an appetizer." He withdrew partway. "But tonight, I'm eating a full meal."

I wrapped my legs around his waist and held onto his shoulders as he turned the molten heat in my core into bubbling lava. He tangled his hand in my hair, and pulled hard, forcing my head back so that he could lave my breasts with his teeth and tongue. He sucked on my nipples, and until that moment I hadn't realized how sore they still were from the clamps last night. I cried out, half out of my mind with the pleasure-pain combination.

He mumbled against my flesh. "You're mine, Sugar. All mine."

"Yours, Sir," I agreed. "Completely yours." My orgasm loomed close, and then it crashed over me. I cried out, and my whole body shook.

Seconds later, he shouted and came, and he held me close until we were both breathing normally. Then he said one of the most romantic sentiments a man ever uttered. "I made bacon for you."

David insisted on driving me to work and walking me inside. "This way, I know you're going to leave at six." The elevator dinged, and he pressed his entry code into the keypad.

I'd seen him do this many times. If I wanted, I could get in and out using his code, but that wouldn't have been honest. And besides, it was the principle of the thing—I wanted my own code.

He noticed me watching him. "We need to upgrade our security with biometric scanning instead of just keypad entry."

I lifted a brow and opened the temporarily unlocked door. "Don't go through all that expense on my account. I know how to make a copy of your fingerprint."

The sound he made was a combination of a dry laugh and clearing his throat. "The place Jesse and I broke into had biometric entry parameters. It would have worked better for them if they'd also controlled roof access."

David and Jesse had filled me in on their adventure yesterday, telling me how they'd rappelled onto the target's balcony. I'd been a little jealous—that mission was right up my alley—but I'd swallowed it down and counseled myself to stay the course. Strategic patience was working. "I need to order different rappelling equipment for you guys."

100

"Hey, Sugar. I see you finally made it in. David, I thought you were taking the day off." Jesse stood in the empty lobby, a meaty file folder in his hand. He looked like he'd come from Dean's office.

"I am, but Autumn isn't. It's bullshit that we can't get the same days off." He kissed my cheek, but from the tension in the hand he wrapped around my arm, I knew he was struggling not to rise to Jesse's bait. "I'll see you at six, Sugar. Be good."

"I'll try, Sir. There are no guarantees in life, and I'd hate to disappoint you, but I'll give it my best effort. Perhaps flowers and chocolates might be a good incentive?"

Shaking his head, David left. I knew he was going to wait until I was out of earshot to laugh.

Jesse motioned in the direction of his office. "Give me twenty minutes, and then I'll go over the report protocols with you."

"Sounds great." I grinned. It felt great to finally be part of the team.

Following Jesse down the hall, I headed to my new office. Yesterday I'd identified several hiding places, and today I wanted to make use of them. For two days, I'd been carrying around five thousand dollars in cash and the fraud evidence I'd uncovered in Brick Dixon's office safe.

It didn't take long for me to see that my office door was open. Jesse must have noticed my frown. "Frankie finished fixing the hole in the drywall she made yesterday, and Dean repainted. He hates messes."

"I could have done that." In fact, I wanted to be the one to fix the drywall. It would have given me a chance to create another hiding place. When Jesse scooted past me to continue to his office, I put my hand on his arm. "Listen, Jesse, I have a favor to ask."

He paused. "Sure."

"Stop calling me Sugar. It drives David crazy."

Clouds of indecision floated through his clear blue eyes as he pondered my request. He chewed his lip. "Does it bother you?"

When he'd first started doing it, I'd been amused by David's reaction, but the fun had worn off—for me, at least. "It bothers David."

"But you're fine with it?" He pressed that point.

"I don't actually care. You don't mean it the same way he does. However it bothers him, and he's your friend. I'd appreciate if you could just call me Autumn."

He nodded thoughtfully, which wasn't acceptance. "Sorry, Sugar. No can do. I'd be a crappy friend if I didn't take every opportunity to bust his chops and keep him grounded. You make him too happy, and that means he's liable to forget himself, and that's dangerous in our line of work. Someone has to look out for him, and that's my job. Plus, it's fun, and I like to have fun." With that convoluted line of reasoning, he winked and continued to his office.

Rather than try to figure out what he meant, I set to work making a hidey-hole. Jesse would eventually come around, and I'd work on Dean as well. They could only spend so long goading David. Now that I was the office manager in reality, they'd let go of their passive-aggressive baiting and move onto the next thing.

The building was old, originally built around the time of the Great Depression, and so I walked the floor and listened for a squeak. When the subfloor wasn't firmly in place, it often came loose at the corners, and that produced a squeak. Unfortunately Dean's attention to detail meant the subfloor was firmly in place. I found no squeaks. Next I examined the edges of the floor because I knew they'd used interlocking hardwood, each nailed to the subfloor. If there was a weakness, it'd be at the leading edge.

My close study only made me realize that I'd have to pry off the molding in order to get at the floor. With a sigh, I unscrewed the vent cover for the cold air return. This void wouldn't have a duct where I could store my goods, so I pounded a nail into the stud to the left of the opening. Then I emptied everything from my bag except the items I wanted to hide. Sacrificing my purse, I hanged it from the nail and replaced the vent cover. I didn't always carry a bag or purse, and David probably wouldn't notice that I was coming home without it.

Thankfully I was able to complete my covert mission in time for my meeting. Jesse walked me through filing mission and expense reports for the job he'd done with David, and he tasked me with reviewing previous files to make sure nothing was missing. "Sometimes Dean forgets to turn in receipts, and it kills us at tax time."

I frowned. "Doesn't your accountant go over all that?"

"Yeah, but Skyler seems to miss a lot, probably because we don't give her access to mission reports." He tapped a few keys to close the files we'd been studying. "If you can see a mission report that mentions staying at a hotel we didn't plan to stay at, then you can double check to see if there's a receipt. Dean likes to throw them in his glove box and forget they exist."

"That doesn't seem like Dean. He's very meticulous."

Jesse laughed. "When it comes to the actual mission, manscaping, or the dress code, yeah. When it comes to accounting, no. He's not a numbers guy. That's David or me, and we're both tired of cleaning up Dean's bookkeeping messes. That's now your job."

"Financial janitor. Got it." Items started aligning themselves on my mental to-do list, and I rose to leave.

Before I could take a step, Jesse had one more thing. "Did you bake me that cake yet?"

I winced and tried to project regret. "Sorry. David occupied all my time. I'll try to get to it tomorrow night. What kind would you like?"

He frowned at one of his monitors. "Surprise me."

I took that as my cue to leave.

Absorbed in the fascinating world of travel receipts and mission reports, I nearly missed hearing my phone when it rang a few hours later. Since it was David's ringtone, I fumbled for the phone, which, thanks to my ingenious storage solution, was in my desk drawer because I no longer had a purse.

"Hi, Sir. How's your day off?"

"I think I'm busier when I stay home."

I didn't know what he had to do. Since my skills were underutilized here, I'd been using that pent-up frustration to keep the apartment clean. His wood had never been so polished. "Did you get through all the shows you recorded?"

"As a matter of fact, no. I've been shopping."

Anyone who says that shopping is a woman thing is an idiot. Most men I knew shopped way more than I did. However his tone clued me into possible items on his list. "Sex toys?"

"Just one. You're going to love it. I also picked up scallops. I'm going to make you an awesome dinner, which I will feed to you while you're naked, bound, and sitting on my lap."

Tonight's scene, I knew, would focus on satisfying his desires, and I was more than okay with that. Though he couldn't see it, I grinned. "That sounds heavenly."

"Are you busy now?"

"Yes. You guys have an incredible amount of paperwork for each mission, and some of you are better at completing it than others. It's good you have me to pick up the slack. I may have to kick Dean's butt, though."

David laughed. "Good luck, Sugar. Listen, I know this is maybe a little quick, but I've invited your family to dinner this weekend."

No words came to mind. Emotions, complex and heavy, weighted down my chest. He'd been pushing me to do this for a month, and I hadn't. I wasn't ready. I might never be ready.

"Sugar?"

"I wish you hadn't, Sir."

"One day, you'll look back on all this and thank me."

I wasn't so sure, but I kept the outrage and recriminations to myself. "I have to get back to work. I'll see you at six."

"I love you, Sugar."

I knew he did, and his misguided sense of affection drove him to do these things. That's why I would eventually forgive him. It didn't mean I liked or accepted his actions. We'd talk later, and I'd convince him to rescind the offer to my parents and brother. I could handle seeing Jessica. I exhaled hard. "I love you too, Sir."

The shortened day came to a close before I was ready to leave. The buzzer on the door sounded a half hour earlier than I expected, and I hurried to answer it. I didn't know why David would ring the bell when he had an access code. Maybe his arms were full with a bouquet of flowers and a box of chocolates. It might be cheesy and cliché, but that was the kind of gesture that would melt my heart. I had simple needs when it came to romance which was good because romance wasn't second nature to David.

At least the rest of the team was in the gym, so there would be no eye rolling or snarky comments that would only serve to dissuade David from spoiling his sub in front of them. As he spent most of his time with them, that would suck for me.

I peered at the surveillance feed to find Chloe Dixon on the other side of the door. A quick glance at the clock showed that I had fifteen minutes to get her out of there before David would likely show up for real. I opened the door, and she fell against me.

Blue eyes wide and highlighted tresses in disarray, she latched her fists onto the front of my blouse. "He's going to kill me. Please, it didn't work. I need all copies of the papers you took."

I pried her hands loose and led her down the hall to my office. "Let's sit down and talk." I guided her to a chair—they hadn't quite removed all the meeting furniture—and pulled another one close. Remaining calm, I exuded confidence and competence. "Tell me what happened."

"Brick, he was pissed when he found your note. At first he threw me out, and I was happy about that. I'd already packed my things and put them in storage, so all I needed to do was leave. I could send divorce papers by mail. It could all be handled through attorneys." She steepled her hands over her nose and mouth, and she tried to steady her breathing. "But something happened. You took something you shouldn't have."

I had no idea what she was talking about. Technically I'd stolen all the evidence in my possession. Some would

106

argue that I shouldn't have taken anything. "What do you mean?"

"A map. He was always looking up legends and local lore. He had dreams of finding buried treasure. I used to think it was cute, kind of endearing, but over time, every time he'd come up empty, he'd get angry and take it out on me. It stopped being fun." She sniffled, and her eyes darted toward the door at the sound of people talking in the hall.

I took her hand in mine. "It's okay. You're safe here. That's the rest of the team."

She appeared mollified for now. "This time is different. He's convinced he has actual proof that there's treasure. He thinks this is the mother lode." She lifted her shirt, revealing a network of fresh bruises on her ribs and stomach. "The night before last, he found me. He dragged me from my parents' house—I thought I wouldn't have to hide—beat me, and locked me in a closet. He said he'd never let me go. He left his goon guarding me, and when he opened the door to let me out to use the restroom, I grabbed his gun and shot him. Then I ran. I need the map. Just give back the map, and he'll let me go."

The appeal in her luminous blue eyes tugged at my heartstrings. I'd failed this woman, and she'd endured torture because of it. And now she was convinced that finding a map would help her situation. I knew it was an excuse, and that Brick Dixon might kill her rather than let her go. Still, there had been no map among the papers I'd taken. "Chloe, I didn't take a map. I only have forged title papers for stolen cars. That's all."

A fat tear dropped from her eye. "Did you see a map in there at all?"

"Yes, but I put it back. I had no idea what it was, and I didn't see how it could be used for leverage."

Her face fell, and she sobbed in earnest.

I rubbed her shoulder and made soothing sounds even though my insides were in turmoil. Not only had I fucked things up for Chloe, but I was going to be in hot water with David. I had to come clean, and he was going to have to fix my mistake. This was going to sideline me for months, perhaps years. Yeah, I was feeling sorry for both Chloe and myself. I'm good at multitasking like that.

The phone rang, but I let it go to voicemail.

"If I don't bring him the map, he's going to kill me." She choked on the words, and I believed that she feared for her life. "There's nowhere I can hide."

"You're not going back there. We'll take care of you. I told you that I'd make this right, and I will."

She hiccupped. "How? How can you possibly find that map? Someone else must have stolen it."

I knew how thieves worked. "We find the thief. I'll need a list of his treasure hunting associates. They're our primary suspects. Think, Chloe. I need to know everything you know about his friends and his previous forays."

She peered at me, and hope kindled in her features. "You think you can find it?"

"Yes." I had no freaking clue whether I could find the thief, but if determination factored into the equation, then I was sure to come out a winner. Besides I wasn't convinced that finding the map was actually in the plan. Getting her away from Brick Dixon was my first priority.

A loud, clunky thud, like metal hitting metal, distracted me from continuing with my assurance. I had no idea what shenanigans those three were up to now, but I suspected that David had arrived a little early. I poked my head into the hall because I needed to head

108

off David. He needed to blow up at me in private and be calm for Chloe.

Jesse nearly ran me over. He pushed me back into my office and continued without apologizing. Peeved at his treatment and intent on giving him the third degree, I followed him to the reception area.

"What the hell, Jesse?"

Jesse dragged the meeting table that had previously been in my office to the middle of the reception area and turned it on its side.

Dean threw a heavy jacket at me, and I recognized a bulletproof vest. "Put that on. We're under attack." He held his phone to his ear. "Clear the building. I'll take care of this end." Then he shoved the phone into his pocket.

I held it up doubtfully. This was not the time for one of their stupid preparedness exercises. "A raid drill? Are you serious? Who the hell would attack your office in the middle of a busy city?"

"I don't fucking know." Dean's jaw set hard, but he ground out the words. "But put the fucking vest on."

Frankie appeared carrying guns of all sizes. Frankie handed two of them to Dean. Another heavy thud came from the security door. I jumped at the noise and scrambled to put on the vest. This wasn't a drill, and they weren't playing around. My brain snapped into crisis mode. "I have a client in my office."

Frankie nailed me with a glare, her lips pressed into a thin line. "Client? Who the hell is your client?"

I glanced down the hall, and I was thankful that Chloe had remained in my office. "Chloe Dixon. She wants to divorce her abusive husband, but he's having some issues with letting her go."

Dean and Jesse swore, and Frankie hissed. "Please tell me she's not married to Brick Dixon."

Chloe chose that moment to join us. In the midst of three vest-clad, gun-toting mercenaries and a wanna-be (me), she looked so small and forlorn, beautiful even with mascara tracks running down her face. She gazed at the steel door separating her from certain death. "That's him. He's found me."

I put my arm around her, and I didn't back down from Frankie's glare. "Have you called the police?"

"That's not going to save us." Dean pushed Chloe and me out of the reception area. "He's in bed with many influential politicians. He's the most powerful crime boss in the city. If the police show up, it won't be until this is all over."

I hadn't known. This was the sort of thing that didn't pop up on an internet search. Still it wouldn't have deterred me from taking the case. Under Dean's insistence, I stumbled into the hallway. "Well, he also steals high end luxury cars from other states and resells them here. I'm pretty sure it's also a money laundering scheme. I have proof about the cars, but not the laundering."

Dean's expression didn't give away his thoughts, but he kept pushing us until we reached the door to the private stairs that led to the gym on the third floor. "We'll discuss it later. Right now, you need to get her out of here. The roof access is through a panel in the ceiling of the internal stairwell. Get a ladder from the closet and go to the roof. Take the ladder up with you, and close the access. Hide up there. Lay low and stay out of sight. It'll be the safest place for you." He pressed a semi-automatic into my hand.

I didn't have a holster, so I made sure the safety was on and tucked it into the waistband of my pants in back. "I know how to use this."

110

"I'm hoping it doesn't come to that."

I grabbed Dean's arm before he could leave. "Dean, what about David? He's going to be here any minute. He can't walk in on this."

He twisted out of my hold and headed back down the hall. "He's here already. We have two floors of civilians to get to safety."

Another thud came from the front door, but this one had a metallic ring that hadn't been there before. I wasted no time in getting the ladder and rushing to the stairwell. I'd only used it to access the gym on the floor below, though I had noticed the access panel to the roof before. It was on my list of things to explore when I was better established here. I set up the ladder, urged Chloe to climb it after me, and shoved with all my might to open the heavy panel. The hot sun blazed down on me the moment I poked my head out of the hatch and looked around the roof. It was flat, covered with black tar, and a low brick wall ringed the perimeter. I scanned to make sure the area wasn't compromised, though I didn't see how thugs were going to get up here. Even the fire escape didn't come up this high. If we were on the fourth floor when fire broke out, we'd have to jump down to the third floor in order to use it.

As I pulled the ladder up through the opening, I heard the *rat-a-tat-tat* of gunfire, and my heart leapt into my throat. My rational mind argued that Dean, Frankie, and Jesse could take care of themselves, but my other rational mind wondered how they could survive this attack.

Chloe screamed and scrambled across the roof.

I closed the hatch as quietly as I could—I didn't want to draw attention to our location—and I scrambled after her. Grabbing her by the arms, I shook her. "No screaming. Keep your wits about you, Chloe."

"He's going to kill me. He's going to kill us all." Her eyes glazed over with fear, and I realized that she was useless in a crisis.

That was okay. I was strong, a survivor. I'd faced down someone bent on murdering me, and I had triumphed. I could do this. "Chloe, listen to me. We're going to use the ladder to get to the next building. We're going to escape that way. Follow me, and do what I say. Got it?"

She nodded, though resignation registered deep in her eyes. She had no faith that I would be able to get her to safety. I took that personally.

The buildings in this part of town were close enough to one another that the twelve-foot ladder could fit the span between them, though just barely. Lifting the far end of a ladder took more strength and dexterity than I'd anticipated, and I nearly dropped it twice. As I went for a third try, I heard the telltale sign of helicopter blades. Looking up, I prayed to see the Channel Four traffic copter, but no giant logo greeted me from the bottom. As a matter of fact, the helicopter had no markings whatsoever.

As we watched, four heavy duty ropes dropped from its open doors, and black-clad men descended like spiders onto the roof. Each man wore a balaclava to disguise his features. They toted some scary looking guns. Since I'd never used a gun in the commission of a crime, I couldn't say what they were, but they looked semi-automatic.

Chloe screamed, and I dropped the ladder. It bounced off the side of the building, ricocheted from the neighbor's brick, and clattered uselessly to the cement below. I exhaled and spread my hands wide to show that I was unarmed. While I had a gun, there was no way I could take down four trained killers with just a Glock. However I was not going down without a fight. I knew how to bump and roll.

"We're unarmed." I'm not sure they heard me over the loud helicopter blades. Didn't they make stealth helicopters for bad guys now? I shoved Chloe behind me, but she didn't stay put.

"Brick sent them. They're going to kill me."

It seemed to me that if they wanted a map they thought we had, then killing us wouldn't be in their best interest. "I'm sure they just want to talk."

"I'm not going back." She grabbed the gun from my waistband. "He's not getting that treasure."

Before I could take the gun back to hide it or to put it down to show the bad guys we weren't a threat, she barreled toward them. I shouted. "The safety is on." It was all I could think to say because I couldn't believe she would do something so stupid.

They opened fire, and I hit the deck. Bullets whizzed by, high-pitched sounds that sang terrible melodies. Heat seared my leg and slammed into my side, but the pain barely registered. I screamed Chloe's name, but it was too late.

Frayed Knot

"What the hell do you mean—the building is under attack?" I cursed rush hour traffic as I sputtered into the phone. I'd spent the day catching up on bills and preparing for a romantic dinner and scene with my sub.

"Ziwei from the flower shop called when she saw six suspicious looking people get on the elevator. Jesse checked the surveillance feed, and we noticed they were armed. Six pieces of muscle with guns do not pay us social calls." Dean shouted something to Jesse or Frankie. I recognized the sounds of them preparing for the worst.

"Autumn—where is she?" I feared for my sub, not because I thought she'd be scared, but because I was terrified that she'd throw herself into the fight. She cared for Dean, Frankie, and Jesse, and she fiercely protected those she loved.

"She's coming out of her office now. Don't worry. I have a vest for her." He raised his volume. "Put this on. We're under attack."

I heard Autumn's doubtful reply. Trust my woman to not freak out. I loved her ability to remain calm in a stressful situation. "Make her get out of there, Dean. She might be one hell of a safecracker, but she's not combat-ready." Fuck rush hour. I drove on the shoulder and cut people off. Life would be easier if my SUV converted into a motorcycle. "I'll be there in four minutes. I have arms in the back." I kept them hidden where a normal motorist put a spare tire.

"Clear the building. I'll take care of this end."

We leased the bottom two floors to businesses and doctor's offices, and those people needed to be protected. I shoved my phone into my inside pocket, parked on the sidewalk a block away because that's as close as I could get, and grabbed my bulletproof vest from the back. I shoved a Sig Sauer P226 into my shoulder holster and extra ammunition into my pocket. Then I grabbed my fully automatic MPX and broke into a full run in the direction of SAFE Security. Pedestrians shouted, crying out in surprise and alarm, and they moved out of my way.

Starting in the flower shop, I shouted to Ziwei. "Gas leak. Clear the building. Now."

Ziwei was the first person who'd rented a storefront from us. She'd served three tours in Afghanistan. Now she was a florist with her own shop. She wasn't stupid. She'd met us, knew what we did. I watched her demeanor change. "Yes, sir. I'll get everyone on the first floor out."

I had no doubt she would. I headed to the second floor, but it was the end of the day, and both businesses closed at five. I pounded on doors and shouted that there was a gas leak and the building needed to be evacuated immediately. Just to be sure, I broke down the door to the ophthalmologist's office. They were fond of staying after hours to do billing and other business-y stuff. Breaking down a door wasn't as easy as it looked in the movies. One had to identify the weak point to the door and kick really fucking hard. In this case, the double doors were made from sturdy plexiglass. I grabbed the welcome sign posted on top of a stanchion, and I used the base as a battering ram.

I barged in, shouting identification. "It's David Eastridge, your landlord. There's a gas leak in the building, and everybody needs to get out immediately. Is anyone in here?"

A woman slowly rose from behind the counter where they fit people for glasses and contacts. Boxes were strewn around her. She'd been stocking the shelves. She eyeballed my MPX. "I thought you were a murderer."

I motioned for her to get out. "Is anyone else here?"

"No. It's just me. Can I grab my purse?"

"Yes. How about the laser surgery place?"

"They're closed. Doctor Farina is on vacation."

Just then, I heard a helicopter. It sounded like it was on top of the building. Thinking back to Rybakov's place, I knew the roof was also our most vulnerable entry point. I wished I knew what the hell was going on at SAFE Security, but we'd soundproofed between the floors for security purposes. I rushed to the window.

"Are you coming?" The woman paused at the door.

"In a bit. You go ahead. Get as far from the building as you can." The fire escape was outside the window. The fire code didn't consider it a viable means for evacuating a building anymore, but the building was historic, and so we'd been forced to reinforce rather than remove it. I tried to slide the window open, but it was stuck. Some asshole had painted the sash shut.

With a great heave, I got the fucking thing open. The screen presented another challenge, but I had a pocket knife. I slit the damn barrier and crawled out onto the fire escape.

I looked skyward in time to see four men dropped from the helicopter, using tension lines to land on the roof. From the way they were dressed and armed, I knew that Dean, Frankie, and Jesse had their hands full. The sharp crack of rapid gunfire came from the roof. They wouldn't be shooting unless someone was up there, and I sure as hell wasn't going to let them fire their weapons at anyone on my watch. I scrambled up the fire escape, but the thing only went to the third floor. This wasn't going to stop me. I used window ledges and architectural features to pull myself to the roof. The moment I toppled over the low wall that lined the roof, I realized that Autumn was up there. She was crouched over the fallen body of a small woman, and she held out a hand to stop the mercenaries from advancing.

"You're making a huge mistake. We don't have the map."

Her plea didn't work. These men had their orders, and they weren't going to listen to anything she or the blonde had to say. Autumn liked to refer to me as a mercenary, but she didn't know the real difference between what I did and what a mercenary did. Like the four of us at SAFE Security, mercs were for hire, but, unlike us, they carried out their assigned job without prejudice. At SAFE Security, we kept the mission in mind, but we listened to reason, and we never hurt an innocent.

Two shots rang out, and Autumn fell backward. Stone cold calm flooded my veins, and as they advanced on my fallen sub, and I aimed. Figuring that they were wearing Kevlar, I targeted the vulnerable spots—head, neck, femoral artery. Four shots, and four bodies hit the roof. Then I turned my firepower on the helicopter, and the lone occupant, the pilot, fled.

Hand on heart, Autumn ran toward me. "Sir! Ohmygod, Sir! You're okay." She threw her arms around me, squeezing me hard. A shock of relief ran through me. I felt the stiffness of her vest as I caught her, and then I saw the Glock tucked in the back waistband of her pants. She hadn't thought to use it against her attackers.

"Who gave you this?" I relieved her of the weapon, and I tried for a little levity because she looked like she was seconds from falling apart. "You're going to shoot your ass off, Sugar."

"I hope not, Sir. That's your favorite part." She took the gun back. Her hands and voice shook. "You're already armed. Dean gave this to me. I know how and when to use it, and you know it. We've been to the gun range together. I'm even better at hitting center than you are."

Looking over at the dead mercenaries on my roof, I had to disagree. "Shooting at a range isn't the same thing." Then I stopped. The woman on the roof wasn't moving. I noted that she was dead, but I couldn't dwell on the fact. "I don't have time to argue with you. What's the situation like inside?"

"I'm not sure. I heard gunfire about ten minutes ago, before we got to the roof." She glanced at her companion, and tears brightened her eyes. "Chloe Dixon. She wanted to leave her husband, but he didn't want to let her go."

Wheels turned, and one clicked into place. "Brick Dixon's wife?" Brick Dixon was the most powerful crime boss in Kansas City. He ran the criminal side of the city because he owned key politicians, a few cops, and a couple of judges. We had, until now, steered clear of him. Our business interests did not tend to overlap.

She nodded.

"Stay here." I opened the hatch that led to the fourth floor and eased myself through it.

"I had a ladder." Autumn gestured to the side of the building. "But I dropped it."

I lowered myself until my hands were the only thing holding me, and then I jumped the remaining four feet. A straight jump from the roof would have led to broken legs, and I didn't want to take myself out of commission when my best friends needed me. Plus I liked to be stealthy when I didn't know what lay ahead.

The report of a single gunshot echoed down the hall and into the stairwell. I hurried toward it, firearm poised to take out anyone who threatened those I loved.

I found Frankie and Dean standing over two men, tying them off with zip ties. Two more were already bound, and the remaining two lay unmoving on the floor of the reception room. At least one table and all the drywall were riddled with bullet holes. Jesse stood watch, keeping his gun trained on the foursome they'd captured. I addressed him. "Status?"

"Clear. Six entered, and none left. You came from the roof?"

"Affirmative. Autumn was beset by four mercs. I neutralized them, but not before they killed Dixon's wife."

Dean finished tying his man and stood. "I have no fucking idea what she was doing here or why he'd send ten mercenaries after her. I didn't even know she was here until these guys attacked."

Neither did I. "Autumn said something about a map. She was telling the mercs that she didn't have it." I'd been watching the reactions of our four living assailants. One of them closed his eyes and leaned back against the wall, a clear sign of disappointment. I noticed that he had a bullet wound on his thigh. I aimed my kick just below it.

119

"What fucking map is worth shooting up my place of business?"

Rather than flinch, he glared. "Your associate stole something that belongs to my employer, and he would like to have it back."

Frankie snorted. "Grayson Cuyler, I love how you asked. Maybe throw in a 'please' or something next time."

Though I didn't voice my concern, doubt clouded my mind. I remembered Autumn saying that she was going to break into a car dealership and go joyriding. Brick Dixon owned a dealership not far from here. I looked to Dean. "How fast before the police get here?"

He shrugged. "I'm sure they aren't hurrying."

I wanted to get back to Autumn, but the name Frankie had said rang a familiar bell. Grayson Cuyler was known for being effective in achieving his missions. He'd left an illustrious, albeit mysterious, career in Special Forces to be a bodyguard for a billionaire. We'd met once many years ago when I'd been a starry-eyed recruit, and he'd challenged me to reach my full potential. It was disheartening to see him here.

He looked me up and down, assessing the threat I might pose and giving no indication he recognized the man I'd become. Then he lifted his chin. "Seriously—no map?"

I shook my head. "Not only that, no clue what you're talking about."

"Where's Chloe?"

"Dead. One of your team shot her on the roof."

He closed his eyes and rested his head against the wall.

This was interesting. If he had a romantic interest in Chloe Dixon, it might explain what he was doing here. I'd never thought of Cuyler as someone who could be bought. "You used to be a star. How did you end up being a crime boss's hired muscle? And going after his poor, defenseless wife? That's low."

His eyelids parted, and he nailed me with a steely stare. "Poor? Defenseless? Her name used to be McMurphy, you know."

McMurphy was the name of the second most powerful Irish mob in Kansas City. That put things in perspective. There was no way Chloe Dixon had been an innocent in all of this.

"I don't imagine any of you will last too long in jail." Frankie threw that bait out casually as she recounted the number of firearms she'd confiscated from the intruders. We all knew Dixon's lawyers would somehow get them free on a manufactured technicality.

Cuyler's expression didn't crack.

"One family is going to be out for revenge, and the other will be doing damage control." Frankie paused to study our illustrious captive. "The police are three minutes out. If you're going to cut a deal with us, the time to talk is now. What does Dixon really want out of this?"

The man next to Cuyler laughed. He was a big guy with the sharp point of a star tattoo sticking out of the collar of his shirt. I waited for him to try to mock us, but he only shook his head. I wished we were set up for interrogations, but we had no holding cells and no way to separate these guys for questioning.

Cuyler scowled. "Your other female operative survived?"

Seeing as how she was the only female member of my crew, I glanced at Frankie. She matched his scowl.

I answered Cuyler. "You're referring to our receptionist?"

121

Cuyler seemed like he wanted to say more. "You seriously didn't add a second woman to your team?"

"Nope, and don't think of threatening our receptionist. She's a civilian."

He glanced away for a second. "I'm going to say something then. Chloe and Brick, they had their problems, but he would never hurt her. She shouldn't have been harmed."

Dean's eyes narrowed. He exchanged a glance with Jesse, and then he gave me a silent signal.

"I'm going to get Autumn down from the roof." With that, I returned to the stairwell and called for my sub.

She lifted the hatch immediately and peered through it. "You're okay?"

"I'm okay."

"Jesse? Dean? Frankie?"

"They're all fine. The bad guys lost. Come down from there."

Autumn grimaced. "Sir, I was going to use the ladder as a bridge to the next building, and we were going to escape that way, but when the helicopter came, they startled me into dropping it. You're going to have to catch me."

I held my arms up. "Feet first, Sugar." I wrapped my arms around her legs as soon as I could reach, and I urged her to let go of the hatch. She slid down me until her hands rested on my shoulders. "Thank you, Sir. I'm so sorry about this."

I didn't know what she had to be sorry about, but I was sure it was plenty. I led her to Frankie's office because it was closer, and I pushed her onto a chair. "Sit. Breathe. I'll get you some water."

She let out a tenuous laugh completely void of mirth. "I'd like something stronger."

Frankie kept cheap bourbon in her desk drawer. I opened the drawer, and Autumn had the bottle before I could reach for it. She twisted off the cap and took a long swig. The tears welling in her eyes spilled over, and Autumn hissed. "That tastes like fire. I may have sprouted chest hair."

Under other circumstances, I'd check or make some kind of despairing joke. Instead I took the bottle from her, replaced the cap, and put it away. "I need you to tell me everything that happened today with Chloe Dixon."

Her gaze sidled away.

"Autumn." Towering over her, I used my firmest Dom voice, and she flinched. "Tell me everything right now."

"Dean and Frankie are babysitting." Jesse came in, closed the door, and perched on the edge of Frankie's desk and next to Autumn. "Sugar, what happened?"

If it was possible, she looked even less thrilled at the idea of confessing to Jesse. "I messed up. This is my fault."

He pulled her into a tight hug, pressing her cheek to his chest. "This is not your fault. You couldn't have known that ten mercs were tailing her."

I felt like punching Jesse for touching her. Though the emotion was unfamiliar, I recognized the green-eyed monster. It didn't make me feel better, but I settled for glaring at him. "Why don't you let her debrief before you pass judgment?"

Jesse threw me a puzzled look and released Autumn. He squeezed her shoulder. "Go ahead. Try to recall every detail, everything she said, every impression you had. You have good instincts."

She looked to me, seeking assurances I wasn't going to give until I knew the whole story. My instincts screamed that she wasn't as innocent as Jesse believed.

Though I loved Autumn, I wasn't blind to her faults, and keeping secrets was one habit she couldn't quite shake.

Eventually she swallowed and lowered her gaze. "The day before Frankie and Dean came back, when you guys were still in Phoenix, Chloe Dixon came here asking to hire a bodyguard. Nobody was here, and she was crying, so I took her into the conference room and tried to calm her down. She told me that her parents were sick, and her husband was abusive and wouldn't let her go see them. She said she wanted to leave him, visit her parents one last time, and disappear. I thought it was unfair that she should have to give up her parents because her husband was a controlling asshole, so I told her that I could fix it. I said I'd get leverage, and that he'd have to give her a divorce."

If I was ever going to have a heart attack from shock, it would be now. I knew she wanted more responsibility around here, but I never dreamed she'd go this far. I didn't bother to hide my incredulity and displeasure. "You took a case?"

She nodded stiffly.

"On your own. Without permission. Without consulting me. Without training to know what the fuck you were doing." I hurled these obvious conditions at her, and they hit her like falls on a metal-tipped flogger.

Jesse stood beside her as if he was considering shielding her from my wrath. "David, let her finish."

"I'm sorry, Sir. I thought it would work out. At first, it did." Her gaze sought mine, but I gave no quarter, and she dropped it to focus on her hands folded in her lap. "I didn't know he was a local crime lord. Even then, I'm not sure it would have stopped me. She showed me her bruises."

That's when I noticed the bullet lodged in her vest, the rip in her pant leg, and the blood caking her exposed skin. "You're hurt." I moved her arm, but she pushed my hands away.

"Chloe is dead." She closed her eyes. More tears leaked out, and she swiped them away angrily. "When I told you that I was going to break into a dealership and go joyriding, I wasn't kidding. He had a Temberley 207-C. It took me some time, but I got it open. I had a 107-E Series when I was younger. Wonderful safe." She cleared her throat and the glimmer of nostalgia was lost in her guilt and grief.

Hindsight put her declaration into perspective. Only Autumn would consider breaking into a safe a form of joyriding. She'd probably been on cloud nine that whole night.

"Inside was evidence that he's been stealing high-end vehicles from other states, assigning them new VIN's, and reselling them as pre-owned luxury cars. It's a common trick. My dad had a buddy in Idaho who did the same thing. So I took the titles, and I left him a Polaroid with a note saying that I'd keep them safe if he left Chloe alone. Chloe was overjoyed. I thought I'd done a good thing. She left him for two days, but when she came here tonight, she said that he'd tracked her down because a map was missing. She needed to get it back so he'd leave her alone, but I don't have it. I saw a map in the safe, but I didn't take it because it didn't look important." Autumn paused and took several shaky breaths.

"What happened on the roof?"

"She panicked. She grabbed my gun and ran toward the guys that came down from the helicopter, and they opened fire." This time, she swallowed and put her head in her hands. "They shot Chloe."

I couldn't let guilt and grief overwhelm her right now. Later, when things had settled down, I'd provide a safe place for her to fall apart. Right now I had to pick her story apart to make sure she left nothing out. "But when I got there, you had the gun in your waistband."

"I went to her. Dean gave me a vest, but she had nothing. I wasn't sure if they'd seen the gun or if they'd shot her because she'd run at them. Chloe fell on the gun. I shielded her with my body, and I hid the gun behind me in case I needed to use it. Against the four of them, I didn't see where it was going to help." She flexed her fists, and then she looked up at Jesse, her eyes wide with a silent appeal. "When I broke into Dixon's office, I borrowed your thumb drive with the password hacking program, and I copied as many files as I could. I put it back exactly where I found it."

Hidden in her confession were many transgressions. In addition to taking on a case she had no right or training to take on, she'd broken into Jesse's office and stolen his property. It was one thing for her to break into my office and use my things, but somehow I'd thought that Jesse, Frankie, and Dean's offices were beyond the limits of what she considered fair game.

Jesse curled his lips inward, which made him look grim and forbidding, but Autumn didn't shrink away. I guessed at what he was thinking. She'd violated his space and his trust, and once someone broke Jesse's trust, he was finished with them. After a long time, he nodded, and it wasn't the kind that showed acceptance. "I'm going to see if Dean or Frankie need any help."

Autumn looked to me, an unspoken appeal clouding her beautiful green eyes. "I hid the documents in my office. There's no map."

126

"We'll get to those later." I didn't see where this map was our priority. "Let me look at your leg."

She turned it away from me. "It's fine. I'm bruised, that's all. Nothing to worry about."

The sound of a footstep had me looking up. Dean hovered in the doorway. "Does she know anything helpful?"

"That's a matter of opinion." Despite her reassurance, I worried about her wounds. However she wasn't actively bleeding, so I dropped the subject for now. "She took a case without telling anybody, and to say that it blew up in her face is putting it mildly."

"It blew up in all our faces." Dean sighed and looked mournfully in the direction of the lobby. "You're lucky this happened when we were here. Another two days, and David and I would be out on a job."

I didn't want to ask whether he blamed me for this. Perhaps if I'd given her more responsibility earlier, she wouldn't have taken this chance. Or maybe it didn't make a difference. Autumn tended to do what she wanted without thinking about how her actions could affect others. Rather than discuss that sticky topic, I took a leaf from Autumn's book and redirected his attention. "Did you get anything more out of our guests?"

"Bloodstains are impossible to get out of drywall and hardwood. I'm going to have to redo the entire lobby." Dean hissed another breath. "Autumn has been after me to make it more welcoming. She said it was austere and cold."

At this Autumn started. "I hope you don't think I did this so you'd redecorate the reception area. I—" She broke off, and tears started anew.

"For that answer, I'm going to have to withhold your man card for another month." I wanted to comfort

Autumn, but I was too pissed at her for needlessly endangering our lives. So I kind of ignored her and settled for attempted levity. "I meant information, not decorating ideas."

Dean shrugged. "I have no incentive to prove my manliness to you." A noise in the hall distracted him. "Police are here. Keep her out of the lobby. Prep her to play the terrified receptionist."

It didn't take long for Autumn to get her cover story straight, and she didn't ask why we'd decided to keep most of the information from the police. Eight hours later KCPD had cleared the crime scene. They'd questioned each of us separately, including Autumn, and processed the evidence. Bodies were carted away in ambulances, and the surviving intruders were taken away in cruisers. I was sure they'd be free before they were formally booked, and I knew charges would never be filed.

As the last crime scene person left, I surveyed the damage. Most of the bloodstains were on the floor, which could be cleaned, but the bullet holes in the walls would take more than just a scrub to fix. I felt responsible for this mess, which I resented. "Let's clean up, and I'll run to the home improvement store in a few hours."

Autumn emerged from her office—I hadn't wanted to leave her unattended in Frankie's office—and tentative steps brought her to my side. She didn't slip her hand into mine, and for that I was grateful. Through her rash, shortsighted actions, she'd put us all at risk. Much as we were doing, she surveyed the damage. "I'll clean it up."

Dean's jaw set hard, his nostrils flared, and his lips thinned. "You've done enough. David will take you home."

Reacting to the steel in his tone, she bowed her head. "Dean, I didn't mean for any of this to happen."

Dean's eyes, normally light green, darkened with fury, and his quiet, measured response simmered with repressed rage. "That doesn't make this okay. You did something you had no right to do, and you put us all at risk. If we didn't have the training and experience we do, we'd all be dead right now. David would be planning four funerals."

Autumn winced. She brought her arms up, wrapping them around her torso to give her the comfort I couldn't bring myself to offer. I was simply too pissed to touch her.

Frankie picked up where Dean left off. "Seven people died here today—needlessly. This could have been prevented."

And then Jesse added his two cents. "We have procedures and protocols that you know nothing about."

Autumn opened her mouth to explain again, but Jesse held up a hand.

"Go home. We'll be in touch about when we'll meet to review the situation." He turned away from her and headed down the hall that led to the supply closet.

Before she could try again, I grabbed her arm. "Let's go."

Meek and compliant, she followed me through the mangled door to the elevator. I drove her to our apartment. The streets were empty, and the half moon shone brightly in the sky. We said nothing for the entire fifteen minute ride. Rather than park, I stopped at the door to our building. "Go inside. Dinner is ready. Luckily I put it in the refrigerator. Heat up some food and go to bed."

Hand on the door, she paused, and though she didn't look at me, I saw the misery in her eyes. "Are you going back to the office?"

"Yes. I don't know how long I'll be."

"Sir, I—"

"Don't. I can't talk about this with you right now. I don't think I've ever been so very angry with another human being before."

She stiffened. "I see."

I didn't know if she did or didn't, but I wasn't going to have it out with her in the street at two in the morning, and I definitely wasn't going to dive into this discussion until I'd cooled down. "Keep the doors locked, and turn on the security alarm."

I watched until she was in the building, and then I went back to SAFE Security headquarters. The blood on the floor had been mopped up. Dean's insistence on having the floors resealed last summer turned out to be fortuitous. None of the blood had seeped into the wood.

Frankie swept up the last of the shards of what had been the table in our smaller conference room while Jesse and Dean extracted bullets from the walls.

"If they went in deep enough, we should leave them there." Jesse looked to me, his brows lifted in question.

"Negative." Bent over to access a low hole, Dean responded. "We have to make sure they didn't damage the wiring. It's a good thing no plumbing runs through here."

I didn't want to get involved in another disagreement between Jesse and Dean, but it looked like I was being called on to mediate.

Frankie saved me. "Evaluate them on an individual basis. If you get electrocuted when you touch it, then take it out. If not, let it alone. We can even frame one in honor of our first shootout here."

I set to work extracting bullets. "You say that like we're going to have more."

130

"With Autumn here, that's a distinct possibility." She tied off a heavy duty construction trash bag and threw it into a stack of three others.

I realized they'd talked while I'd been taking Autumn home. "If you want to fire her, I'm not going to stand in your way. If you'll recall, it wasn't my idea to hire her."

"Way to stand up for your sub." Disapproval dripped from Jesse's sarcasm, and I snapped.

In two strides, I closed the distance. Then I jerked him up from his crouched position and slammed him against the wall. "Why the fuck do you care?"

Surprise made Jesse's jaw drop, but reflex had him throwing a punch to my midsection. With a grunt, I returned the favor. Before I knew it, we were in an all-out brawl. I channeled every ounce of rage I felt at finding out that my best friends were in danger and the woman I loved had put them there, and I used it against Jesse. I'm sure he vented some pent-up anger on me as well. We were evenly matched on the best days, but I had one more source of vexation in my arsenal—I was tired of him fawning over Autumn.

We grappled, rolling around the extra-wide hall and putting a few more holes in the drywall, until Frankie and Dean pulled us apart. Dean held me immobile while Frankie stood between Jesse and me. We faced each other, chests heaving with exertion.

Frankie nailed me with her worst scowl. "What the hell is wrong with you two?"

I jerked free of Dean, and he must have known I wouldn't attack Jesse again because he didn't fight me. I jabbed a finger in the air, mentally stabbing Jesse with the gesture. "She broke into your office, stole your equipment, and then she nearly got you killed—and you're still in love with her."

Okay, it was a stupid thing to say. I could argue that she'd done all those things to me, and I was still in love with her. However we'd come to an understanding, one that would have to be expanded to include a "don't kill us" clause.

Jesse peered at me as if I'd lost my mind. "I'm not in love with Autumn."

"Bullshit. You didn't want her to know you were the honeypot in Phoenix, and you've been kissing up to her since we've been back. You touch her any chance you get, and you call her Sugar."

Now Frankie was looking at me as if I was crazy. "Dean calls her that as well. They do it to get your goat." She parked her hands on her hips, which I knew was preparation to intervene in case I went after Jesse again. "It looks like they got it."

Crossing his arms over his chest, Jesse shrugged. "If it bothers you that much, I'll stop calling her Sugar. But the other stuff—I don't kiss up to anyone."

It wasn't enough of a concession. "Again, bullshit. Whenever she calls, you go running. 'I'll train you on this. I'll show you that.' And then there's the fact that you didn't really get upset with her when she told you that she'd broken into your office. I know how you are about people getting into your experimental stuff. You'd kick any of our asses if we did that."

"Pardon me for being happy to have someone else pick up the slack around here." Jesse spit that at all of us. "Look, I love the work we do, and you guys are my family. But you all suck when it comes to the business end of the business, especially you and Dean. Frankie isn't bad, but she just does her part. That means the rest of it falls on me."

Dean scoffed at that. "We have an accountant."

"You pay her to come in once a month. We need a day-to-day person." He strode across the space and planted himself inches from me. "If I was nice to Autumn, it's because not only is she lifting a huge burden, but she's your girlfriend. I held back when she told me that she'd broken into my office because I didn't want to piss you off. If I'd had my way, I would have ripped her a new one, and then I'd have fired her."

Any relief I felt at knowing Jesse didn't harbor a crush on Autumn was short lived. It looked like her time here had come to an abrupt end, but I failed to find the joy I thought this moment would bring. I'd wanted her to decide to leave. Forcing her out hadn't been the plan.

But Jesse's initial reaction still didn't make sense. "You agree that she should be fired, but you're getting on me for not arguing to keep her?"

"Yeah." He shrugged. "If you advocated for her now, then when we tell her that she's fired, at least you could say you tried. Now what are you going to do? Chances are, this is the end of the road for you guys, and that sucks. You're never going to find another woman who will put up with you the way she does." He ran his hand over his hair. "If you'd argued to keep her, I probably would have backed you on it."

Dean went back to removing bullets from the drywall. "So you see? Jesse, as always, has your back. And I'm not going to stop calling her Sugar. I like the way you narrow your eyes every time I say it. I need these small pleasures in life."

Maybe later, when I was thinking clearly, I'd reconsider whether Autumn should continue to work for SAFE Security. As soon as I had the thought, I felt my brain looking for reasons to give her another chance. Following Dean's example, I went back to work. Though I didn't apologize to Jesse, I knew we were square. As we prepped the walls for repair, Jesse and I recounted the things Autumn had told us about Chloe Dixon.

Some Mistakes are Worse Than Others

Entering the apartment brought on a fresh wave of sobbing. David had prepared a romantic meal—scallops, scalloped potatoes, and gently steamed baby carrots—and he'd set the table with lots of candles. A thick floor pillow sat unused next to his chair, and I knew he'd planned to feed me while I knelt at his feet. And when he couldn't stand it any longer, he'd pull me into his lap to finish the meal.

Rose petals were scattered on the table and floor, and a trail led into the bedroom. I followed it to find the bedroom set for a scene. Cuffs dangled from the headboard. A spreader bar waited at the foot of the bed. Vibrators and dildos in various sizes were set out on a towel he'd placed on the nightstand. David had a fascination with using those kinds of implements on me, and I loved it as well. I noticed a new toy with three prongs. One would vibrate in my pussy, the next would impale my ass, and the last little arm would stimulate my clit. I bet he planned to use this on me and forbid me from coming.

I wasn't hungry, so I cleaned up the dishes he'd left in the kitchen and got ready for bed. Standing naked in front of the mirror in the bathroom, I examined the huge bruise on my side. It looked so much like the one Chloe had shown me only a few hours earlier. Only mine was the result of something that had saved my life and hers had been the result of her husband's rage.

Taking a deep breath, I tested it to make sure a rib hadn't been fractured. It hurt a little, but I determined that I was just bruised. Next I attended to my leg. I'd been terrified when the bullets had started flying, and I'd barely noticed this injury. I studied the angry scratch on my leg that would probably turn into a scar. The skin had been gouged, and it hurt like a really bad sunburn. I'd endured these small pains as a sort-of penance for my part in last night's fiasco. Now I dressed the wound and put an ice pack on my ribs.

Being in the bedroom with all those toys out, mocking me for fucking up the sensual night David had planned for us, was too much. I took a blanket out to the sofa and lay in the dark, waiting for David to come home. I'd already explained, and now I owed him one hell of an apology. I didn't know if he'd ever forgive me. Putting Jesse, Frankie, and Dean's lives in danger—even though I hadn't meant for that to happen—might prove too much for him to pardon.

With those heavy thoughts, I fell asleep and dreamed of Chloe dying in my arms. Rivers of blood ran over the title papers I'd taken from her husband's safe. I tried to mop up the mess, but the towel in my hand turned out to be the treasure map I hadn't taken. As I looked at the thing, it came to life. It sprang from my hand and ran away, rivulets of blood marking its trail. I woke suddenly, sweating and shaking, to find myself all alone and the mid-morning sunlight filling the room.

David hadn't come home.

I went through my normal morning routine, hoping at each stage that he'd walk through that door, but he didn't. I called his cell, but he didn't pick that up either. If he was on assignment, I wouldn't have been surprised, but he wasn't. He was home, and he was so angry that he was avoiding me. So I texted him that I'd be out visiting Summer, and he could come home to shower and change without running into me.

Summer's room was empty when I arrived. The schedule on her calendar said that she had physical therapy, so I went to the PT room in search of her. She'd progressed so far in just a few months, but I wasn't surprised. Like me, Summer was a survivor. We'd grown up learning to thrive on the strength of our will and wits.

The PT room looked like a gym for the most part, though the row of therapy tables and the machinery next to them gave away the true purpose of the place. I scanned, looking for her at the equipment where she spent most of her time, but she was nowhere to be found.

"Hi, Autumn." Miles O'Reilly, her regular therapist, appeared at my side. The top of his head came up to my shoulder, so I could see his thinning hair at the crown. Though he was short, he sported the physique of a man who'd dedicated his life to physical fitness. He pushed his round, wire-rimmed glasses to the bridge of his nose. "Looking for Jessica?"

From the sympathetic way he peered at me, I wondered exactly how much of our story he knew. Pity wasn't something I wanted from anyone. "Yeah. Her calendar said she had a session right now."

"Just finished up. I worked her hard, and she's in the hot tub so those muscles don't tighten back up." His gentle smile was at odds with his sadistic streak. Summer had told me more than once that he gave no mercy when it came to pushing her to achieve more.

I returned his smile. "Thanks."

Summer saw me before I saw her. "Autumn, what a nice surprise. I didn't know you were coming today."

It was a surprise because I hadn't answered her calls since the last time I'd been here. I perched on the edge of her hot tub. "I didn't know I was coming."

She put her hot, wet hand over mine and regarded me with a somber gaze. "I'm glad you're here. I want to apologize for last time. You weren't ready, and my therapist says that I can't force you to be ready."

If she was discussing me with her physical therapists, then the look Miles O'Reilly gave me made sense. Narrowing my eyes to slits, I glared. "You're talking about private matters to Miles?"

She laughed. "No, silly. Nikki Eliachevsky is my shrink. I started seeing her when we moved here so that I could begin to sort out my parental issues. You'd like her. If you want, I can give you her contact information. She's a great listener."

I had David, and he was a great listener. I dismissed all the things I hadn't told him because, in all likelihood, I wouldn't tell them to a shrink either. Yeah, I had issues with trust. Maybe one day I'd tell David everything, but that day was not today. I smiled uncomfortably. "That's okay. David helped me. I'm okay with calling you Jessica." Now I just needed to do that in my thoughts as well. It was hard because I'd been calling her Summer for so long.

"That's great progress."

"Yeah. Look at you, though. You're walking like an old lady. That's even better progress." Don't like the subject? Change it, I always say.

Jessica knew me better than anyone. She was wise to my favorite coping mechanism. She stood up, flashing her bathing-suited body to the whole room. For a woman who'd spent the past three years in a coma, she was looking good. "Hand me a towel?"

I snagged one from the cart and brought it back to her. "Let me help you out of there."

"Nope. I can do it myself." She navigated the three steps like an amateur. I stood nearby, ready to catch her at any moment, but she made it down, dried off, and wrapped the towel around her waist. "Dean and Jesse came by yesterday morning. Those two are even worse than you."

I knew the guys—and even Frankie—visited on a semi-regular basis. I liked that they'd embraced Jessica as part of their extended family, though now that I was sure to be ejected, I wondered if they'd dump her by the wayside as well. "What did they do?"

"They wouldn't listen to me. Dean felt he needed to hold onto my arm, which makes it hard to dry off, so Jesse decided he'd do the honors." She threw a wicked grin in my direction. "Have I ever thanked you for bringing them into our lives? I know I don't have a snowball's chance in hell, but having two handsome, muscular men fawn over a woman does wonders for her self-esteem."

I laughed.

"And they're entertaining. Dean likes to crack jokes and tell racy stories, and Jesse can talk about pretty much every subject under the sun. Did you know he stumbled upon a cache of stolen paintings?"

Since he'd stumbled upon them with David and I'd filed the mission report, complete with photos of the paintings they didn't retrieve, I did know that. However the Jesse I knew wasn't much of a talker. He could communicate a wealth of information with a look, but he seldom said much otherwise.

Jessica looked tired, so I brought her walker closer and held it so that it wouldn't roll away on the ceramic floor. "It's good you like them. They may have an opening for an office manager really soon. You'd like working there."

Jessica knew they'd been treating me as a receptionist. She'd been the one to urge me to be patient with David. She took a step forward, pushing the walker on its rollers. Her smiled vanished. "They can't hire an office manager. That has to be your position. You've worked so hard and waited so long."

I hadn't shared news of my promotion with her yet. "I was the office manager for almost a full day. They called me into a meeting the day before yesterday and explained my new duties."

She stopped walking and stared at me, waiting for the full story. She probably also needed a break from the trail she was blazing. "Why aren't you there now?"

"Let's go to your room, and I can tell you how badly I've messed it all up."

A half hour later Jessica lay in bed and fought gravity's effects on her eyelids. She'd listened to my whole story. I was right that she was proud of my initiative—right up until it blew up in all our faces.

She jerked awake. "Holy shit, Autumn. When you mess up, you certainly go big. Remember the first time you stole a car? It ended up belonging to the owner of the chop shop Dad—I mean Gene Bowen—sent us to."

I remembered all right. It was difficult to forget being threatened by a bald man twice my size with ink covering nearly every square inch of his skin. Every time I saw him after that, his face was still twisted in that angry growl. It was like someone had tapped him on the back while he was yelling, and his face had been frozen that way. I was alive today because I'd talked myself out of being killed and into a part time job. Or maybe he had a soft spot for fourteen-year-old girls who didn't crack under pressure. Either way, that job had vanished two months later when Dad, who I still thought of as his alias Brian Sullivan and not the legal Gene Bowen, moved us out of the state in the middle of the night.

"I'm not sure I can talk my way out of this one. I went behind their backs, and it didn't have a happy ending." I'd envisioned this going much differently.

Jessica pursed her lips. "Would they have reacted differently if things hadn't ended so horribly? I'm not so sure they would have been as overjoyed as you're thinking."

I didn't see why not. A successful mission was a successful mission. I bristled at her question. "They would have known I could handle helping with missions. I could coordinate them from a home base. Maybe I could go on some with them, like if they need a safe opened quickly or a lock picked cleanly." My skill set was perfect for a band of honorable mercenaries.

"I don't think they doubt that you can handle yourself, but you're not really one of them yet."

I resented her for saying that, and my nose got stuffy, a sure sign I was about to cry again.

Jessica held her hand out to me. "Autumn, I don't mean to hurt your feelings. I'm just trying to make you consider that their point of view might not be what you think it is. Dean isn't very tolerant when it comes to the way we were raised. He always gets that quiet and disapproving look on his face whenever I try to share an adventure I've had that is sort of like one he's had, only mine weren't sanctioned by the government. And Jesse... He feels sorry for us. I hate that. Frankie, maybe, is the most understanding one, next to David. But that doesn't mean they're going to be okay with the fact that you took a job without first getting their approval."

The shame and guilt I'd been feeling threatened to overwhelm me. I curled up in the chair next to her bed, tucking my knees into my chest and wrapping my arms around my body. "You know what's even worse than losing all the friends I've made?"

Her green eyes, so like mine, widened. "David wouldn't break up with you over this. He loves you."

I hadn't thought David would be the one to end it. No, he'd stick with me to the bitter end even if he couldn't look me in the eyes anymore. I pushed that thought out of my head because I didn't have the strength to deal with it right now. "Chloe. She died without ever being free of her abusive husband. When it all went to shit, the last thing she said was that he couldn't have that treasure."

She'd wanted to keep the treasure from him, a payback for the hell he'd put her through. It'd be the perfect payback for the hell he'd put her through. All of a sudden, I wanted that treasure. Not for me—I'd donate it to a museum or use it to set up some kind of memorial fund in her name. Okay, maybe I'd squirrel away some of it as a rainy day fund, but most of it would go to charity. I had a picture of the map on my phone, and that was a start. I sat up straighter as I began planning how I was going to begin this quest.

"Oh, crap. I know that look. Autumn, don't do something stupid to try to make up for the other stupid thing you did." Jessica's voice, thin and high because she was exhausted and worried, penetrated my planning fog.

"I'm going to find that treasure before Brick Dixon does. I'm going to do it for Chloe. It's what she wanted. She said so with her dying breath, so that makes it her last wish." I got to my feet. "You're worn out, Jessica. I know PT really kicks your butt, and you've been fighting to stay awake to listen to my trauma drama. I don't have much to go on with this treasure thing, so I'm going to start researching."

Before she could respond, David's ringtone sang from my phone, and I picked up immediately. "Hi, Sir." I didn't ask how his day was because I already knew it sucked. "Did you make it home yet?"

"No. I was here all night, and then I crashed on Jesse's couch for a few hours." He had done that before—worked all night and slept over at Jesse's.

"Oh. I'm glad you got some sleep."

"Yeah. Listen, there's a meeting in a half hour to discuss next steps. You need to be here for it."

I heard the finality in his voice. They'd already decided my fate. "You're firing me."

"Autumn, we need you to come in and tell us all what happened. There are some questions that need answers." He responded quietly and without rising to my bait.

I wanted to press for more information, but Jessica's admonition to be patient and to consider that they couldn't appreciate my point of view was fresh in my head. "Yes, David. I'll be there." I slid the phone into my pocket and looked over at Jessica to find her sound asleep. I pressed a kiss to her forehead and closed her door as I left.

I was late. It was a running joke with David—with anyone who knew me—that I had a loose interpretation of what it meant to be on time. The first few times I'd met David, I'd appeared later than the agreed-upon time. If I'd been home, getting to the SAFE Security offices in a half hour wouldn't have been an issue. Because I was in a suburb visiting Jessica, and I hadn't factored in the effect of mid-afternoon traffic coming into the city, there was no way I would make it to the building in under an hour.

Twenty minutes after the start of the meeting—which was still ten minutes earlier than I'd predicted—I rushed into the sandstone building and into the private elevator that led to the fourth floor. When the doors opened, I found that they'd replaced the ruined door with something even more heavy duty. I ran my fingers over the naked steel, noting the smooth texture, and I tried to guess the gauge of steel. It had to be at least an eight, which meant it would stop a bullet.

As I fumbled with the keypad—they'd most likely changed the code—the door opened. Dean regarded me with absolutely no expression on his face. Still his appearance told me enough. Dark half moons marked the underside of his eyes, and stubble stained his cheeks and chin. His eyes, though, were clear and hard like emeralds.

I tried for a smile. It flickered once before faltering. "Hi, Dean."

"We had to change the access code when we installed the new door." His tone neither apologized nor offered me the new digits.

"Makes sense." Actually it was advisable to change the code on a regular basis. "I'm sorry I'm late."

144

"You can wait in the conference room." He closed the door, and the sound of locks engaging echoed through the narrow, empty lobby.

They'd done a lot of work since early this morning. The floor was clean, though a section of molding blood had seeped into was missing, and the destroyed table had been removed. They'd filled the holes in the walls and mudded over them. In a few days, they'd be able to paint. I should have been allowed to stay and help with the repairs.

I kept that comment to myself and made my way to the conference room without encountering anyone else. Dean didn't follow me, though he watched to make sure I went where he told me to go.

The conference room was empty. Nobody had put out snacks or made coffee, as I liked to do when I knew they'd be using the room. Part of me wanted to go find David, but my better sense made me stay put. Messing up right now could be detrimental to my continued employment prospects.

Working for myself or working for someone lazy was so much easier than working for people with standards and expectations.

Since I was alone for the time being, I put on a pot of coffee. While that was percolating, I arranged some cookies and pastries on a platter. They weren't my homemade ones, but they'd do.

"You don't have to do that." David set a tablet on the table and came to me. He set his hands on my shoulders, and I melted into his touch. He kissed my neck, a firm greeting from my Sir.

"I have some lemonade in the refrigerator."

"Just sit down. I'm glad you made it on time."

"I'm twenty minutes late. I was visiting Jessica when you called."

He steered me toward the chair next to his. "Actually you're ten minutes early. I know how you operate."

Stunts like this did not provide incentive for me to stress about being tardy. I never knew when David made allowances for my tendency to underestimate how long it would take to get from point A to point B. As I took my seat, the rest of the crew came in. Each carried a tablet or a file folder, and in Jesse's hand, I recognized the file I'd made on Chloe that I'd put in my desk drawer. Now I knew they'd searched my office. I did not see anyone with my bag that contained the titles and the five thousand Chloe had paid out to me.

I felt it was wise to lay all my cards on the table right now. "Do you want me to get the titles I took from Brick Dixon's safe?"

Frankie poured a mug of java and added her usual four sugars. In the field she wasn't picky. She'd drink it black if no sugar was available. "That'd be great." Like her coffee, her tone was too sweet.

I hurried. The screwdriver in my lower right drawer wasn't where I'd left it. Whoever had gone through my desk wanted me to know they'd been there. This sharp slap came from Jesse. When I'd violated his personal space by breaking into his office, I hadn't left a trace. He wanted me to know that he'd never do something so insidious to me. I found the tool in another drawer.

Dwelling on that slight wasn't going to get me anywhere, so I climbed onto the filing cabinet and unscrewed the vent.

"Good hiding spot." Frankie leaned against my open door and watched me work. "Jesse and David both said you were good at finding unexpected places to hide things. We searched everywhere for those titles, but none of us considered that you'd use the vent."

"It's a cold air return." I extracted the bag and set it on the cabinet below. "Putting things in vents is tricky because you have to think about the temperature and whether the moving air will make a sound when it hits what you've hidden. A cold air return is an empty space with a vent cover. You put a nail into the stud, and you can hang a bag from it."

"And even when the vents are cleaned, your treasure won't be disturbed." Frankie took the bag and peered inside. "Clever. I wonder how many hidden things you've left behind over the years?"

"Nothing important." We never had much in the way of material possessions. Brian Sullivan had been keen on selling off whatever we didn't need, and so Summer and I knew better than to form attachments to too many things. We returned to the conference room, and Frankie unpacked my bag. She set the titles in one pile and the cash in another.

David stared at the money. "Where did you get that?"

"It was the fee Chloe paid me. She wanted to use cash so that Brick couldn't stop payment." I gazed wistfully at the money, the first paycheck I'd actually earned since I'd been here. "Five thousand. You can use it toward paying for the repairs to the lobby."

Dean waved away my offer and tapped away at his tablet. "We've already made an insurance claim, and the new door cost double what you've got there."

Doors that expensive weren't found at the local home improvement chain store. "Did you have it in storage?"

He responded without looking up. "I'd been meaning to change out the old one for a while now."

The first time I'd visited the SAFE Security office, I'd recounted a story where I'd broken into a law firm that had the same security door. They'd been suing a friend of my dad in a civil suit. We'd been paid to make the evidence disappear. I'd forgotten the exact details, but I remembered the door. My father had short circuited the locking mechanism with a shock from a large battery.

Of course I heard the censure in his tone. He hadn't thought the security upgrade necessary until now.

"Let's get started." David folded his hands over his midsection and turned his attention to me. "Walk us through your first meeting with Chloe Dixon."

I hadn't known we were going to rehash things I'd already told David, Jesse, and to some extent, Dean. Frankie was the only one to whom I hadn't directly confessed, but I was confident they'd told her everything already. I bit the inside of my cheek to keep from mouthing off, but it didn't work. "This is an interrogation? You're going to have me retell it over and over so you can look for inaccuracies?" In my statement to the police, they'd made me omit several details. Essentially they'd coached me in lying to the police.

Dean didn't mince words. "Yes."

Since David had asked the question, I knew his mind, so I looked to Jesse and Frankie to see where they stood on the issue of this tactic. Jesse regarded me with a steady, stony stare, and Frankie lifted her brow to indicate I should answer the question. It looked like they were a united front, which didn't make me feel very good at all. I was once again an outsider. All the work I'd done to earn a place in their hearts had been wiped out with one well-intentioned act.

I opened my mouth and let the words pour out. This factual account included my impressions and thoughts,

148

and I related it in excruciating detail. Dean only looked up from taking notes on his tablet when I described the pristine state of Chloe's manicure the final time we met. I placed the color somewhere in the peach family, but as I wasn't one for painting my nails, I couldn't be sure about the exact shade.

"She got a manicure before she came to see you?" Frankie interjected this, her first question, into my narrative.

"I guess so. I didn't ask."

Dean shifted. "If Brick had beaten her and locked her in a closet, a manicure wouldn't have held up."

Normally I'd expect David to pipe in with some kind of sarcastic comment like, "You would know," but he simply agreed with Dean.

I looked from Frankie to Dean before concentrating on David. Jesse was still avoiding my gaze. "You think she lied to me?"

David lifted a shoulder and let it drop. "At this point we don't know."

I thought about the fact that the bruises on her ribs looked a lot like the one I had from being shot in a Kevlar vest. It's possible that the bruises she'd shown me at our first meeting hadn't been the result of a beating. After grappling with Frankie, I had fingerprint bruises on my arm where she'd grabbed me.

"Please continue." Dean issued that command in a very dominant tone.

I finished up my tale, ending with Chloe dying on the rooftop while I tried to shield her body with my own. As I thought about her last, rattling breath and light fading from her eyes, my nose stuffed up and tears welled in my eyes.

David handed me a tissue, but he didn't otherwise offer comfort.

Jesse finally looked up, his brows wrinkled and his lips curled with almost vicious impatience. "What steps did you take to corroborate her story?"

The whole time I'd known him, which was almost as long as I'd known David, Jesse had not spoken a single harsh word to me. His tone hit me as hard as a physical blow, but I took a deep breath and pretended it hadn't hurt. "I looked up Brick Dixon and found that he owns a chain of car dealerships."

His expression didn't change, but I forced myself to meet his iron glare. That's when I noticed a bruise darkening his cheek. "But you didn't look up Chloe Dixon in any of the databases?"

I didn't know anything about a database. "I looked on the internet. All the hits were of her at different charity events for Dixon Motors."

"Did you run a background check on Chloe or Brick Dixon?"

I also didn't know the first thing about running a background check. "No. I can tell when people are lying to me."

"Always double check." Frankie pinched the bridge of her nose and rubbed her eyes. "Someone always beats a lie detector, and that includes the human kind."

"You didn't catch on when Stephanie Ciechelski lied to you." Dean lobbed that bomb into the air. Stephanie Ciechelski was the woman who'd framed me for embezzlement and tried to kill me.

They were baiting me, and though I knew why, I found their tactics unfair. This was my breaking point. "Because you're perfect and you've never made a mistake? I'm not wrong about the car theft ring."

150

Dean closed the cover on his tablet and regarded me with a fierce scowl. "I didn't nearly get us all killed. That was you."

My chest ached. He could have just punched me instead. Any kind of response eluded me.

Jesse attacked next. "You ignored every protocol we have in place for vetting potential clients. We have those in place for a reason."

As if they'd rehearsed it, Frankie lit into me. "Seven people died here last night, six of them killed by me, Dean, and David."

David rounded out the recriminations. "You broke into Jesse's office, violating his trust and making us all doubt that we can trust you to respect our privacy and our personal space. It's one thing when you break into my office. Due to the unique nature of our relationship, I expected it. It's quite another when you ignore the boundaries Frankie, Jesse, or Dean set by locking a door."

The listing of my sins piled up. Behind each item was a quiet fury and a sense of betrayal. I already felt guilty about what happened with Chloe, and I hated that they were all so irate. I knew where this was going, and I berated myself for allowing myself to become attached to these people. As much as I wanted it, I'd never truly belong here.

Silent seconds stretched minutes into miles. Finally I stood. "You're right, of course. I'll make this easier for everyone and resign." Yeah, I was quitting, but I couldn't bring myself to use that word. Growing up, I'd learned what had to be done when I'd overstayed my welcome.

They looked to David for leadership, but he was busy watching me put the five thousand into my bag. It was payment for services I'd rendered, which had cost my job, and since Dean had turned it down, I felt entitled to it. Nobody stopped me.

David followed me to the elevator. "Sugar, are you sure about this?"

I know he felt betrayed by my careless actions, but I also felt betrayed by the fact that he sided completely with Dean, Frankie, and Jesse. Yeah, they were his friends, but I was his girlfriend. At the very least, he should have tried to help them to see my side.

I pressed the button to call the car to the fourth floor, and I didn't look at him. "It's what you've always wanted."

"You're not doing this for me."

"I'm not?" Not bothering to disguise the misery I felt, I faced him. "You didn't stand up for me at all in there. If I continued to fight for a place here, and you continued to let them walk all over me, then there's no way we'd survive this."

The elevator dinged, and David wrapped his hand around my wrist to keep me from stepping forward. "They didn't walk all over you. We were right to be critical of your actions. You had no right to do what you did, not only because it wasn't your job, but because you have no training in what we do. You put us all at an unnecessary risk."

This was an old argument. I didn't see a real difference. They chose clients like I chose a target, based on need and the thrill of the challenge. I twisted out of his grasp. "I know I made a mistake. I forgot that I was dealing with a bunch of perfect people who never fucked up anything in their lives." I stepped into the car and pushed the button for the first floor.

David clapped his hand over the sensor to stop the door from closing. He pressed his lips together like he wanted to prevent himself from feeding the growing acrimony. "I'll be home for dinner. We'll talk then."

I thought we'd said enough. I met the firm steel in his dark eyes, and I rejected the implicit command. He could talk all he wanted, but I didn't have to be there to listen to it. "I won't be there."

"Don't test me tonight. I'm not in the mood for games."

Holding out against his Dominance was difficult under the best of circumstances. Right now, I wanted to submit to him. I wanted to give in and let him hold me while we both got over the pain and melancholy, but I knew I'd hate myself in the morning. I dropped my gaze to hide the tears I didn't want him to see. "Neither am I."

Perhaps he mistook my admission for acquiescence, but he let the door go. I left, not clear where I would go next, and I drove around the city. At one point traffic forced me to stop, and a glance to the side shook me from my fog of self-pity. Books spines, painted on the side of a building, presented a striking image. Invisible Man caught my eye first. I'd read this years ago, and now I wished I could retreat from the rubble of my world and become invisible.

Next my gaze was drawn to Silent Spring. I didn't know what that was about, but in my current state, I imagined packing what I could carry and disappearing from this life. I'd change my name and live off the grid. Nobody would find me. Except for the sounds of nature, all my springs would be silent from now on.

Lastly I studied the plain brown spine of The Adventures of Huckleberry Finn. I'd swiped a leather bound copy of that book from a job in Michigan, and I'd been in the midst of reading it to Summer when David had brought dangerous, thrilling, and deadly adventure into my life. I'd never finished it.

It dawned on me that this was the parking structure for the public library. They had computers and books in there, and they probably had volumes of local lore. This was the perfect place to begin my search for the treasure Chloe hadn't wanted to fall into Brick's hands. I parked and went inside the library.

Calling up the map in the picture gallery on my phone, I studied it for landmarks. Rivers ran rampant through the whole thing, though something about it seemed familiar. Most people couldn't look at a map of a watershed and identify the specific river. Symbols that looked like rocks marked several places, and numbers were hand written along some of the rivers. I really hoped this wasn't a map of a cave system.

I zoomed in on the top edge, and in faint script next to a dot, it read *Kirbeysvill*. That was a start. I fed that name into the computer, and I came away with suggestions for alternate spellings. It didn't take long to find a town named Kirbyville in southern Missouri, located between the Bull Shoals and the Table Rock lakes. From there I followed the treasure map south, but nothing showed up on my internet search. Taney County appeared to consist of a lot of open countryside in the Ozarks. I'd never been there, and my acquaintance with them was passing at best. I'd always pictured a barren wasteland, and boy, was I wrong.

The images blew me away. It looked a lot like Michigan's Upper Peninsula, a place Jessica and I had visited several times before the accident that put her in a coma. The first time we'd gone camping because people spoke so fondly of it, but we hadn't been impressed. It reminded us of those times we didn't have anywhere to call home. We'd done a lot of camping growing up. After one night, we'd booked a hotel room for the rest of our vacation.

Digging into the issue of treasure brought forth a trove of local legends, everything from thieves who terrorized the countryside to caches of buried gold that some old coot hid before he kicked the bucket. Even narrowing it down to the legends of treasure purported to be in Taney County, I came away with two possibilities. It was either Alf Bolin's buried loot or a horde of Spanish gold. And here I thought the US had bought this part of the country from the French. Go figure.

I was about to dive into how Spanish gold might get to Missouri, but a tap on my shoulder distracted me. A tall, willowy man who looked like he'd spent the last sixty years with his nose buried in books smiled regretfully. "We close in ten minutes. If you're going to check out a book, please do so now. Otherwise you have five minutes before the computers automatically shut down. The library opens tomorrow at nine."

I had a town and a state, but somehow I couldn't dredge up enough emotion to be excited about my progress.

The apartment was dark when I entered. City lights twinkled through the windows. Though it was a breathtaking vista, it failed to draw me closer. David and I had parted on unsteady terms, and part of me hoped that he'd be here. Perhaps he was in bed, exhausted after not getting enough sleep the night before. Not wanting to wake him, I slipped my shoes off and set them next to the door.

"You're three hours late for dinner." His voice came from the sofa. I squinted in the dim light, but I wasn't able to make out his outline until he moved.

My eyes adjusted to the darkness. "I thought maybe you'd gone to bed." I glided closer, stopping far enough away so that he couldn't easily reach me.

He turned on the lamp next to the sofa, and when he settled back, he had a glass of wine in hand. "Have a seat."

I parked myself in the chair on the other side of the coffee table and looked at him. He'd changed into his pajamas, a soft gray cotton shirt and green plaid pants, and his feet were bare. Under other circumstances I'd kneel at his feet and ask for permission to sit on his lap. "I don't want to fight with you."

"So you ignored my order to be here for dinner? That's not a great start." He sipped his wine.

"David, I sincerely don't want to talk about work. I've said all I have to say. It's as resolved as it's going to get. Besides, you got what you wanted."

A cornucopia of reactions flittered across his face, but he opted to honor my wish to not argue. "Where were you?"

"The library."

"Doing what?"

"Reading, mostly. I researched the treasure map."

A warning lit his eyes, a flashing neon sign that advertised his suspicion that I'd lied to them this afternoon. "You said you didn't have the map."

It was great to know how much he trusted me. "I have a picture of it. It's not a map in an X-marks-the-spot kind of way. It's more of a vague puzzle." A puzzle that I was determined to solve.

The light faded as he accepted my explanation. He finished off his wine. "Have you eaten? I picked up some takeout for you."

My dinner had consisted of half a pack of breath mints I'd found in my purse and a pack of crackers from a vending machine. This whole uncomfortably polite situation made my stomach churn. "I'm tired."

"Then let's get ready for bed." He stood and held a hand out to me.

Longing, pure and unrelenting, burned like indigestion. Turning my face away, I refused his invitation. "I'll sleep on the sofa."

"No, you won't." He wrapped a hand around my upper arm. "There's no reason for you not to sleep in our bed."

It wasn't our bed. It belonged to David. He'd bought it years before he'd met me. He'd probably slept with other women in it. This apartment, the car I drove, even the clothes on my back—it all belonged to him. "David, I need some space."

He wrapped his other hand around my arm and hauled me to him in direct opposition to my request. A feverish fierceness had taken over his bearing. "Sir. Say it."

I didn't want to use his title. I didn't want to reaffirm that part of our relationship because I truly didn't feel like I belonged to him or with him. I loved him, but that wasn't quite the same thing. Ending this relationship would kill me, and I wasn't quite ready to die.

"Damnit, Autumn. I'm not going to let you walk out of here without one hell of a fight, which you will lose because I'm not willing to give up on us. Not now, not ever."

He'd released me once before. Though his declaration sounded a little stalker-ish, it wasn't. This was his way of telling me that he was serious in his commitment. Another time it might come off as romantic, but right now it didn't sway me. Right now, his insistence that I honor our dynamic pissed me off. It looked like we were going to fight after all.

Channeling my inner Domme, I met his fierce look with something steady and cool. "Let go of me. I said I needed space, and I'd like you to respect my choice."

"You're still mad because you think I didn't stick up for you."

"You didn't."

"I did. We weren't going to fire you."

I gaped at that. "But you were fine with letting me quit?"

"I never wanted you to work there. You're the one who talked your way into a job, and you're the one who quit."

Once again, he'd failed to fight for me. The way they'd all looked to David when I'd resigned made much more sense. Using a move Frankie had taught me, I ripped my arms from his hold. Rather than following it up with a punch or kick, I slammed my open palms against his chest. "I left there because you weren't willing to fight for me, not even a little bit. When they started in on me, you not only didn't defend me at all—you joined in with their ridicule."

"It was constructive criticism of your mission. You broke rules, and you failed miserably. Yes, we are all pissed at you for what you did. You betrayed all of us, Autumn. What you did was incredibly stupid and short-sighted. Don't expect sympathy or platitudes when you put us all at risk."

Yes, I'd messed up, but nobody was harder on me than myself. I didn't need them compounding my feelings of self-hate. "You didn't say a single word in my defense, David, and for that, I'll never forgive you."

158

"You'll never forgive me? You know what, Sugar? I'm having a hard time forgiving *you*. Do you have any idea how terrified I was when Dean called to tell me that you were under attack?" A bundle of rage, he whirled and paced to the bank of windows. He had his back to me, and so I watched his reflection spit venom in my direction.

"I've been part of some harry missions that have gone sideways before, but I've never been as afraid as I was then. All I could think about was that I couldn't lose you. I used all my training to stay focused and do my part, trusting that my team would do their part. The whole time, I vacillated between worrying about them and fearing for your life. When I heard gunfire and I saw a body lying on the roof, I shot four men even though I knew that body wasn't yours. I went for kill shots because I couldn't take the chance that they'd hurt you."

They'd been about to shoot me. If he hadn't intervened, I had no doubt that I wouldn't be standing here right now. Still I refused to be swayed because we'd already been over what I'd done wrong. "Don't make this about you."

He turned around, leaning his back against the window. "Right, because this is about you, about how you're mad at us for ganging up on you, about how you're mad at me because I didn't stop you from quitting your job—which, for the record, you weren't doing when you took that case."

"I didn't mean for any of this to happen." I shouted because I hated how he dismissed my pain so easily. If my emotions didn't matter to him, then I didn't matter either. "I thought it was a simple case of empowering a woman in a domestic abuse situation. I mean, who the hell sends ten mercenaries after a woman and a map?

That's overkill, even for a vindictive mobster." I closed my eyes because now I was getting off track. "You never fight for me, David. You let me walk away from you once, and now you're letting me walk away from a job because you don't want me to have it. You're only supportive of me when I'm doing what you want me to do."

He shook his head. "I let you work at SAFE Security. How is that not being supportive of something *you* wanted to do?"

I hated how he'd learned to turn an argument back on me. This was supposed to be my talent. "You waited for me to fail, and then you opened the door for me to leave. You made it possible to get exactly what you wanted without having to take the responsibility for the decision."

He gave up any pretense of not being equally affected. Closing the distance, he put his face inches from mine. In all respects he dominated my personal space without physically touching me. "I'm the one who convinced them not to fire you. They hadn't decided in your favor, Sugar. They looked at how you betrayed us and voted to eject your sweet little ass."

"Because you're all so perfect." I sneered the line of reasoning Jessica had given me because it was the only thing I could think of. "None of you have ever messed up and put the others at risk. I'm the only one who has ever fucked up on that epic level."

"Not even close, Sugar. When we take a mission, the others know what we're doing. They know the score, and they're prepared for the fallout. You blindsided us. We weren't ready to take on organized crime. You lied to us, and that's why they wanted you gone. But I advocated for you. I said you had to have a good reason for withholding information. I'm the one who convinced them to give you a second chance." As he yelled, he took small steps forward, forcing me back until I hit the door to our bedroom.

I pushed him away, but he didn't budge, and that fueled my blind fury. "None of you sounded like you wanted me around anymore. You all said such nasty things."

"They could probably do without seeing you for a few weeks. Dean motioned to suspend you for a month, but Frankie and Jesse talked him down to two weeks. You should have accepted the criticism and apologized. Instead you got on your fucking soapbox and quit. They weren't going to persuade you to stay. I was the only person in that room who'd advocated for you to stay. When you quit, you sided with them and made me look like a fucking idiot."

Right then, I hated him for turning this around to dismiss my explanation and make it look like I'd screwed him over multiple times. "I only did it because you wouldn't let me do anything in the office. I wanted to show you that I could be a valuable member of the team, but you consistently ignore any value I have outside of the kitchen or the bedroom."

I'd scored a direct hit with that one, but it didn't bring the satisfaction I'd sought. The wrong kind of sparks flew from his eyes, a storm he kept tightly under wraps. "If I'm such a caveman, why are you still here?" He opened the bedroom door and pushed past me on his way to the bathroom.

Mouth agape, I stared after him until I heard the sound of water running. Then I kicked into high gear. I dragged my single suitcase from the closet and dumped as many clothes into it as I could fit. Because David had taken me shopping several times since I'd moved in with him, I now had more clothes than would fit, so I selected mostly the items with which I'd arrived. There were some newer things that I really liked, and I figured he wouldn't care if I kept them.

Toothbrush in hand, David came into the bedroom. "What are you doing?"

"You made a good point." In fact he'd made several good points, but I didn't want to think about that right now. I needed him to acknowledge my point of view. "There's no reason for me to still be here."

"Don't be obtuse." He waved his toothbrush at me, as if he was the Tooth Fairy and he could magically make me do what he said. "It was sarcasm, the only logical way to respond to your assertion that I only value you for sex and muffins."

Since he was out of the bathroom, I slipped in and gathered my personal hygiene items. "I told you I didn't want to fight with you tonight. I told you that I needed space. But like you always do, you ignored what I need and did what you wanted."

He closed his hands around my wrists, gently restraining me from packing. "I never ignore what you need, Sugar, but I admit to not always giving you what you want. We needed to have this fight. We needed to lay it all out on the table."

We'd done that, and one thing was glaringly clear to me. "I love you, David. But you hurt me today. You hurt me badly, and it still hurts. I asked you for time and space, and you gave me neither. I can't stay here with you tonight because you don't understand exactly what you've done to me." With a pointed look to his hands on my wrists, I used my safeword. "Red."

"You can't safeword during an argument."

162

"It's also been said that you can't argue with a safeword. Let go of me."

His hands slipped away, the whisper of a caress I needed to stop wanting. "At least stay here. I'll sleep on the couch."

Physically and emotionally exhausted, I consented to that arrangement.

An hour later, I adjusted my position for the ten hundredth time. I hated arguing with David. I hated that we'd fought, and I hated that he wasn't sleeping next to me. While he was on the sofa because I'd basically threatened to leave unless he gave me some space, it seemed like the start of the end of us. Add to this snippets of legends I'd read at the library, and ideas about Spanish gold and Civil War bandits pummeled my brain while doubt and grief chipped away at my heart.

I needed David next to me because I didn't know if it would be our last night together, so I crept into the living room. It was dark, and I didn't know if he'd be awake, wrestling with unhappiness as I was, or if he'd surrendered to exhaustion.

As I came closer, the sound of his even breathing told me all I needed to know. I couldn't see anything more than his outline, but I recognized that his blanket had fallen to the floor. I bent to pick it up—I didn't want him getting cold—and he moaned. The desperate noise arrested my intention, and I took a closer look. He moaned again, and this time he tossed his head and kicked restlessly. I recognized the sounds of a nightmare. Summer used to have them all the time.

I rubbed his chest, but he didn't awaken. When he groaned, a loud, unsettling sound, I shook his shoulder. "David, wake up."

He jerked and grabbed my hand. I let him hold it because he seemed to need an anchor to the real world.

I didn't think he'd admit to having a nightmare, so I settled for the next best truth. "You weren't breathing right."

Sitting up, he washed the memory of that awful dream from his mind by rubbing his face. "I'm okay."

He needed to come to bed, and not just because I needed him there. Since he was tired and probably disoriented from his bad dream, it didn't take much coaxing to get him to agree. Once I had him where I wanted, I somehow couldn't get comfortable. This would be so much easier if he'd touch me. David liked to snuggle. When we were in bed, even if we didn't have sex, some part of him was in physical contact with some part of me.

In my quest to fall asleep, I tossed and turned, and I may have bumped into him a couple of times. I apologized, and he accused me of attempted revenge.

"Sugar, did you get me in here just to beat up on me?"

When he called me by that term of endearment, I knew he wasn't really mad. Still I felt compelled to point out that I'd already apologized. "I said I was sorry."

I tried to stay still. Perhaps once he fell asleep, he wouldn't notice me wiggling around in search of a position that wouldn't bother my hip, lower back, shoulder, or any other part of me that objected. After a time, I moved again, and that's when I realized the sheet was twisted around my legs. I turned again, and I bent down to push at the knot.

"Fucking hell."

Even though my elbow might have come into abrupt contact with his chest while I was trying to get free, I couldn't stop the sarcasm. "I didn't realize you were so delicate." Since he was awake anyway, I sat up and straightened the covers.

His legs must have been uncovered as well because he moved at the wrong time, and I clipped him in the jaw. "Damnit, Sugar. You made your point."

I hadn't hit him very hard at all, but I'd noticed a bruise there earlier when we'd been arguing. I'd wanted to ask him about it, but the opportunity never arose. Right now, his attitude wasn't helping me to calm down and get to sleep, and I desperately wanted him to take me in his arms and hold me one last time. I rolled to face him and found myself half on top of him. "I'm not making a point. I'm trying to fix the blankets so that we can go to sleep."

He put his hand on my knee, holding it with the same pressure he used when he restrained my wrists during sex. A shudder ran through my body, and I took a chance that he might respond like the virile male he was. I kissed him softly, an invitation I hoped he would accept.

He released my knee and brought his hand up to stroke my cheek, a tender caress that made my battered heart sing. We deepened the kiss, and passion took over. I wanted to give myself to him one last time, and so I concentrated on his pleasure. But he had always been a generous lover, and when I refused to see to myself, he flipped us over so that he was on top, and he gave himself to me.

His lips skimmed my cheeks and eyelids. "I want you to come, Sugar."

A climax wasn't something I sought. I wanted him to touch me, to hold me, to tell me that this wasn't the end even though it seemed that way. I tried to tell him that, but the words got stuck in my throat. This man knew my body so well, and he made sure I climaxed just before he did.

Afterward he collapsed on top of me. I hugged him to me, taking what I really wanted. A few moments later, he kissed my forehead and rolled back to his side of the bed where his even breathing told me that he was asleep.

I stayed still for a few hours, drifting off every now and again only to jerk awake with my heart racing. This was how I used to sleep whenever I knew Dad was going to move us again—ready at any moment to abandon the life I'd created and start over.

Eventually there was no point in pursuing sleep. I threw on some clothes and went into the kitchen. I owed Jesse a cake, and no matter where my life's journey took me next, I wanted to make sure my debts in this part were paid in full. These people had been good to me. They'd supported my attempt to have a normal life, right up until it had nearly cost them their lives.

As I mixed ingredients to make muffins, I realized that David had been right in his assessment of my actions. I'd been rash and careless. No amount of baked goods could make up for what I'd done, but it was all I had to give. Perhaps one day they'd remember me, and instead of thinking of the ways in which I'd hurt and betrayed them, they'd recall the way in which these sweet cinnamon rolls melted on their tongues.

When David woke up, bright-eyed from a good night's sleep, he sauntered into the kitchen. In a pressed shirt and fine pants, he surveyed the mess with a bewildered expression. His tie hung loosely around his neck. Normally I would tie it for him, but my hands were gooey.

"Good morning, Sugar."

"Good morning." I almost used his title, but I refrained. I had to start weaning myself away from him sometime. I'd become too attached. I'd thought my dad was crazy for always moving on once we were established in a place, but now I knew he was preparing us for the normal pattern of life.

David, I knew, wasn't going to let me go that easily even though the writing was on the wall. I felt the gentle pressure of his hands on my shoulders, and he turned me to face him, but he didn't otherwise touch me. "Sugar, yesterday was pretty rough. You were angry, and you never use my title when you're angry. That bothers me. It's spiteful and disrespectful. It's fine for you to be mad, but it's not fine for you to toss out the rules of our relationship every time you feel like being passive-aggressive."

He was totally right. I'd wanted him to call me out on my bratty behavior for quite a while, but he hadn't got around to it. There seemed to be no point now. I looked at the floor because I couldn't meet his gaze, and I felt I had to be honest. "I'm sorry, Sir. It's not because I'm angry, though. I'm kind of past angry. It's because I don't think we're going to survive this."

His lips parted and his eyes widened. "Why not? Have you stopped loving me? Was your affection conditional on you working at SAFE Security?"

"No." I'd never stop loving him. When I was old and alone, I'd warm myself with memories of our few precious months together.

"Then where does this doubt come from?"

I needed to finish prepping the cinnamon rolls so they'd be done before he went to work, so I turned my back on him and continued being honest as I started the process of breaking away from my Sir. "Working with you was a path to showing you that I had something valuable to contribute. It was a way to keep us connected. Now that's all gone, and after today I'm never baking again. That leaves sex as the glue holding us together, and that'll eventually not be enough."

"Sugar, that's not all we have." He was quiet for a moment, probably thinking about all the ways I was right despite his wish that I was wrong.

I arrived at a decision. Yesterday I'd wanted to go after that treasure for Chloe, and that hadn't changed today. However I had a new reason for pursuing this action—I needed this to prove to myself that I wasn't a complete screw up, that I could do something valuable without messing it up. "I'm going after that treasure. I've done some research, and I've narrowed it down to either Alf Bolin's booty or buried Spanish gold. I need to do more research, but I'm nearly there. Something is nagging at me, and once I realize what it is, I'll know where to look."

"Can we talk about this when I get back? I should only be gone two or three days." I glanced over my shoulder in time to see him frown. "Right now, I want to talk about us."

The timer for my muffins dinged, and I exchanged them for the cinnamon rolls. I hadn't made these for David before, but I knew he'd love them. They appealed to his sweet tooth, and I hoped he'd think of me every time he ate one from now on. "I don't know what else there is to say, Sir."

He didn't accept my brush-off. If anything my attempt fed his Dominant streak. He leaned in close, caging me between his body and the edge of the counter. The scent of his soap and aftershave mingled with the smell of sugar and flour that I couldn't get out of my nose. More than that, this was the aroma of the man I loved. I closed my eyes and let myself draw strength and comfort from his nearness. Once he left for work, I'd pack my things and be on my way. He might come after me because I couldn't go far with Summer stuck here, but then again, he might be happier with me not in his life.

Though he didn't touch me, I could imagine the feel of his fingertips caressing the side of my face. I opened my eyes, and his steady gaze, stronger than rope or chains, held mine captive. "Sugar, relationships change and people change. It's not easy, but we'll adapt because that's what you and I do—we adapt, we solve problems, and we overcome obstacles. You and I will last because we'll do those things together. This is a curveball. Things didn't go as expected. It sucks, but you can't let it destroy everything we're building together. I love you, Sugar. You and I aren't our careers. Those come and go, but we are eternal."

Holy crap. I'd teased him for not being very romantic, but that wasn't fair. Without trying, David frequently said and did things that swept me away. Right now, he managed to eviscerate arguments and reasoning I hadn't voiced. More than anything, I wanted the life he described. I slipped my arms around his neck, and he held me until the cinnamon rolls were ready.

Coffee With a Crime Lord

The curtains glowed caramel brown, a product of the yellow city lights and the dark tan hue I'd selected from three choices a decorator had offered. An unholy silence echoed through the apartment somehow managed to percuss on the bones of my inner ear. I adjusted the spare blanket Autumn liked to keep over the back of the sofa so that it covered more of my torso. On cooler evenings she'd curl up under it while watching television or reading. Right now I couldn't find a way to arrange it so that I was neither too warm nor too cold.

My pillow also wasn't doing the trick, though I had no problem with it normally. On the mantle over the fireplace, a clock ticked, slow etchings marking the seconds of my penance.

I'd hurt her.

She wanted space.

She'd even begun packing a suitcase. My heart had nearly stopped when I'd come from the bathroom to see what she was doing. I'd expected her to be angry with me, and I hadn't wanted to go to sleep without resolving this issue. Never sleep on an argument, right? Isn't that one of those axioms for how to make a relationship last?

In my mind, I'd envisioned an ugly fight, one in which both of us said things in the heat of the moment. It wouldn't be pretty, but at the end of it, I'd hold her in my arms, and we'd move forward together. Nothing had turned out like I'd wanted. The fight hadn't been as epic as I'd hoped because she was more hurt than angry, especially when I explained our reasons for being upset with her. I hadn't counted on that backfiring so spectacularly. I'd counted on my firecracker of a woman to light into me. I hadn't realized the depth of the pain smoldering in her heart.

I wanted to make it go away, but she wouldn't let me near her.

I must have eventually fallen asleep because I dreamed that I woke up alone. I rushed to the bedroom to find the bed neatly made. I ripped open her drawers, and each was empty. Her half of the closet had been cleared out. Even the places where she'd hidden her prized possessions—photographs and mementos from her youth—were bare. I looked out the window and caught a glimpse of the back of her head as she crossed the street. A ratty duffel bag was slung over her shoulder, and she headed for the bus stop.

This was my last chance. I had to salvage this. I'd never love another woman the way I loved Autumn. She was everything to me. I ran, but the floors were suddenly made from quicksand. The air had turned soupy, and I couldn't breathe. Suffocating and drowning, I fought to get out of the apartment, but every time I made it to the door, I found myself back at the window. I beat on the glass and shouted. I tried to say her name, but nonsense came out of my mouth.

"David? David, wake up."

I jerked awake. Sweat soaked my chest even though the blanket had fallen to the floor.

Light spilled from the hallway, and Autumn was bent over the sofa, shaking my shoulder. A line creased between her eyes. "You weren't breathing right."

I sat up, planting my bare feet on the floor, and scrubbed a hand over my face. "I'm okay."

"The sofa is too short for you. Come to bed."

There was no way in hell I was going to let her sleep on the couch. "I'm giving you space."

She plopped onto the cushion next to me. "You're leaving tomorrow. I'll have plenty of space then."

I'd heard plenty of jokes about women changing their minds all the time, but that hadn't been my experience with Autumn. Mulish was her middle name. "You sure?"

"Yeah."

I grabbed my pillow and followed her into the bedroom. Determined to give her as much space as I could on a queen mattress, I stayed on my half. She turned out the light, and a few seconds later the bed dipped. She settled on her side, facing away from me, and plumped her pillow. A few seconds later she rolled to her back. Since she didn't resituate her body first, she somehow managed to pinch the skin on my arm.

Without making a big deal, I moved my arm to ease the pressure.

She turned again, and this time her knee caught me with a sharp jab to the side of my thigh. "Sorry."

"Sugar, did you get me in here just to beat up on me?"

"I said I was sorry." She huffed, rolled to her stomach, and abused her pillow some more before laying her head on it. Not a full minute later, she flopped to her back, and the point of her elbow made violent contact with my ribs, and I think she was tangled in the covers.

"Fucking hell."

Rolling violently, she dislodged the hold the sheet and blanket had on her. "I didn't realize you were so delicate." Her shadow rose as she sat up in bed. The covers lifted, bringing a cool breeze as they floated back down. Then they lifted again, and this time her fist caught me on the jaw where Jesse had punched me earlier. She didn't hit me hard, but the bruise was fresh and tender.

"Damnit, Sugar. You made your point."

She whirled on me, ruining all the effort she'd put into straightening out the sheet and comforter by rolling so that she was half on top of me. Her face inches from mine, she hissed. "I'm not making a point. I'm trying to fix the blankets so that we can go to sleep."

Her knee was dangerously close to my balls, and given her sudden klutziness, I feared for my boys. I put a hand down to block her trajectory. "I'd prefer if you put more distance between your knee and my balls. In your quest to find the perfect sleeping position, you've kicked, pinched, elbowed, and punched me. I'd hate to see what happens when you're actually trying."

She exhaled hard, which sounded a lot like another hiss. For a few seconds she didn't move. It was too dark for me to see her eyes, and so I had no inkling what nefarious plan was brewing in that gorgeously intelligent brain of hers. Then she shifted, moving her body so that it was mostly on top of mine. Her lips brushed mine, a tentative foray that had my heart beating faster.

Taking a chance with my future potency, I released my hold on her leg. I caressed her cheek, a soft encouragement and an assurance that I would heal the emotional pain I'd caused. She deepened the kiss, unleashing a storm. With a mighty roar of thunder, what had begun as gentle turned violent. She ripped at my shirt, and once that was gone, she scratched my chest.

Passion built as she ran her hands and mouth over my skin, alternating kisses and caresses with scratches and nips. I relieved her of the shirt and panties she'd been wearing, and I touched every inch of her sensuous, soft skin. The more brutal she became, the gentler I touched her. She needed to understand that I was her Dom, and I would always give her what she needed.

Without asking permission she positioned my cockhead at her entrance and sank down the length. Sitting astride me, she rocked her hips, fucking me to a furious, impossible rhythm. If she kept this up, I was going to come before she did. Perhaps that was her intent? If I came and she didn't, it would reinforce her earlier assertion that I didn't give her what she needed.

She needed to know that I loved her, that I cared about her, and that I was in control.

Ignoring the growing heat in my core, I ran my palms up her thighs and across her stomach, reveling in the silky feel of her skin. Then I kneaded her breasts and rolled her nipples until she gasped. Suddenly I sat up and captured her lips in a hot kiss that let her know I was done playing. In one swift move, I flipped us so that she was beneath me. Now I set the rhythm, and I slowed things down.

"David, please." She met my thrusts, going a little quicker to urge me faster.

I hooked my arm under her right leg and forced her to hold still. "Sugar, don't play games. Nothing you do or say will make me spank you, punish you, or deny you an orgasm. You're going to come."

Her head thrashed from side to side, a vehement refusal. "I won't. You can't make me."

With another caress, I swept a lock of hair from her forehead. In the dim city lights bleeding through the curtains, I locked my gaze with hers, and at the end of each thrust, I twisted my hips in a move that drove her crazy. We battled silently until her eyes rolled back and her body convulsed. Her velvet pussy squeezed around my cock. I couldn't resist such sweetness. The inferno at the base of my spine detonated, and I buried myself deep to empty my seed.

I collapsed on her, and I didn't bother to roll to the side to spare her my weight. I wanted her to know that I was here, and that I'd fight for her—even if I had to fight her. She lay under me, her body trembling and her arms wrapped around my shoulders.

There was so much I wanted to say to her. Sitting in my desk drawer at work were two tickets to a house I'd rented on a private beach. I'd planned to take her there, spend a week naked, and I'd even bought a ring because she'd once told me that she wanted a romantic proposal on a tropical beach. But how could I tell her any of that when she wouldn't even look at me?

Exhausted from the events of the past thirty-six hours, I didn't want to move. Summoning the last vestiges of energy, I kissed her forehead, and then I rolled over and fell asleep.

The next morning, I awoke to the aroma of baked goods. My nose twitched and my stomach grumbled an encouragement to get my ass out of bed. Since I was naked, I got dressed first. I grabbed a white shirt and gray pants that matched the jacket Autumn had picked up from the cleaners a few days ago. When it came to my tie, I draped it around my neck because I preferred when Autumn tied it for me.

The kitchen looked like five episodes of Bakery Wars had taped while I'd been sleeping. I glanced at the clock to double check the time because there was no way I'd overslept. The clock chimed eight-thirty, confirming that I was not running late.

Autumn surveyed my attire, and when her gaze came to rest on my tie, she held up her hands. They were covered in flour and sticky with the filling she was using on the cinnamon rolls. I tied my own tie while she went back to mixing and rolling. Then I slipped my arms around her waist and kissed her cheek.

"Good morning, Sugar."

"Good morning." She didn't address me by title, but I couldn't let that slide. I had a job today, and I wasn't going be able to focus on that if I couldn't get my mind away from Autumn.

I very gently turned her to face me. Her dark, silky hair was pulled back in a ponytail, and she had smudges of flour on her forehead and temple. Circles darkened the translucent skin under her brilliant green eyes, making them even more striking, and I realized that her night hadn't been as restful as mine. She needed my dominance in order to help get her emotions under control. "Sugar, yesterday was pretty rough. You were angry, and you never use my title when you're angry. That bothers me. It's spiteful and disrespectful. It's fine for you to be mad, but it's not fine for you to toss out the rules of our relationship every time you feel like being passive-aggressive."

Her gaze dropped, and the frantic energy of her mood plummeted as well. "I'm sorry, Sir. It's not because

I'm angry, though. I'm kind of past angry. It's because I'm not sure we're going to survive this."

My heart sank, leveling off right about where her mood had gone. "Why not? Have you stopped loving me? Was your affection conditional on you working at SAFE Security?"

"No." She didn't lift her gaze defiantly, and she didn't offer an explanation.

"Then where does this doubt come from?"

She turned back to the counter and resumed spreading the brown, gooey substance that gave flavor to the cinnamon roll. "Working with you was a path to showing you that I had something valuable to contribute. It was a way to keep us connected. Now that's all gone, and after today I'm never baking again. That leaves sex as the glue holding us together, and that'll eventually not be enough."

Normally I'd make her face me when we talked, but right now I was glad her back was to me. Thinking back over how we'd met and how our relationship had evolved, I realized that working together was the one common thread winding through our story. From the start our personal relationship was predicated on our working one. I'd never thought about it like that before.

"Sugar, that's not all we have." My brain scrambled for something to say that would actually salve the situation, but she was faster.

"I'm going after that treasure. I've done some research, and I've narrowed it down to either Alf Bolin's booty or buried Spanish gold. I need to do more research, but I'm nearly there. Something is nagging at me, and once I realize what it is, I'll know where to look."

Autumn changed subjects faster than anyone I knew, and I was winging this without the benefit of caffeine.

"Can we talk about this when I get back? I should only be gone for three days at the most. Right now, I want to talk about us."

A timer dinged. She snagged an oven mitt and took a steaming rack of muffins from the oven, and then she slid the sheet of cinnamon rolls inside. "I don't know what else there is to say, Sir." She whispered my title, a verbal caress that packed a melancholic punch.

Parking my hands on either side of her body, I caged her against the counter. I didn't know what to say either, but I went with what was in my heart. "Sugar, relationships change and people change. It's not easy, but we'll adapt because that's what you and I do—we adapt, we solve problems, and we overcome obstacles. You and I will last because we'll do those things together. This is a curveball. Things didn't go as expected. It sucks, but you can't let it destroy everything we're building together. I love you, Sugar. You and I aren't our careers. Those come and go, but we are eternal."

Emotion choked whatever she might have said, so she slipped her arms around my waist and rested her cheek against my chest. I held her until a rude buzzer made her pull away. "I'd better get those before it burns. That's your breakfast."

She drizzled a homemade liquid frosting over them. The second that sugary concoction hit the heated buns and that aroma hit my nose, my stomach growled loudly. With a pleased smile, she plated two of them and presented the offering to me—on her knees, as a good sub should do.

Joy thrummed through my bloodstream, and I accepted the goodies. "Thanks, Sugar. Have you eaten yet?"

"Yes, Sir. If it's all right with you, I'd like to frost Jesse's cake."

"Sure." I'd rather she sit on my lap and feed me, but I didn't have time for where that would lead. Due to the chaos in the office yesterday, Dean and I weren't quite ready for our next job. We'd been hired to ferret out a security threat at an oil executive's weekend retreat.

"I owe Jesse a cake. He said to surprise him, so I went with plain yellow and chocolate frosting."

I sat at the counter on the living room side where I'd placed three barstools. "This is for when he had to listen to us having phone sex?"

"Yes, Sir. I've made your muffins as well." She'd made enough muffins to last all of us an entire week. She spun the platter as she smoothed the frosting. "I've packed up some for you to take into work, and I was going to take some over to the rehab center later when I go see Jessica."

"My flight leaves at one. Text me when you get home tonight."

She glanced up, but instead of replying, she frowned. "I'm not cut out to be a housewife."

I licked the last crumb from my finger. "I never thought you were."

"I'm going to find this treasure, and then I'm going to look for a job."

This was the third time she'd mentioned the treasure, and I finally realized that she was serious. "Please don't do anything dangerous unless I'm with you."

She laughed, the first hint of mirth I'd seen in far too long. "I'll try."

Frankie's eyes rolled skyward as she savored a bite of a pumpkin spice muffin. "Damn these are good. I'd call

Autumn and thank her, but I don't think she'll speak to me."

Dean started on his second muffin. "And here I was, thinking we'd never see another bite of her baked goods again. Where's Jesse?"

In the midst of carefully selecting my fourth muffin— I'd cheated and had two while driving in—I paused. "He's probably hiding his cake."

The subject of Dean's query chose that moment to join us in the conference room. He snagged a muffin and frowned. "I earned that cake."

A devilish grin turned up the corners of Dean's mouth. "Don't say that too loud. If David hears, he might beat you up again."

Plopping onto a chair, Jesse peeled the paper from his treat. "In his dreams. I won that fight. Seriously, though—how is she? I didn't expect her to go home and spend the night in the kitchen."

I shrugged, more because I wasn't ready to get maudlin right now. "She's okay. We had a big fight. We talked. We made up."

"You make it sound so simple." Frankie sipped coffee. "Did she take a swing at you?"

Still unsure whether her midnight violence had been intentional, I shook my head. "It wasn't simple. At one point I had to stop her from packing a bag and leaving."

"That's when you talked and made up?" Dean frowned, one of his most menacing expressions, and I figured he was worried about whether I'd be able to focus on our upcoming job.

"No. That's when I agreed to sleep on the sofa. Before too long she came out and asked me to come to bed. In the morning we talked. She was thinking we wouldn't survive this, and I assured her we would."

Frankie studied the half eaten muffin in front of her, and then she looked toward Jesse. "You said you earned the cake. Does that mean she owed it to you, like this is a debt she's paying?"

"Yeah. She felt sorry for me because I got stuck listening to her and David having phone sex. Her baking more than makes up for that kind of trauma." Jesse would have continued, but a three-toned chime sounded.

Frankie groaned. "I hate that thing. If Autumn was here, we wouldn't have to have it on. The notification would just go to her."

The three of them turned a combination of impatient glares and icy stares on me. Okay, Autumn wasn't the only one who wanted to punish me for her not working here. I rose, adjusted my tie, and smoothed my lapels. "If you wanted her to stay on, then you should have spoken up yesterday. I was under the impression that you were relieved she quit. Right now she's researching that treasure, not lamenting an unsuitable job she used to have."

Dean nearly busted a gut, he laughed so hard. "You think treasure hunting is a safer pursuit?"

I thought it was a pointless pursuit. It would occupy her mind and her imagination until she settled on a different career. I had no doubt that Autumn would change her job many times in the coming years. She had an inquisitive mind and a restless spirit, and I aimed to indulge her in almost anything she wanted to try.

The security camera revealed Brick Dixon on the other side of our new security door. He had a rectangular head that seemed to have been put directly on his square body. I wondered how someone so unprepossessing could have landed a dish like Chloe. Since she was the daughter of another local crime boss, it might have been an arranged marriage, a deal between two rival parties. I pushed the intercom button. "Can I help you?"

He stared at the intercom, and then his gaze lifted to the camera embedded in the wall. "I'm alone and unarmed. I just want to talk about what happened with my wife."

Opening the door to a known criminal who'd sent ten mercenaries after his wife wasn't a wise course of action. I'd rather meet him in a neutral location, but then I reflected that he was taking one hell of a chance coming here. I pushed the button again. "It's all in the police report."

He rolled his head from side to side, and I heard what sounded like a neck cracking, but for the life of me, I couldn't see that he had a neck. "I'm not stupid."

A person did not amass the wealth and power this man had by being stupid. I wanted a second, third, and fourth opinion on this problem. "Hang on for a sec."

I jogged back to the conference room to find Dean and Frankie in a heated debate over who got the last chocolate chip muffin. I grabbed a plastic spoon from the counter and did my best to cut it in half. "Brick Dixon is here. He wants to talk."

Jesse jumped to his feet. "He rang the bell and asked? That's different."

Halfway down the hall, Frankie said, "I'll check security footage to make sure he's alone."

Dean pulled on his suit jacket. He liked to look his best when confronting murderous thugs. "I'll help Frankie. You keep watch."

When Jesse joined me, he had Kevlar vests in hand. These were trim, meant to be worn under clothes, and so we stripped out of our shirts and put them on. If Autumn were here, she'd be watching with an appreciative gleam in her eyes. Jesse was dressed before I had my shirt buttoned. "This is why T-shirts are preferable."

After a few minutes Frankie and Dean returned. I knew without asking that they were also wearing vests. Well, I knew Frankie was wearing one because it flattened her chest. She motioned to the door. "He's alone. Go ahead and let him in."

Jesse opened the door. With his badass military bearing, he presented a formidable figure. "Come in, Mr. Dixon."

Brick Dixon sauntered across the threshold, his movements surprisingly agile for a man who seemed to have been molded by the makers of Minecraft. He looked around the lobby, no doubt noting where we'd patched the drywall that had yet to be painted. "Thank you for meeting with me."

"This way." I steered him toward the conference room.

He paused in the doorway. "Looks like you were in the middle of a meeting already." Then he continued to a place that didn't have a muffin or a mug of coffee. He motioned toward the bin Autumn had sent with me that morning. "May I?"

I wanted to refuse. This scum didn't deserve to eat anything over which my sub had labored. But Dean answered first. "Sure. Would you like coffee or water?"

"Water is fine. I'm trying to cut down on the caffeine. Chloe says—said—it makes me too jumpy." He pressed his fingertips to the table. "I can't believe she's gone."

I bit back a comment about how he probably shouldn't have sent his crew to murder her, and from the expression on my friends' faces, I think they were doing the same thing.

183

Dean set a stack of papers on the table, and then he sat down. As he was our unofficial leader, that was our cue to follow suit. He motioned to the papers. "Those belong to you."

Dixon slid them closer and looked them over. Then he nodded. "Thanks. I appreciate it. Listen, I'm gonna level with you. I know who you are and what you do. Since your business and my business don't usually overlap, I kinda just ignore you, like I'm sure you do with me."

Dean steepled his hands on the table and leaned forward. "Mr. Dixon, it doesn't seem like you're ignoring us anymore."

Dixon studied Dean, and then he nodded. "You must be Alloway. Grayson said you were the one in charge. He said he knew you way back when you were just starting out." Then his gaze moved to Frankie. "Sikara, I heard great things about you. If you ever get tired of working here, you come see me."

Frankie had that gift many women had where she could tell someone to fuck off without opening her mouth or changing her expression. She used it now.

Dixon chuckled, and his gaze slid to Jesse. "You must be Foraker. I don't have anything on you, but Grayson said you know your way around a package of zip ties." Without waiting for a response, he addressed me. "And you're Eastridge. I wanted to thank you."

This was unexpected, though it was probably also backhanded. I lifted my eyebrows. "For?"

"For taking care of business for me. They were just supposed to stop the other crew. Chloe wasn't supposed to get hurt. Even though she probably had it coming, they knew she was off limits. I couldn't let a mistake like

184

that slide. An organization can't operate if people don't follow the rules. Nobody harms Chloe."

Thinking back to Autumn's accounting of Chloe's story and the accompanying bruises, I snorted. "Except you."

Dixon shook a finger at me. "No. Not me. That's one of the reasons I'm here. You met Chloe. She's dramatic, my wife, a real actress. She had it all—beauty, brains, and charm. She could get anyone to believe anything she wanted. It's a talent."

I shook my head. "I never met her. None of us did."

Dixon's face, already hot, turned a darker shade of red. He sipped his water. Then he slammed his fist on the stack of title papers. "How did these get here if you never met Chloe? How did she come to perish on your roof if you never met her?"

Dean cleared his throat. "Mr. Dixon, Chloe came here when we were all out on a job. She convinced our former receptionist to take her case. If she'd talked to any of us, we would have turned her away. We don't take jobs like this."

Dixon didn't take his attention from Dean for a second. "I want to talk to this receptionist."

That wasn't going to happen. I fielded this one. "No."

The color of his face edged toward purple. "Some broad out there thinks I beat my wife and had her killed. That is not what happened."

I hated people who abused others. Autumn had told me everything about her meetings with Chloe, and I used that information now. "What about the bruises on her arms and ribs?"

Dixon waved my question away. "Paintball, I'd guess. She put in a wicked course in the south corner of our property in the Ozarks."

It still didn't add up. "What about her sick parents?"

"Her parents are in excellent health, though losing their oldest daughter might change that. Her mom won't eat, and her dad just walks around the house shaking his head." Dixon pursed his lips. "They retired to Florida, but they come up in the summer and stay with us."

This made no sense whatsoever. "Then why did she want help leaving you?"

He chuckled. "She didn't want to leave me. She wanted that fucking map I took away from her. She was so obsessed with the thing that Grayson almost left her. You shoulda seen how pissed she was when your receptionist didn't bring back the map. He had to keep her under guard for two days until she promised not to kill the receptionist. Of course, at the time, we thought it was one of you."

"Chloe and Grayson were lovers?" Frankie's face scrunched up, and she frowned so severely that her chin had an upside-down V.

"He was her Dom. I didn't go in for all that stuff, but I liked to watch sometimes, and he had a good head on his shoulders. Mostly. I don't know what he was thinking, coming in here with a six-man force." Dixon nibbled on a muffin. "Damn, this is tasty. Where'd you get it from? The bakery on Fifth?"

"I made them." It was close enough to the truth. They'd been baked at my apartment.

"You're good. You ever get tired of working here, I could use another chef." Dixon swallowed. "Listen, it's obvious none of you knew Chloe. I'd really like to have a few minutes with your receptionist."

"She quit." Jesse crossed his arms over his chest in a deceptively casual pose. "She's not military. She signed on to file papers and make coffee, maybe learn a little billing. Once this all went down, she was finished."

Dixon ate his muffin slowly and in silence. Only when the last crumb was gone did he speak. "She can break into my dealership, finesse open my safe without leaving a scratch, and she's intimidated by a few guns?"

Jesse wasn't going to budge. "Yep."

Dixon picked up his water bottle and stood. "I could use someone with those skills."

Molten fury sent my blood pressure through the roof. I shot to my feet. "Stay away from her."

Dean smoothly slid between Dixon and me. He motioned toward the door. "I'll be sure to let her know that Mrs. Dixon's story isn't what she thought it was. If you'll excuse us, we need to get back to work. Let me show you out."

Dixon nodded once at each of us. He gathered his stack of titles. "No hard feelings, fellas. I just wanted to set the record straight. My Chloe was a good woman, if a tad on the obsessive-compulsive side."

Once he was gone, Frankie threw an ounce of sympathy my way. "I'm sure he just thinks you're protective of our former receptionist. It's good you were the one to get up in his grill about possibly mistreating Chloe."

"Yeah," Jesse added, a wry grin on his face. "You're one of those misogynistic guys who thinks all women are weak and in need of protection."

I know he meant to tease me or goad me into reacting, but I seriously considered his statement. Autumn had consistently proved she didn't need protection, but that didn't change the fact that I had a deep need to protect her. Was it sexist of me to want her

187

in a safe, boring job when she repeatedly communicated that she had other dreams for her life?

In a word, yes.

I stared at the greatly diminished pile of muffins and thought about the tremulous resolve in her tone when she'd declared this the last batch she'd ever bake. "Did we make a mistake in letting her quit?"

Jesse stood and faced me. "We made a mistake in not explaining our debriefing process to her beforehand. We made a mistake in going after her as aggressively as we'd go after each other."

"We were too angry to have a productive meeting." Frankie stared at the last quarter of the chocolate chip muffin on the table in front of where Dean had been sitting.

Back from ejecting our party crasher, Dean snagged the last of his muffin before Frankie could make a play for it. "We stupidly let you have the final say on everything concerning her. She worked for us all, not just for you."

I heard the censure in what Dean said because he'd essentially agreed with the voice in my head. "I'll call and let her know that we don't accept her resignation."

Misery Loves Margaritas

"No, thank you." My refusal was met with silence, which I interpreted as confusion. After a much needed nap this morning, I'd picked Jessica up from the rehab center, and we'd strolled through a nearby park. Now we were chilling at an outdoor café. Jessica gave me the what-did-he-offer look, and I motioned for her to wait a minute while I explained my position to David. "I'm going after this treasure. I have to do this for Chloe. I failed her, and it was her dying wish."

"Sugar, there's more to the story than you know. Just wait until I get home, and I'll tell you everything. Or you can meet with Frankie. She can fill you in. We had the most bizarre visitor today." The bustle of a busy airport surrounded the sound of David's voice. He'd been scheduled to leave earlier, but Dean had pushed back the flight for some reason.

There was nothing they could say that would change what I knew in my heart to be true. However I appreciated the effort he was making to show that he had listened to the concerns I'd raised last night and that he understood their import. "Sir, I appreciate that you advocated for me. Really it means the world. But I need to do this."

"All right, Sugar. My flight leaves in a few minutes, so we'll discuss this when I get home. I love you. Have fun with Jessica tonight."

Jessica slurped the rest of her frappe and set the cup on the table. "What did Loverboy want?"

A fly landed on the edge of my iced tea and began cleaning its feet. With a grimace, I pushed it away. "He offered to rehire me. I guess they've found they can't live without me."

"This is what you've wanted. Why turn it down?"

I shrugged. "I want to go after the treasure. Chloe's dying wish and all that."

Jessica fished in her bag and came out with sunglasses, which she put in her hair like a headband. "You're not that sentimental. I know you feel bad about what happened, but it wasn't your fault, which I know you know."

I threw enough money on the table to cover the bill and a tip. "I don't want to go back to what I left. David had too much control over what I was allowed to do, and I didn't really have any recourse. If I go back, it'll be on my terms."

She got to her feet, and though she struggled I didn't reach out to help. She'd come a long way, and I honored her progress. "Good for you. Working together under those conditions put an unnecessary strain on your relationship. You've had one foot out the door since we've moved here. Sometimes I think you only stay because he's paying for my rehab."

The thought had crossed my mind, but I rejected the idea that was my main motivation. "I love him." Of course, after my nap I'd packed my old duffel bag so that I could leave at a moment's notice. David and I had reached a tentative peace, but I was used to changing locations and identities when a situation started to sour.

Jessica slung the strap of her bag so that it hung across her body—the best way to ward off pickpockets—and dragged her walker closer. This week she wasn't leaning against it so heavily. People who didn't know about her iron will were shocked at how quickly she was recovering. "You've loved a lot of things, and you've left them all behind."

I scoffed at that. "I moved out here to be with him. I could have stayed in Michigan. I had an apartment and friends." My apartment had been tiny and in the bad part of town, but people generally let me be.

"When's the last time you called Julianne?"

Julianne Terry had been Jessica's friend before the accident, and during the three years I waited for her to wake up, she'd become mine as well. I slung my bag over my shoulder the same way Jessica had. "Let's go. The finger painting thing you wanted to go to should be starting soon."

She followed me out of the café and onto the sidewalk. "That's what I thought. I haven't called her either. We suck at friendship."

"I'll call her tonight."

Jessica didn't comment because neither of us knew if we'd follow through. We were both conditioned to abandon our old identity and all the trappings that belonged with it, including friends and possessions.

The owner of the art supply store hosted therapeutic art lessons the last Wednesday of each month at Breckenridge Rehab Center. Before the accident, Jessica had been a pretty amazing artist. Now she struggled with fine motor control, and Deshaun Johnson, the art guy, had invited her to this event sponsored by his store.

As we walked down the block, I scanned the storefronts. "What's it called?"

"Art Attack. I think the entrance is around the corner."

Indeed it was. People drizzled into the door propped open with a bucket labeled CLAY, and most of them were very small. We were among the only patrons inside who were not accompanied by a child. Large pieces of white chart paper were placed at intervals along two rows of tables. As kids wiggled and jumped while peering longingly at the papers, I eyed them doubtfully.

Jessica led us deeper into the store, and I noted which items were closest to the door and easiest to steal. Then I scoped out the register and a hallway likely to lead to a room with a safe or strongbox. I didn't do this on purpose or because I planned to shoplift. Old habits were difficult to kick.

"Jess—you came! It's great to see you out and about." A man hugged Jessica before I could see his face. From my vantage point, which included sightlines of his bare arms and the lines of his chest visible through his tank top, he looked like he gave great hugs. Muscles glistened in the bright florescent light. Mentally I undressed him and compared him to David. Then I threw in a shirtless Jesse and Dean just for fun. Was it getting hot in there, or was that just me?

As he pulled away, I noted the multitude of black braids spilling to his shoulders where colorful beads danced and clinked. He kept his arm around Jessica and faced me with his hand extended. "And this lovely lady must be your sister, Autumn. I'm Deshaun Johnson."

As I shook his hand—firm handshake—I noted the strong line of his jaw and the wide planes of his handsome face. No wonder Jessica wanted to come to this event. "It's great to meet you. I'm glad Jessica is getting back into art. She's really talented."

"So I've seen." He motioned to a nearby paper. "Let's get you set up here. Autumn, you get to paint too." With one hand on my back, he guided me to the place next to where Jessica was already dipping her finger into a pot of blue paint.

The little kids swarming the place gave me pause. "That's okay. I like to watch."

His sandpapery chuckle managed to have a melody. "Nonsense. Everybody paints today." He handed me a pot with a verdant green. "This matches your eyes, which are the same shade as Jessica's. I mixed it specifically for her, but she won't mind sharing."

I accepted the pot. Deshaun, a charming grin lighting his face, left to deal with the line we'd cut. Then I contemplated the blank paper and tried to figure out what to make. I glanced at Jessica's paper to find her already blending colors and smoothing lines. "I can see why you wanted to come here."

"I never pass up a chance to get paint stains under my nails."

I smiled at my big sister. "Yeah, paint stains. That's what you want to get under your nails."

Her wicked laugh made joy bubble in my heart. It was great to see her embracing life.

"Aren't you a little old for this?" The brittle and disapproving voice of a woman holding the hands of two elementary-aged children interrupted any kind of off-color reply I might have made.

Without missing a beat, Jessica poked a blue finger in the air inches from the woman's blouse. "Our childhood was stolen by a bad man, so back off."

I think I was as shocked as the woman. Holding the hands of her kids a little tighter, she steered them to the other set of tables. Eyes wide, I regarded Jessica.

She snapped at me. "What?"

"I wish you wouldn't call him a bad man."

Taking the unused pot of green from me, she poured small pools in three places on her paper. "Do you remember when we used to stop by playgrounds outside of schools when they were in session?"

While we'd watched from hiding places, we used to pick out a girl and tell why we wanted to be her. Jessica might say, "I want to be the girl who scored the winning goal in the soccer game, and everybody would give me high-fives." I would follow with, "I want to be the girl on the monkey bars. I'd hang upside down and play clapping games with my best friend."

As we got older the location of the game changed. We'd sit in a mall, a park, or on the curb during a street fair. Incidentally these were all places where it was easy to find things to steal that Dad could fence.

I poured a dollop of white on my white paper. Once it spread out, it would be invisible like we had been. "I remember."

"We should have been on those playgrounds. That was stolen from us."

Shrinking back from her vitriol, I added a dot of black to the white base. "We played on playgrounds and built sandcastles at the beach."

"Even when we played with other kids, they were strangers. We rarely saw the same kids more than two or three times before we had to move on."

Careful not to mix it too much, I swirled the black dot in the white paint, creating a spiral. I loved spirals. They were so mathematically precise, a breathtaking Fibonacci sequence if they were done right.

But Jessica wasn't done. She leaned close and whispered. "Imagine us here as kids."

I didn't want to, but from the moment she told me to, it crashed into my mind and flickered like a forgotten television salvaged from the trash heap. While we painted, Dad would have been chatting up the shop owner. We would have been stuffing our pockets with art supplies or anything salable while he provided the distraction. If either of us wanted to make him extra proud, we would have sneaked behind the counter and slipped some cash from the register. The whole experience would have been spoiled by a requirement that we take enough to pay for our next meal.

If we didn't manage to make enough, we went without that meal. Once we were a little older, Jessica and I added food to our list of things to steal, and we'd never again had to go to bed without dinner.

As these forgotten memories—ones I hadn't necessarily buried, but ones that I didn't care to think about—came rushing back, I painted. The result was supposed to be an image of two little girls swinging at night on an abandoned playground, a single unbroken streetlight providing an eerie spotlight. The fact that my people didn't quite resemble humans had more to do with my lack of talent than making them a symbol of how we'd spent our lives not being part of human society. We were always on the outside looking in, envying random girls for their friends and the fact they belonged somewhere.

Even with David, I felt like I was on the outside looking in. I kept waiting for the con I was pulling on him to clarify in my brain, but it kept getting lost in mushy feelings and dreams of the future. Meanwhile I went through the motions of being his girlfriend and his submissive. Did I love him? Yes. But at every turn, I doubted that he truly loved me because I didn't think he really knew me. What if this was just another façade I'd created?

I'd even weaseled my way into a job at SAFE Security, but that didn't make me part of the team. Dean, Jesse, and Frankie tolerated me because I was in David's life. I was right to quit. I couldn't go back there and pretend I belonged where I didn't. Though I could scam my way into their hearts, it would just be another lie in the long string of lies that passed for my life. Love and affection—the ultimate scams.

Did I belong in David's life? I honestly didn't know. A huge part of me couldn't see how I belonged in my own life.

I looked at Jessica's picture. Even with finger paints, she'd managed to create something remarkable. She'd drawn a woman gazing into the distance, her hand up to shield her eyes from the sun's glare. A halo of yellow circled the woman, successive rings fading into the background.

She studied mine. "Finger painting is great therapy."

I wanted to cry for those lonely girls almost lost in shades of black and white. "I hate him."

She took my hand. Paint squished between us, mixing her brighter colors with my dark and dismal ones. "So do I."

The day passed quietly. I took Jessica to dinner at a place that specialized in Tex-Mex. In light of my near-breakdown, which Jessica referred to as a breakthrough, I pigged out on food and margaritas. Emotions as black as mine needed to be drowned in handmade nachos and a variety of salsa choices.

"He always had money for the ponies." We'd been comparing the merits of the fiery salsa to the mild, but Jessica had no problem following this out-of-the-blue observation.

"Yep. He was addicted to gambling. Leon said that's how he got involved with unsavory characters in the first place." She scooped a huge helping of fiery salsa onto a chip.

Leon was our little brother, and he also happened to be an FBI agent who specialized in kidnappings. He was another person I had spent the last four months avoiding. Like Sylvia and Warren, he was someone who made me uncomfortable because his presence forced me to question everything about my life that I'd accepted as unassailable.

The server came to the table with a refill for our nacho basket and a huge plate piled high with chili con queso, more nachos, quesadillas, flautas, guacamole, and sour cream. I snagged a chicken flauta and dug in. Flavors danced on my tongue, and I stoked the fire with a healthy sip of my margarita.

"Wouldn't it be cool to find Spanish gold?"

"It's not Spanish gold." Jessica spooned some chili con queso onto her plate. "If I remember correctly from all those Spanish history books I read when we lived in Port Charlotte—or was it Fort Pierce?—the Spanish were hyper-vigilant with their records way back then. Someone would have found it by now."

The same could be said of the local treasure, though not with regard to the record-keeping. I dimly remembered the summer Jessica had spent reading anything about Spanish exploration when we lived in

Florida. That was the year I'd stumbled upon Descartes biography. "You think it's Alf Bolin's buried treasure?"

She shrugged. "I'm not a believer in buried treasure. Sunken, sure, but not buried. First off, things underground have a tendency to decay. You bury a pile of cash, come back in fifty years, and it's worm food. But—do you remember when we lived in Alabama and BS used to take us to the track?"

"BS?"

"Brian Sullivan. I can't call him Dad, and Gene isn't working for me. It implies we're on friendly terms, when in reality, if I had it to do over again, I'd drive a tractor trailer over his car. Then I'd back up and do it again. If that doesn't give me the level of satisfaction I want, I might set him on fire. It also speaks to my passive-aggressive need to call him on his bullshit." She used a chip to scoop up some con queso, but all of it didn't quite make it into her mouth. Dip dribbled down her chin, and she wiped it away with her napkin. "The coordination will come back. I'm working as hard on fine motor skills as on the gross ones. Before you know it, I'll be able to pick your pocket without you noticing."

I gave her the pity laugh. She'd always had skilled hands. The same skills that made her a great thief had made her an incredible artist. "Was that Birmingham?"

"Yes." She slipped into her Alabama accent. "There was a guy who used to sit three rows up from BS. Super old, like a bag of wrinkles, and really obese. He was always there, marking up his betting sheet. He kept track of every race, but he didn't bet. He used to buy popcorn and pretzels for me every week, and I'd sit with him and listen to his stories. He had a ton of them, but they were reruns. He told the same ones every week."

I had no memory of this, but I didn't doubt it happened. Jessica and I used to scam people at the track by offering to run errands for them so they wouldn't have to miss a race. While they were occupied, and such sweet little girls couldn't have nefarious intentions, we'd shortchange them.

"I want to say his name was Benny. Anyway, he used to tell about his great-grandfather who was part of a gang of bandits during the Civil War. They were a mean bunch, raping and killing willy-nilly. At the time, I felt sorry for Willy."

I giggled at this. People looked at us because I was too loud, but I didn't care. A pleasant buzz made me extra happy.

"He said it was Art Brolin's gang out of Missouri in the Ozarks. I bet it's the same guy. Benny said that before his great-grandfather was killed by Brolin for cheating at cards, he confessed to his wife that the crew had dug out some tunnel and lined it with all sorts of traps. He said it could be found fifty paces from Murder Rocks. That's an ominous name." Jessica motioned to the server for another refill of our drinks. She bit into a quesadilla wedge. "I love cheese. I think I dreamed about it when I was in the coma. I have vague memories of waking up and asking for cheese, but those were probably dreams too."

"You had a tube down your throat. You couldn't talk." Murder Rocks was the name of the rock formation where Alf Bolin and his gang used to lie in wait to accost travelers. It reportedly had a great view of the road in both directions. I'm not sure I believed all that much in buried treasure, but I wanted to see if I could find anything. Chloe seemed to think her husband believed something was there. Plus the booby trap part of it appealed to the adventurer in me. "I have a map, and I have a pretty good idea where it points. Are you up for a road trip?"

"Let me check my schedule." Jessica made a show of looking at the calendar on her phone. "Wide open. Let's do it. I'll bring my cane, but you might end up giving me a piggyback ride anyway."

The server brought another margarita, and we toasted to our new adventure.

Mid-sip, Jessica nodded at a man at a nearby table. "He keeps looking at us. I was trying to figure out if he was checking out you or me, but I don't think he's decided."

Jessica and I resembled one another to a point. We had the same oval shape to our faces, high cheekbones, and green eyes. But where my eyes were almond shaped, Jessica's were big and round—perfect for playing off the innocent look. She also had been blessed with soft, unfreckled skin. I had a sprinkling across my nose and my upper cheeks. We had the same hairstyle, so if someone didn't look too closely, we could almost pass for twins.

Throwing caution to the wind, I openly studied Staring Guy. He was sitting, so I couldn't figure out his exact height, but he wasn't short. I couldn't see the color of his eyes, but they had a nice shape. He had a squarish face softened by the angles of his cheeks, the arch of his brows, and the strong line of his jaw. He had a rugged handsomeness that invited a closer look, even if his shuttered expression did not. Something about him seemed familiar, but the impression was too vague, and so I dismissed it entirely. He wore a tight cotton shirt that showed off his broad shoulders and tapered physique.

"He works out."

"I wonder if he does PT. It might not be such a drain if I had that guy putting his hands all over me."

"You want me to invite him over?" One mention of my boyfriend, and I would no longer be a consideration.

She shook her head. "I'm not ready."

"It's not serious."

"Still not ready." She lifted her drink. "However I am ready for more food and the rest of this margarita."

Ninety minutes later, we stumbled into the parking lot. The manager had ordered a taxi to take us home. While I was definitely drunk, Jessica was nearly horizontal. Two and a half margaritas had knocked her on her ass, while four hadn't done as much damage to me.

She sprawled on the bench outside the restaurant, her eyes closed and a huge smile pasted on her face. "Ya know, I'm such a lightweight now. I miss smoking."

Before her coma, Jessica had gone through about a half of a pack a day. One of her health and wellness goals was to not pick up the habit again. I strove to be supportive. "You've been clean for three-and-a-half years. Don't blow it."

A peal of giggles nearly knocked her off the bench. I pulled her so that she leaned her head against my shoulder. "Brea, you're so funny. 'Don't blow it.' You made a pun."

I hadn't meant to, but it struck me as extraordinarily funny, and I joined in the laughter. During our dinner, we'd changed my name. It didn't feel right to keep the name someone who'd stolen my life had given to me. Jessica had even said a short eulogy for Autumn Sullivan. *She tried to have a normal life, but she didn't know how.* A few minutes later—or not, because my brain seemed to shut off for short stretches—I held my stomach.

Jessica rolled so that her head lolled on the back of the bench. "Don't throw up on me."

"It's sore from laughing." I watched the stars twinkling in the sky, and it occurred to me that they were actually cell towers and satellites. For a second, I felt the rotation of the Earth and the pull of gravity on the soles of my feet. "I gotta break up with David."

Without moving or opening her eyes, Jessica responded. "You do what you gotta do, sister. We can both move in with Sylvia and Warren." She flapped her arm.

"What are you doing?"

"Trying to pat your leg."

I opened my bag and fumbled for my phone. Even in our inebriated state, Jessica and I had taken precautions to keep from being an easy target for thieves. It took three tries, but I managed to unlock my phone. Calling David proved easier, as I commanded the phone to get him on the line.

"Hi, Sugar. Are you home for the night?"

"Nope. We are still at the restaurant."

"You're not driving home." He hesitated. "I can't come get you. Can you call Frankie or Jesse, or do you need me to?"

"We're waiting for a cab."

"Good. How much have you had to drink?"

My high horse reared its head and led me to my soapbox. I had things to say, and they were damn well going to be said. "That's not what I wanted to talk about, Sir. First I wanta say that I changed my name. I'm Brea now." It was bad when I could hear the slur in my own voice.

"Brea? Like the tar pit?"

"What carpet?"

202

"Tar pit. That place in California where—nevermind. How did you come up with Brea?"

"Well I'm not gonna be Bree-*on*-uh. Maybe if Sylvia had noticed the stalker in the bushes watching her little girls, I might have gone down that path, but then we never woulda met cuz I woulda been the cheerleader prom queen who married the quarterback."

He chuckled, and someone else also laughed. "That would have been unfortunate."

"I think so. Is that Dean laughing?"

"Yes, Sugar. You're on speaker because I don't have my hands free."

"You wouldn't-a been plastic." Jessica hiccupped. "I would have kicked your shallow ass."

"You would have." I patted Jessica's hand. At least I aimed for her hand. I might have landed on the bench. "What was I saying?"

David's cough sounded a lot like a chuckle. "You're not a Breanna."

"Nope. We shortened it, but Jessica didn't like Bree, and she doesn't wanna be called Jess. Got it?"

"Got it, Sugar."

"Okay, so that's the first thing. The second thing is that I have mostly liked being your sub."

"That's great. I've mostly liked having you as my sub."

It struck me that he couldn't have been completely happy with our relationship either. "So you agree. We have to break up."

"No, Sugar. That's not what I said. We do not have to break up." He was either lifting something heavy or gritting his teeth for another reason.

I struggled with a fit of the giggles. "This is one of the reasons I love you, Sir."

"I love you too, Sugar. How about we talk about this when I get home? Or even tomorrow, when you're sober?"

"Nope. We're breaking up right now. I already have my bag packed. I did it this morning after you left." After my nap I'd carefully put all my important belongings into my duffel bag because I thought I should leave before I overstayed my welcome. Now I intended to leave because I wasn't the same person who'd moved into the apartment.

"Sugar, I'm not finding this at all amusing."

That sobered me enough to banish the giggle fit. Firing all four of the alcohol-soaked cylinders in my brain, I struggled to focus on the important part of my message. "You're right, Sir. It's not amusing. It's very, very sad, but you're mostly good and sometimes an asshole."

"Autumn—"

"That's not my name, Sir."

"Please let's talk about this when I get home in three days. I'll get out the flogger, and you can SAM as much as you want."

That was just like him. "Sir, I'm deadly serious. You always want to do things on your schedule, but you can't treat people like that. My emotions don't ad—adh—stick to your timeline even though they're sticky and messy. You wanted me to change my name, but I wasn't ready. You wanted me to call my parents and you say that they're hurting too, but you know what? I'm mad at them. Sometimes I hate them. Even when we first met, you went too far. I should have been able to share parts of my life with you when I chose to share them, but you dug and dug. You were like a hound dog after a raccoon. And it matters, Sir. You took important things away from me, and you had no right to do that. You say my feelings are valid, but you only want me to feel them when you want me to feel them. I'm not here for your fucking convenience. I'm a fucking person."

"Sugar, I'm sorry. But that still isn't a reason to break up. We can talk about these things when I get home."

I shook my head and the world spun. Jessica slid off the bench until she sat on my foot, and then she rested her head on my lap. "You don't know who you are. That's the last one."

"Yes. I don't know who I am. And so, you see, that's why I can't be with you. I'm not Autumn, and so I'm not gonna let you walk all over me anymore."

"Brea, you're not exactly being fair." Again he sounded like he was lifting heavy things.

"I hate fairs. We used to have to work them. People are easier to scam in places like that."

He exhaled hard, and I finally recognized that he was furious. "Sugar, I've never walked all over you. We will discuss this in detail when I get home."

I tried shaking my head again, but nausea stopped me from getting anywhere significant. "You walked all over Autumn. She was a pathetic person, but it wasn't her fault. She wanted to belong, but she went about it all wrong. At first she didn't know how. Then she was afraid to try. Then she thought she had to listen to her Sir and wait for him to decide she was worthy of truly belonging. Her whole life, she waited outside the playground, watching other kids have the life that was stolen from her. Brea isn't going to do that. She's gonna play on the playground. She's gonna sing songs and hang upside down on the monkey bars. And that's why we broke up, Sir. It's not because I stopped loving you because I won't ever stop loving you. Okay?"

"No. It's not okay. This isn't over."

"It has to be, Sir. Autumn is dead, and you can't have a real relationship with a corpse. Well, you can, but that's kind of gross."

Jessica snagged my phone and pressed the button to end the call. "Sometimes you just gotta hang up."

The night became inordinately warm all of a sudden, and I knew what that meant—I was about to get sick. I tried to get up, but Jessica must have still been on my foot, which had fallen asleep. I pitched forward, and strong hands caught me.

"Whoa, there. I've got you." He put an arm around my shoulders.

That pins and needles feeling shot up my leg, and I groaned. The sweet smell of this guy's aftershave made me gag, and I felt too hot. I bent over and lost some of my dinner.

The man wiped my mouth, and the sweet smell got stronger. Vaguely it registered in my mind that this was our taxi driver, and he'd take us home. I must have passed out because that's all I remember.

Breakups and Other Bombshells

"What the hell just happened?" Willing my hand to remain steady, I carefully lifted a bundle of wires so that I could see what was hidden beneath them.

Dean sprayed coolant on the timer. It was made from cheap parts, and if they overheated while we were this close—the first step in detonation—we were in big trouble. "Your girlfriend broke up with you while you disabled a bomb situated forty feet from an oil executive whose life has been reliably threatened by eco-terrorists."

I willed my hands not to shake. The mercury tilt switch didn't require much help from gravity to make it trigger the bomb. Instead of being the kind with the mercury at one end and the electrical contacts at the other, the mercury was already touching one of the contacts. It sat mere millimeters from the other contact. If I tilted the device or even vibrated it too much, the circuit would close, and we'd all be toast.

"I haven't disabled it yet." If this bomb hadn't been planted inside the pool house of the oil baron who had engaged us to provide security for this three-day retreat, I would have cleared the area and detonated the bomb.

But clearing the area wasn't possible. Our client wanted nothing, not even a bomb, to disrupt her retreat.

Disabling it was a three-step process, requiring me to separate the explosive material from the timing mechanism and the fuse. Of course no obliging terrorist—which is what I called anyone who used intimidation and violence—had provided a countdown, so we didn't know how much time we had.

One of the things I'd failed to pack after I'd exited the military was the heavy space suit designed to protect me in the event the bomb detonated while I worked on it. Right now I wished Dean and I were both sweating under the weight of the hundred-pound suit.

"You will. Think about Brea later. Right now concentrate on what you're doing."

Three of the longest minutes later, we placed the explosive material into a vat of water, rendering it useless. Our client, Rozenn Gaelle didn't want us going after the eco-terrorists or even reporting the incident. She feared the effect that kind of publicity would have on the delicate deal she was using this retreat to negotiate. I didn't know anything about the deal, and I didn't much care. We'd run a background check on this woman and her company, and she'd come out relatively clean.

"It has to be someone here." Dean leaned against an ornate, wrought iron fence and surveyed the partygoers. "We swept this entire place before anyone arrived."

Though we'd run checks on all the people on the guest list, four last-minute changes had been made, and we hadn't found out about them until guests began arriving. "Jesse and Frankie are running checks now."

I wanted to ask one of them to check on Autumn. Brea. Damn it, I didn't care what she called herself. She was my Sugar. However I couldn't pull Frankie or Jesse

208

from their jobs to track down my inebriated would-be ex-girlfriend. Just in case she texted and I missed it, I pulled out my phone to check messages.

Dean guessed the direction of my thoughts, not that it would take a genius. "She's at home passed out on top of the covers."

"On top?"

"From the amount of slurring in her words, she wasn't going to be vertical for much longer. I imagine her and Jessica stumbling into the elevator and bumping into the walls in the hall. Your one neighbor who complains about the noise will come out and scowl at her, and she'll giggle at his sour expression as she fumbles with the key to unlock the door. She might not even make it all the way to the bedroom."

I peered at Dean. "You've really thought about this."

He shrugged. "It was less stressful than thinking about what would happen if you fucked up with the bomb."

"I never fuck up with ordinance." Having been trained for over a year in EOD—explosive ordinance disposal—I knew everything from common to classified ways to dispose of explosive ordinance. The method we'd used was far from safe or the most efficient, but we were limited by our employer. If I hadn't felt I could disarm it, I wouldn't have cared what our employer wanted. I would have cleared the place and detonated the bomb, and our employer would have needed to build a new pool house.

"Thank goodness your EOD skills are far superior to your relationship skills." Dean watched a woman cross the patio. Though she was attractive, that had nothing to do with his vigilance. She was one of the last-minute additions. We'd divided the four unexpected persons. I watched two, and so did Dean.

If we hadn't been on the job, I would have punched him. Not only would it have been a great way to respond to his jab, but I could have blown off some of the pent-up stress. This morning I'd been happy and full of muffin-y goodness. How far I'd fallen in just a few short hours. "There is nothing wrong with my relationship skills."

"Brea is the third woman with whom you've tried to have a long-term relationship, and she dumped you for the same reason all the others did—because sometimes you're a controlling asshole. There is a limit to what you can and can't control when it comes to another person."

I knew that, and I disagreed that I'd overstepped my bounds. "I don't try to control her emotions. I help her deal with difficult and emotional issues. That's all."

Dean folded a stick of gum into his mouth. "By giving her tasks and deadlines about when and how she has to accept the fact that her entire life isn't what she thought it was? You can't do that. You might want to because you hate that she's in pain, but you can't fix it for her. It sucks, but you have to accept that she needs to do this in her own time and in her own way. Otherwise she'll always be emotionally fucked up."

Again I didn't see it the same way he did. Autumn—Brea—needed me to push her because her first instinct was to bury her head in the sand and pretend nobody was shooting at her. "I *can* do that. It was working."

"She disagrees, and buddy—her opinion is the only one that counts here." He broke from his firm, all business stance to smile and nod at the attractive guest in a one-piece bathing suit with a translucent wrap tied around her waist. She might think he was flirting, but he was actually using her response to gather data. The fact that she kept glancing toward the pool house had moved her to the top of our suspect list.

Her gaze roamed his figure dismissively, but it lingered on me.

"My opinion should count." Though we'd only been together for five months, we'd been through hell and back. I knew her tender heart and her emotional fortitude better than anyone.

If Dean agreed, he gave no indication. "This didn't come out of nowhere. You said you fought last night. Take me through what happened."

Though I didn't want to—the content of our disagreement seemed private—I did. I related the entire ugly ordeal, even when I'd thrown at her that she could leave if she wasn't happy in our relationship.

At the end of my story, he exhaled hard, but he said nothing.

"You see? We were fine when I left."

Though his green eyes were shadowed because we were away from the lights blazing near the pool, disapproval emanated from them. "She said her only value to you was sex and baking, so you had sex with her and praised her for making treats for all your friends."

It wasn't like that. She'd thrown that at me in the heat of argument. The sex had been our way of reconnecting, and she tended to bake a few times each week. I didn't have to voice the fact that I disagreed with his assessment for Dean to know it.

"She is pissed at you, David. She doesn't have a lot, not as a support system, and her life was never an open book. She's hurt and angry because you forced your way into her life faster than she was ready to let you in, and she hates herself for a lot of reasons. Notice the way she's already starting to separate herself into different identities. It's not multiple personalities, but it's how she's coping. I have no idea if that's fucked up or sheer genius."

I wasn't sure either. This wasn't an avoidance strategy she'd used since we'd met. "I need to call her."

"Wait until tomorrow, when she's sober."

Forcing the mess of my love life to the back of my mind, I concentrated on my job. The woman who'd flirted with Dean checked her watch and frowned in the direction of the pool house. She walked toward it, though she kept out of the blast perimeter I'd estimated. "Let's proposition her."

Dean frowned, but not at my suggestion. He knew I meant it was time to nab our suspect. "One of us needs to stay out here in case we're wrong."

Though I was confident that we'd found our bomber, I wasn't going to start being careless. "We don't have to take her out of view. She's already separated herself from the group. I'll steer her toward the pool house."

Without waiting or discussing the rest of the plan—we'd worked together long enough to know the exact course of action to take—I sauntered across the patio and stopped near the woman.

Her suggestive smile welcomed me. "I haven't seen you around here before."

I'd assumed this was her first visit, but I didn't let that new information throw me. "No, ma'am. It's my first time. I'm David." I held out my hand, and she put hers in mine. I lifted it to my lips, intending to inspect her fingers for visual evidence she'd handled the bomb. Her skin smelled faintly of chemicals, but that could have been her hand lotion. Despite her apparel, she hadn't been swimming. I kissed the back of her hand, and then I turned it around to inspect her palm. I found a small burn scar at the base of her thumb and a cut on her finger. Taken alone, this might not mean anything, but I suspected the cut came from handling stripped wire, and the burn was the result of soldering them together.

"Kaylee Sullins." Her eyelids fell to half-mast, and she leaned closer. "Let's skip the small talk, David. Take me to your room."

I glanced around. "The pool house is closer."

"Oh, I couldn't. I mean, what if someone saw or heard us?" Her gaze dropped in fake embarrassment and submission.

Autumn had never done this, not even when I'd hired her to be my submissive. Her reactions were always authentic, and I'd forgotten just how much plastic women grated on my nerves. I crowded into her personal space, forcing her to take a step back. "Behind the pool house."

"No. That's not going to work either." She bit her lip and took a shaky breath. "Let's go to your room."

I looked toward Dean. "We have a deal—any woman we bring back to our room is for the both of us."

Her eyes widened, and her jaw dropped. "That's— That's—Okay. He's cute. Not as handsome as you, but still attractive."

"Great." I took her by the hand and dragged her in the direction of the pool house.

She tugged against me, but she was forced to follow because I gave no quarter. "I said not the pool house."

I reached the door and pushed her inside. My employer had given me a strange look, but I knew she wouldn't question my method in front of her guests. As far as they knew, we were also investors.

In three inch heels, she stumbled backward. Her ankle turned awkwardly, and she tumbled onto the floor. "You're a beast."

213

"You'd better believe it, Ms. Sullins." I snagged a pair of handcuffs—for work, not kink—and dangled them in front of her. "Wait until I really get going."

Crab crawling on three limbs, she scrambled away from me. "Let's go to my room. It's in the main house."

I approached slowly, herding her to the place I wanted. I slapped one cuff around her wrist and the other around the fireplace grate. "This'll do."

"I changed my mind. This is a mistake." She jerked on the cuff, trying to get free. "Undo the handcuff."

"Okay." I patted my jacket pocket and came up empty, so then I made a show of searching my pant pockets. "Hmm. It must be in my room. Let me go look."

"No." She tried to stand, but the way I'd cuffed her and her wobbly ankle made that feat impossible. "Just break it. I have to get out of here."

This was progress. I sank down into an upholstered chair and tapped my finger on my lips. "Why the hurry?"

With a frantic glance toward the kitchenette, she swallowed. "I don't like it here. I'm claustrophobic."

The pool house was larger than many people's homes, and so I chuckled. "You'll have to do better than that." Time was on my side. I didn't have to know when the bomb had been scheduled to go off because the perpetrator did. Judging from her increasingly anxious expression, that time was now.

"Okay, there's a bomb in the kitchen."

I folded my hands over my midsection. "You don't say?" Dean came in quietly, but he stayed out of her sightline.

Pulling on the cuff, she rattled it against the grate. "Don't just sit there! Go see, if you don't believe me."

"I believe you. Now tell me why you planted it."

She gritted her teeth.

"You don't strike me as an eco-terrorist. First off, those shoes are made from alligator skin, your makeup is tested on animals, and the manufacturer of your bathing suit is responsible for dumping chemicals into local water sources in the third-world facility where they're made."

Her brown eyes turned black. "Roz stole my husband. We were married for ten years, and he had the nerve to shack up with her. She invited me as a peace offering, but I'm not interested in peace. I want her, her friends, and my husband dead."

I looked to Dean. "Did you get that?"

He emerged from the shadows across the room. "Yes. I've also notified local law enforcement. They're on their way.

Ms. Sullins looked from me to Dean and back again. "Are you freaking stupid? There's a bomb in here."

A genuine smile lit my face. "Correction—there was a bomb in here. Good thing I disarmed it. You'd be facing murder and destruction of property charges instead of just attempted murder."

By the next morning, Kaylee Sullins was in Federal custody. Despite Rozenn Gaelle's wish that nothing disrupt the weekend retreat she had spent months planning, she had to move her guests away from the pool so that the crime scene could be processed. Dean and I both gave statements.

When the place quieted down around mid-morning, Dean gave me an envelope. "I changed your flight. Now that we know Sullins was behind all the threats, we don't really need to be here."

"Why are you staying?"

"Ms. Gaelle has requested that one of us stay on 'just in case.' There's no reason for you to be here. Go home and straighten things out with Brea." His eyes clouded over, darkening to olive green, and he rubbed the back of his neck. "She's a good person, and I've never seen you this happy before. You guys have some issues to work out, but that comes with the territory—strong personalities and all that."

Flying from Houston to KC took no time at all, and by early afternoon, I pushed open the door to my apartment. "Sugar, I'm home." Dropping my bag by the door, I swept my gaze across the living room, kitchen, and dining room. "Sugar?" I called again, but I knew it was pointless. The apartment had that empty feeling.

Clean dishes lined the dish drainer, and the indicator light on the dishwasher blinked to tell me those were clean as well. Three plates of muffins wrapped in plastic sat out on the counter. In the living room, I found her laptop abandoned on the sofa and a coffee mug on the table with a half inch of java left inside.

Gathering my courage, I went into the bedroom. These little signs that she still lived here meant nothing. Autumn had tons of practice in disappearing from people's lives.

The bedroom looked almost exactly the same. She liked things neat and tidy, and so I made a point to put my clothes in the hamper or a drawer. My shoes were neatly lined up in my closet. The bedcovers were rumpled and pushed down, but that only told me someone had slept there after I had. I opened her underwear drawer to find it empty. Other drawers revealed various levels of depletion, and her closet was missing a few outfits. Her shoe rack showed two pairs of shoes gone.

And her favorite duffel bag sat neatly next to it. I dragged it out and threw it on the bed. Opening it revealed all of the missing clothes, one pair of shoes, and

216

the box of mementos she kept hidden under a loose base in the kitchen that she thought I didn't know about.

She'd said she'd packed, but it didn't make sense to leave it all behind. Even if she'd fled without a single item of clothing, she'd take the box of pictures and trinkets. It meant the world to her. I'd come upon her several times curled up on the sofa and thumbing through the images of her and Jessica.

I called her cell phone, but she didn't pick up. Next I called Jessica, but she didn't pick up either. I had a little more luck when I called the front desk of Breckenridge Rehabilitation Center, and the woman on the other end, Latesha Smith, knew me well. "This is David Eastridge. I'm looking for Jessica Zinn. She's not picking up her cell."

Latesha clucked. "I'm sorry, Mr. Eastridge. Ms. Zinn signed out yesterday. She planned to spend the night with her sister, and she hasn't signed back in, so she should be with Ms. Sullivan. She missed her PT appointment this morning."

It was unlike Jessica to miss physical therapy. She'd come so far, and she was determined to live a normal life within the next six months. I rolled my lips inward as I thought. "Did they happen to say where they were going?"

"I'm sorry, Mr. Eastridge. They did not. I can have Ms. Zinn call you as soon as she gets back."

"That would be great. Listen, can you do me one last favor? Can you see if she cleared out her room?"

Latesha's frown came over the line, loud and clear. "Why would she do that?"

I had no idea why either of them would leave. There was no reason for them to go. "I don't know, Latesha, but before I spend the rest of my day tracking them down, it would be helpful to know if she planned to return or not."

"Let me put you on hold." Minutes passed, and Latesha picked up again. "Mr. Eastridge? All her stuff is where she left it. Is she missing? Should I report it?"

I didn't know if they were missing, but I couldn't think of another way to explain the evidence. "Not yet. Let me do some digging. Please call if you hear anything, okay?"

"Right away, Mr. Eastridge."

"Thanks, Latesha."

My next inclination was to call Frankie and Jesse. Jesse could pull public surveillance recordings to see where they'd gone, and Frankie could go with me to retrace their steps. However they both had work to do, and my personal crisis was probably nothing. Maybe they'd changed their minds about taking a cab home, and they'd gone to a hotel near where they'd eaten?

Autumn's credit cards were on my account, so if she paid that way, I'd be able to see where she'd gone. I signed into the account and looked for the latest entries. It showed a three-hundred dollar charge at an art supply store, and then she'd spent just under ninety dollars at her favorite Tex-Mex place. As the billing statement didn't give an itemized receipt, I printed it out and grabbed the keys to my car. I would visit the last place she went first.

The restaurant wasn't crowded when I pulled into the parking lot. It was the lull between lunch and dinner, so my timing was great. Scanning the parking lot, I noticed Autumn's car sitting alone halfway down a row. I pulled into the empty space next to it and peeked in the windows. Bags full of art supplies filled the cargo space in back, and two large pieces of paper had been rolled up and tossed onto the back seat.

Last night Autumn—Brea—had told me that she'd called for a taxi, but I showed no charge for it. She could have paid in cash, though. I tried to make sure she always had enough cash on her for a small emergency. I went inside the building. The dark interior was lit with colored lights that created a fiesta mood.

"Hi, how many in your party, Sir?" A teenager wearing a red shirt and black pants, the uniform for this place, stood with her hand hovering over the stack of menus. She smiled politely.

"I need to speak to the manager who was on duty last night."

Her smile faded. "I don't know who that was, but I can get you the manager who's here right now."

"That'll do." While I waited, I looked around to see if I could spot any sign that Brea or Jessica had been there.

"Sir? I'm Mirabella Vega. How can I help you?" A small Hispanic woman bustled toward me, a bundle of energy that probably fueled her staff as well. She couldn't have been older than twenty.

"Ms. Vega, my wife and her sister had dinner here last night. My wife's car is parked outside, but neither she nor her sister have turned up." I pulled out my phone and showed Mirabella images of Brea and Jessica. "Jessica, my sister-in-law, is disabled. She uses a walker to get around."

Mirabella took my phone and peered closer at the pictures.

"I also have a transaction number from the credit card they used to pay the bill. I was out of town last night, and when my wife called me, she indicated that someone here had called a taxi for them because they had too much to drink." I extracted the printout from my jacket pocket and handed it to Mirabella.

"Let me look it up." She went to a computer, and I followed her. She typed commands until her deep brown eyes lit. "Now I remember them. Table sixteen. Good tippers. They had the appetizer sampler, variety fajitas, and seven margaritas." Her gaze flicked up to my face. "Between the two of them, not each."

Jessica hadn't imbibed in years, so she was a lightweight, and Brea wasn't one to indulge in more than a glass of wine or a beer every now and again. "Do you know what taxi service picked them up?"

She handed my phone and the credit card statement back. "They didn't wait for the taxi. They went home with the guy from table four. I gave the taxi to another couple who shouldn't have been driving."

I couldn't see Brea or Jessica getting into a car with anyone they didn't know. "Do you have a name for the guy at table four?"

Mirabella shook her head. "He had fish tacos, and he paid in cash."

I didn't give a flying fuck what he'd eaten. Looking around, I noticed the video surveillance cameras. "I'm going to need you to show me where the guy sat and where my wife sat, and then I'm going to need to see your surveillance feed."

Mirabella opened her mouth to argue with my request, but I cut her off.

"Ms. Vega, I can't go into the specifics because they're classified, but my wife and her sister may be in a great deal of trouble. You can either show it to me now, or I can return with the FBI and a warrant in under an hour." I wasn't sure about the timeline, but if those women were missing, one call to their brother Leon, an FBI agent, would open some doors. He wasn't about to let anything happen to them.

She sighed. "Fine. Follow me."

Brea and Jessica had been seated in a table near the center of the room. The table where the man had been

220

seated gave him a clear view of the both of them, and they would also be able to see him. Under normal circumstances, Brea would be aware of anyone watching her, but she'd been drinking, so I couldn't be sure she had been aware of her surroundings.

"Can you describe the guy?"

Mirabella shrugged. "Regular looking white guy, about your height. Really short hair. He didn't strike me as the fish taco type. I would have thought he'd be a con carne guy."

That didn't sound like anyone I knew, and at the same time it sounded like hundreds of people I knew. "I'll see the surveillance footage now."

It didn't take long to cue it up, and it took even less time for me to recognize the guy who'd given them a ride home—Grayson Cuyler.

"Son of a bitch." I dialed Frankie. She picked up immediately. "Grayson Cuyler kidnapped Brea and Jessica."

"Brea?"

"Autumn. She changed her name. Damn it, Frankie. We have to find them." I ran a hand through my hair and willed my mind to stop racing.

"We will." Frankie's voice came through, calm and collected. "Let me ping her phone. It's the easiest way to track her. You call Jesse, and we'll meet at headquarters ASAP."

My First Day as Brea Had a Lot in Common With the Dinosaurs in the Tar Pits

The ache at the base of my skull was matched only by the figurative pounding of a ball peen hammer on my forehead. Even the groan I didn't consciously make ricocheted through my brain like shrapnel. I tried to lift my hand to rub the spots that hurt, but it was stuck behind me. The rough feel of carpet under my cheek jerked me from my semiconscious state. Nowhere in my apartment did we have carpet, and the few rugs we had were soft enough to kneel or lay on.

I opened my eyes to find myself trussed up on the floor of a van. The windows had been darkened, so I couldn't tell whether it was night or day. My pounding head and bleary eyes wished for nighttime. Never had a hangover felt like this, and sharp pain shot through my bad shoulder because I'd been laying on it while my arm was behind my back. From what I could tell, we were alone in the vehicle.

Inches away lay Jessica, similarly trussed, with her eyes closed and her face relaxed in slumber. Only the rhythmic rise and fall of her chest let me know she was asleep and not dead. My ankles were tied together, so I nudged her with my knee. "Jessica."

Nothing. Ignoring the excruciating pain in my shoulder, I scooted closer so that I could kick her harder. "Jessica." Two more insistent jabs, and nothing happened. "Summer."

Her eyes fluttered open. She'd used that name on and off since we were children. It was ingrained in her psyche, and a piece of her would always be Summer. She lifted her head and looked around. "We've been kidnapped?"

"Looks like."

Closing her eyes, she let her head drop. "I have a monster hangover. Every part of my body hurts."

I wasn't in great shape either, and I wished a shot of adrenaline would kick in to give me a boost, but apparently I was immune to having a freakout due to kidnapping. "I'm going to throw up."

One door in the back creaked open, letting in enough light for me to guess that it was early morning. However since the light source came from behind our captor, I couldn't see his face. "No, you're not. That's the aftereffects of the chloroform. It'll fade in a little while."

I groaned. If I'd been feeling good, this would have been a great subterfuge to lull him into a false sense of my weakness and ill health. Unfortunately I felt like hell, and I was in no condition to test my acting chops. "I had Mexican food and four margaritas. I'm going to barf, and it's going to smell like regurgitated Tex-Mex in here forever." My stomach began to roil, and my body heaved—a precursor to the main event.

He must have taken me seriously because I found myself lifted. He set me down on my knees in time for me to pitch forward and let loose a good portion of my last meal. I coughed, and another wave shot forth. I projectiled at least two feet, and I sort of felt a sense of pride about that.

The kidnapper lifted my hair and held a cold water bottle against the back of my neck. "This should help with the nausea."

I appreciated his thoughtfulness, though now that I was outside the van and could get a good look, I recognized him. "You're the guy who was watching us last night. I thought you were kind of into my sister. I guess I was wrong."

He grabbed my arm, and I cried out. Immediately he lifted his hand away. "I barely touched you."

"I have a shoulder injury that makes it really painful when my wrists are tied like this for long periods. Could you switch and tie them in front? It achieves the same end, and it's ever so much less painful on my shoulder."

"Yeah, of course. We need you to be in good shape." He cut the zip tie on my wrists and retied my hands in front. When he finished, he clamped his hand onto my shoulder and massaged it.

"Holy shit, that hurts. Please don't stop." I may have leaned against his chest because my legs weren't steady, but he kept up the therapy on my poor shoulder. I took that time to also study my surroundings. We were in a forest in the middle of nowhere.

Jessica groaned, a wretched noise that had the kidnapper abandoning my massage and pulling her out of the van. Her vomit didn't go as far as mine had, but she made her point. Never put a drunk woman to sleep on her stomach.

"Let it all out. You'll feel better." As he'd done with me, he placed his cold water bottle on the back of her

224

neck. He pulled her hair back from her face, tucking it behind her ears, and then he set her on the bumper. Maybe he did like her after all.

She favored him with a tremulous smile that I knew was totally fake, but he seemed to buy it. "Thank you. What's your name?"

"You can call me Gray." With one swipe of his pocket knife, he cut the zip tie around her wrists.

"Thanks, Gray." She put her hand to her forehead to block out the sun's glare. "I'm a lightweight."

"So I see."

"You were at the restaurant last night." She blinked. Her eyes were watering from the brightness. "Did you bring my bag? I have meds in there that I need to take."

I hopped closer, noting that he hadn't bound her ankles. "She was in a coma for three years." I felt it was necessary medical information that our captors should know.

"That explains the walker. You look entirely too young and too healthy to need one of those." He twisted open the lid of the water and handed it to Jessica. "Swish it in your mouth and spit it out. We need to get you both hydrated."

Jessica did as he said, and then he brought the bottle over to me. I did the same, only with my wrists and ankles bound. Part of me wanted to ask if he thought I was a threat and she wasn't, but I didn't want to draw attention to the fact that she wasn't currently bound. She might be able to get away, even if she couldn't go too far too quickly.

He helped me hop to the van, and I sat on the bumper next to Jessica. Without seeming too obvious (or so I hoped) I studied him. He was handsome in a classical sense, and he had unusual gray eyes, which is probably

225

how he came by his nickname. Mostly I noted his military bearing and the shrewdness in his eyes.

"Okay, Gray. Level with me. Why kidnap us?"

"You're Autumn Sullivan."

That name no longer belonged to me. "My name is Brea."

"You were the receptionist who helped Chloe. She wasn't trying to divorce Brick, by the way. She just wanted the map he'd confiscated. She was sure it led to actual treasure, and she wanted to find it before Brick did." He handed the water to Jessica, and then he fished around in one of the many pockets on his cargo pants. After a few seconds, he produced saltines. "These will be easy on your stomach."

This explanation brought up more questions than it settled, and not the least of which was why he had a couple of plastic wrapped two-packs of saltines in his pocket. Had he raided a soup kitchen? But I stuck with the relevant query. "Why wouldn't they look for it together?"

Gray shrugged as he opened a packet of crackers. "I didn't make a habit of getting involved in their relationship. Both of them were very competitive, and sometimes their rivalry was pretty cutthroat. He's very sorry that things got out of hand."

A woman was dead, and he described it as getting out of hand. "Are you one of the hit men who came after her at SAFE Security?"

"Yes and no. Brick sent four after the map, which he was convinced you had. They came by way of the roof. I led a team on behalf of Chloe that raided the office." He handed a saltine to Jessica and one to me. As we nibbled to settle our stomachs, he continued. "After all that, he

226

found the map in his safe, stuffed between the pages of a contract."

"So now you're working for Brick Dixon?"

"Looks that way."

"So he doesn't beat her? How did she get those horrible bruises?"

Lines crinkled around Gray's eyes as he smiled. "Mostly from paintball. She refused to wear pads. In her defense, she was right about us not landing very many shots. She was great at hiding out and sneak attacks."

While I was relieved to hear that Chloe hadn't been abused, I was growing angry that she'd used me and put people I loved in danger.

"She sounds like a sociopath." A disapproving frown wrinkled Jessica's chin and between her eyes. "People died because she and her husband wanted to play some stupid game with the possibility of buried treasure as a prize."

Gray handed us each another cracker. "She lived life to the fullest."

Any residual sympathy or guilt I had about Chloe Dixon's death evaporated. "So why kidnap us? We don't know where it is. We don't even know if you're going after Spanish gold or Alf Bolin's booty."

"I need someone with your particular set of skills." A voice came from the woods.

I peeked around Gray to see a man whose body was built from a mass of red, stacked squares—Brick Dixon. I wasn't surprised, but I had no idea what he meant. "What skills?"

He stopped next to Gray and looked me over. "You got into my safe without being detected and without leaving a scratch. That's talent. I could use someone like you in my organization."

227

I wished David had recognized my talent with such enthusiasm. Snorting, which I meant derisively, but it just served to remind me that I needed to blow my nose, I responded. "Kidnapping is how you recruit people? That's not effective. Ask nicely, send a card or flowers—those are better methods."

Brick scowled at Gray. "Why aren't they pissing in their pants?"

Jessica fielded that one. "Because—eww. We're housebroken, though now that you mention it, I could use a bathroom. I'd also like to brush my teeth and shower. I'm hungry and in need of a pain reliever, and then I'd like to take a nap to get rid of this raging headache."

If it was possible, Brick's face grew redder. He glared at Jessica. "You've been kidnapped, and you won't be let go until you do exactly what I want. If you refuse, you will be killed and buried where nobody will ever find your body."

Jessica and I exchanged a glance, the kind where we asked if this guy was for real. We decided that he was, but that we were too tired and jaded to care. I faced off against Brick this time. "This ain't our first rodeo. Also— threatening to kill me—that's been done before too," I added helpfully.

Dixon gave up trying to intimidate us. "We're going after Alf Bolin's treasure."

"I knew it." Jessica pumped her fist in the air. "There's no Spanish gold hiding in Missouri."

Jessica had always been better at the research angle, where my strengths lay in figuring out logistics—like when and how to rob someone. "I don't see how my skills are necessary for that. I'm not much for excavating on

228

account of my shoulder, and my sister can't stay on her feet for very long. It's probably best if you let us go now."

Dixon didn't blink. "Bolin hid his treasure behind a trove of deadly traps, and he sealed it in a vault carved from bedrock. That's where you come in handy." He flicked his gaze over Jessica. "I hadn't meant for you to be here, but I can use you as leverage." Now he turned a sickly sweet smile in my direction. "I believe that's the term you used when Chloe was trying to convince you to rob my safe. She was a sly vixen, and she will be missed."

I had to know. "What's our cut?"

This threw him for a loop, and Gray burst out laughing. "They're feisty."

Brick frowned. "You're prisoners, not partners."

I huffed and rolled my eyes, which made me wince because it sent another sharp pain through my head. "I thought you were a businessman."

"Ms. Sullivan, this is not a negotiation." He faced Gray. "Mr. Cuyler, take them to the caretaker's hut. Be careful to stay out of sight of the house. I have my wife's viewing to attend, so I'll return after dinner. Have them properly prepared."

Gray nodded. He watched Brick disappear into the woods, and then he lifted us both back into the van. The doors closed with a finality that drove home how much our witty repartee hadn't impressed Dixon. Of course, Gray seemed to like us. We'd continue to chip away at his armor. Under that thug's skin was a man who didn't like his lot in life and didn't know how to change it. Lucky for him, Jessica and I were experts at changing our circumstances.

The caretaker's hut looked like it hadn't seen anyone who cared about it in a long, long time. The sagging

229

porch was surrounded by overgrown bushes, and kudzu covered much of the exterior.

This time when Gray opened the back doors, he pointed a gun at us. I recognized the same kind of Glock that David had. He motioned for Jessica to get out.

She scooted to the edge of the van and slid to the ground, all the while gazing at him with a wounded expression. "Gray, has it come to this so soon?"

"You two aren't what you seem. I knew if I let you talk enough, you'd tip your hand. I didn't think Eastridge would fall for someone stupid or useless, and I was right." Gone was the man who smiled and sort of seemed open to flirting with Jessica. He threw a bowie knife into the back of the van as he pulled Jessica against him and pressed the gun to her temple. "Cut your legs and arms free."

It's extraordinarily difficult to cut a zip tie around one's own wrists, but I managed to get the job done.

Gray backed up, taking Jessica with him. "Walk in front of us to the house. Be careful on the porch."

As soon as I started toward the house, I heard the van doors slam shut. I turned to make sure he hadn't tossed Jessica back inside. I wasn't stupid—if we were separated, our chances of survival went way down.

Behind me, Gray lifted his chin. "Go."

The porch had a bad case of dry rot. I went slowly, easing my weight forward gradually. A few times a crunching noise had me pulling back and picking a different board to step on. Without waiting for him to say anything, I opened the door and went inside.

At one time, this had been a quaint little house. Someone had wallpapered the living area with a flower print, but the yellow backdrop and the blue flowers had long since faded. The threadbare rugs and dusty furniture had been lovingly selected and arranged, though at the time they probably had been new. Through a doorway to the back of the house, I spied a kitchen. The staircase to my right had a simple banister separating it from the room.

The door closed behind me. "The washroom is the door to the left of the kitchen. Jessica will stay out here with me, and if you try anything, I'll shoot her in the leg. If you keep it up, I'll shoot her in the other leg. Get it?"

I scowled in Gray's direction. "Just when I was starting to like you."

He pushed Jessica into a leather wing chair. "My self-esteem will recover."

The day crawled by. After letting us freshen up, he directed Jessica to make a couple boxes of macaroni and cheese. It proved to be great hangover food. Then he bound us again and locked us in a bedroom on the upper floor. He remembered my shoulder problem and tied my wrists in front of my body instead of behind, and for that I thanked him, but he only grunted in response. Just because our kidnapper had turned surly was no reason to give up the charm offensive. Exhausted and still feeling the effects of the hangover, we slept on that narrow, musty, twin mattress until nightfall.

Jessica woke first, and she nudged me. "Do you think David has noticed you're gone?"

I blinked the sleep from my eyes. Being inches from one another made whispering easy, though it did drive home how a thoughtful kidnapper would have provided toothbrushes. "He's on a job until the day after tomorrow."

"But if he calls, and you don't answer, won't he send Jesse or Frankie to check in on you? They'll suspect something, right?"

She was looking for assurances I couldn't give. Regret sat heavy in my heart—not for breaking up with him, but for the way I'd gone about doing it. He deserved to have a sober, in-person conversation with me, and now I doubted that would happen. I wasn't sure Dixon would let us go after this little adventure was over. Worse—what if he kept us and forced us to do work for him? BS had done that to us, though he'd used his position as our "father," where Dixon would skip the emotional abuse and move right to physical intimidation and abuse.

"I don't know. They're all mad at me, and I'm not sure David would even call me after last night. He might want to give me some time to think about it, or he's expecting me to sober up, call him, and beg for forgiveness."

She rolled to her back. "So we're on our own until tomorrow night."

"What happens tomorrow night?"

"If I'm missing from Breckenridge for thirty-six hours, they'll notify next of kin. When they can't get you, they'll call Sylvia and Warren, and you can bet your sweet ass that they'll move heaven and earth to find us." Jessica closed her eyes. "When we left BS, I was overjoyed to give up a life of crime. But you know what I missed? This kind of excitement and adventure. I know our situation sucks right now, but I know we're going to survive."

I didn't know where she kept her optimism, but I needed an infusion. "How do you know?"

With her eyes still closed, she grinned. "Because we're smart and courageous, Brea. You and I have done some amazing things in our time. This is going to be one of them."

It seemed that my big sister had a plan. "What are you thinking?"

"I think we should help find the treasure. I mean, it's *treasure*. That's pretty freaking awesome."

"With an armed mercenary and a powerful mob boss calling dibs, I don't see how we're going to steal it."

She turned back to face me and grabbed my hands in hers. "We're not going to steal it. Remember the story I told you about that guy at the track in Birmingham? He told me all sorts of stories about the traps Alf Bolin set. All we have to do is make sure our captors are caught in a trap. Bolin did the work for us."

The more I thought about it, the better this plan sounded. After all if David didn't know we were missing, he couldn't know that we needed saving. No matter what happened between us, I knew he'd come running if he knew I was in danger.

With his trusty gun in hand, Gray directed us down the stairs. Dusk had fallen, and we were starving.

"I smell pizza." Bliss was written across Jessica's face. "I'm famished."

"Stay in the living room. You may use the bathroom one at a time, and remember that the other one's life is in your hands."

I rubbed my wrists. Though the zip tie was gone, the hard plastic had cut into my skin, leaving bruises and marks that were sore. "Jessica can go first this time." I plopped onto the wooden rocking chair and snagged a slice of cheese and pepperoni pizza.

Before Jessica's return, Dixon came through the front door. He wore jeans and tennis shoes, which made him appear quite ordinary. Even his face was less red. "She looked absolutely amazing."

Gray tore his gaze from me to assess Dixon. "As always. I'll go tomorrow."

It occurred to me that they'd both been in a relationship with her, and that neither of them was overly aggrieved by her death. I hoped that when I died, someone besides Jessica would be sad that I was gone. The way I was going, though, it didn't seem possible. Perhaps this time when I started over it would be the last time.

Dixon glanced around. "Where is the other one?"

"Bathroom. I just let them out. They can eat while you go over what will happen tonight." Gray's steady stare reminded me a little of David's, which I found rather disconcerting and a little creepy.

Jessica came out, and I jumped up.

"Where are you going?" Dixon's brows drew together.

"Bathroom. I have to pee." I didn't hear much talking while I was in there, and I didn't take too long because I had realized that Gray was deadly serious in his duties. He might have not been a horrid captor, but he wouldn't hesitate to kill us if we proved more trouble than we were worth. I resumed my seat and grabbed another slice. "Okay, what's the plan?"

"The plan is that you unlock the vault." Dixon set several items next to the pizza boxes on the coffee table.

I recognized the tools of my trade—a stethoscope, a pad of paper, and a pencil. It occurred to me that opening a vault was only difficult when you didn't want to damage the vault. "What if we don't find it tonight?"

He chuckled. "I know where it is. That's why I hid the map from Chloe—I didn't want her getting the jump on me, may her soul rest in peace. Having you break into my office safe was a brilliant audition idea."

I pushed aside my disgust at the fact that he seemed to have come to terms with his wife's death pretty quickly. We had business to discuss, and I needed to plan

234

how to save our lives and steal the treasure. "So why not force it open? You could bring cutters or a little C4. I'm sure it's not hard to come by for a man of your resources." These methods were all faster than breaking the combination code.

"I'd prefer that method, but Bolin has rigged the tunnel to explode if the vault door is damaged."

"Oh." That was a good reason to turn to someone with my skill set. "That sucks."

"Legend says that he put in pressure plates that fall away into a deep chasm when you step on the wrong one." Jessica paused in her inhalation of three stacked slices of pizza. "And there's something about a time limit, like they all fall away after a certain number of minutes."

Dixon peered at her strangely. "Is that what the massive clock is for?"

Jessica shrugged. "I only know what I've heard. I also heard that he rigged crossbows to shoot when anyone triggered a tripwire."

"I haven't come across tripwire."

"Well, don't look at me. I thought this was just a tall tale." She resumed eating. "I also heard that he hid the bodies of a bunch of people he'd killed inside. If that's the treasure, it shows that Alf Bolin was truly a deranged individual."

Dixon shifted to face me. "Ms. Sullivan—"

"Zinn. My name is Brea Zinn." As I said it aloud for the first time, I couldn't hold in a giggle. "Holy shit, I'd better marry soon."

"Ms. Zinn." Dixon ignored my outburst of mirth. "What do you know about the treasure?"

I only knew what I'd found in the library. Meeting the challenge in Dixon's harsh eyes, I gave a brief accounting. "Alf Bolin terrorized the people left in this area when all the men were off fighting both sides of the Civil War. He and his gang would hole up at a place called Murder Rocks. They'd rob and kill people traveling down the road. Eventually a Union officer trapped him by posing as a guest in the home of one of his gang. The officer killed Bolin, and the town rejoiced. A hundred years later, they were still celebrating the death of a monster."

He waited two beats for me to continue, but I merely selected another slice of pizza. If this was my last meal, I was not going to save room for later. Then he said, "That's the official account. Don't you know anything more?"

"No." That was a lie. After my talk with Jessica, I knew more about the traps than she'd revealed. The timing trap wasn't for the pressure plates; they were for opening the vault.

"Let me fill in the details. The tunnel entrance is near Murder Rocks, not in any of the places people commonly thought to look. I found it by removing one of the higher rocks using heavy machinery. Back in Bolin's day, it probably took his whole gang to set it in place. It follows a handmade tunnel for about forty feet, which does not contain pressure plates, at which point it opens into what I call the Vault Room." He paused when I took another slice, shock and male judgment written in his gross, beady eyes.

I deserved five slices, and he could go fuck himself.

"I've uncovered evidence that there used to be crossbows on pressure switches—firearms too—but time, critters, and dampness have decommissioned the items hidden in the hand dug part of the tunnel. However the great clock and the vault door are intact, if a little rusty, because they're not in the portion that Bolin dug out. It's

236

a natural cave, a dry one. It's like time stood still for a hundred and fifty years."

After washing down my dinner with a healthy swig of water, I let loose a great burp, probably one of my top ten best. Only Jessica seemed to appreciate the art and talent that went into it. "What makes you think it'll explode? Did you find explosive material?" Back then, they had gunpowder and TNT, but neither held up well over time.

"One of my crew happened upon an explosive. He lost a leg. That's when I took a closer look at things. Someone drilled holes into the bedrock, and they installed vials containing liquid nitro into each one. I can't find how they come loose to disarm them. This is a perilous undertaking."

I sighed. "Then I don't see why we can't work together. I'm willing to split it fifty-fifty."

Dixon shook his head. "If you're successful, you'll leave with your life. If not, you'll both die." He stood and motioned to me. "Let's go."

I looked to Jessica. "Aren't we all going?"

"No. Gray and Jessica will remain here." He lifted his chin at Gray, but even that gesture didn't reveal a neck. "If we're not back by morning, kill her and dispose of the body."

I motioned to my sister. "But she knows the folklore stuff. I don't."

"I am not in need of a research assistant." Dixon withdrew a small gun from his pocket, and he pointed it at me. "Now, Ms. Zinn. Grab your tools, and if you forget anything, making a return trip necessary, I will cut off your sister's foot."

These guys were gruesome. I shot them both a look of pure disgust, but I made sure to get everything. As

Dixon drove us toward Alf Bolin's tunnel, I looked back at the light shining from a single window where my sister remained vulnerable and alone, and there was nothing I could do about it. The first chance I got to use Bolin's traps to my advantage, I was going to seize that opportunity.

Over the River and Through the Woods

The stress was getting to me. In my line of work, I'd become used to hurrying up to get ready and then waiting for a long period of time. But when the life of the woman I loved hung in the balance, the waiting became unendurable torture. The drive to the location of Brea's phone was taking almost three hours, and yes—I was breaking land speed records.

Frankie occupied the passenger seat. She periodically checked the locator on her phone to make sure Brea's phone hadn't moved. In the car following us, Jesse and Leon rounded out our crew. Since Dean was busy on assignment, I'd called Brea and Jessica's brother to help. Though I didn't know him all that well, I knew he'd want to be part of rescuing his sisters. As an FBI agent, he knew how to conduct himself in the field, so I wasn't worried on that end. Plus he could smooth it over if any law enforcement types objected to our unsafe speeds.

I'd warned him that his presence wouldn't affect the operation or our decisions. If we needed to employ questionable or illegal means to assure the safe return of either woman, then Leon would have to look the other way.

Frankie checked her screen again, the light flashing on and off in the gloom of dusk. She said nothing, so I knew the status hadn't changed.

This was getting to be too much. Anxious for the wait to be over, I flipped on the CD player and sang along with the first song that came up. "Tell your mother, I tell your friends, I tell anyone—"

Frankie burst out laughing.

"What's funny?"

"You—singing along to Janet Jackson. I never would have pegged you for someone who'd know the words."

I shot her a withering glare. "Brea listens to her. She likes to dance around while she bakes." She wasn't one for cooking very often, but she baked all the time. Meal preparation was more my area. I was okay with that division of duties. I made a killer glazed salmon, and her chocolate mousse melted in my mouth when I licked it off her stomach.

The luster of Frankie's smile dimmed. "We'll get her back, David. She's important to all of us."

I shook my head because I knew what Brea's response would be—that she wasn't actually important to any of us. It wasn't true, but it was her perception of the truth. Once I had her safe in my arms, I was going to make sure she understood those things in her heart.

Frankie, who usually bubbled over with conversation, squeezed my hand and checked the locator once again. A lifetime later, she sat up straighter. "Half mile ahead on the right. Pull off the road."

The two-lane highway was in the middle of a rural part of the Ozarks, so nobody was around. Still we didn't want to chance tipping off Dixon that we were onto him, so I parked next to the tree line. Frankie pulled camouflage netting from the trunk and covered the car. Jesse pulled up behind us, and Leon helped him conceal their vehicle.

We were already dressed in dark shirts and cargo pants, and now we loaded ourselves with other equipment—firearms, flashlights, and any other preferred gadget.

Frankie gathered us in a circle and showed us screenshots on her phone. "The signal is a half mile down this road. It's a private road that leads to Dixon's Ozark estate. It consists of a main house, a large storage structure, an outdoor pool with cabana. About a mile to the south, there's a dilapidated structure that looks like a house, though I can't tell if it's still Dixon's land. Neighboring estates to the east and west have similar structures and are located three-quarters of a mile away on either side. The north side of the road is state-owned land. There's a small lake and campground about three miles into the forest."

We listened, and I memorized a map of the area. Frankie was taking the lead on this because her head was bound to remain much cooler than my own. In my zeal, I may have ignored protocols that existed to keep us safe and barreled down the driveway, alerting our target to our presence. She also was our unofficial kidnapping specialist, having masterminded the safe return of thirty-six percent of victims she'd been hired to save. While that might not sound like a lot, many kidnap victims were murdered before Frankie got involved. I didn't think about how long Brea and Jessica had been missing because I didn't want to remember gruesome statistics.

"What's the plan?" Leon's dark clothing didn't quite match our SAFE Security uniform. That detail would have bothered Dean. Part of me wished Dean was there instead of Leon, not because I didn't like or trust Leon, but because I knew how Dean thought and moved.

Frankie responded. "Recon, first. Numbers and locations. I'd prefer a sneak and grab."

That was not acceptable. I voted for maximum property destruction. "They can't kidnap two innocent woman and escape repercussions."

Leon cleared his throat. "Once we've liberated my sisters, I'll have the FBI come in and make arrests. They've wanted Dixon for a long time, and kidnapping is a special circumstance that means we won't need warrants to search everything on this property. He won't get away with this. I'll see to it."

Prison was too good for Dixon. I wanted to tie him up and let Brea whack him with a big stick as many times as she wanted. Batting practice would be great PT for Jessica as well. When they finished with him, I'd have a go—if there was anything left. However this wasn't an argument I wanted to have right now. "Let's go."

Frankie led us in single-file formation through the edge of the woods and close to Dixon's house. I leaned close to a tree and used binoculars to assess the situation. Other than the porch, no lights were on, and no cars were parked in the driveway. We crept closer, but our sweep produced no results. This place was completely devoid of human life. I would have thought he'd have servants or a caretaker around, but there was no one.

Jesse traced the signal for Brea's phone to the grass next to the driveway. He picked it up and examined the outside, looking for signs of physical evidence.

"It unlocks with my fingerprint." I pressed my finger over the scanner, and the screen flashed briefly before going dark.

"Battery is almost dead." Jesse fumbled with his phone. In seconds, he'd exchanged the batteries, and Brea's phone chirped happily as it rebooted. He thumbed through her history while I looked over his shoulder. Frankie and Leon kept watch.

"Anything?" Leon's impatience mirrored my own.

"Nothing helpful. Brea isn't much of a picture-taker, and she has no social media accounts." Jesse frowned. "I'm going to have to teach her all the cool things this baby can do."

I'd asked Brea—when she had been Autumn—if she'd wanted to set up social media accounts, but she'd merely frowned and said there was no point.

Frankie gestured to her left. "Let's check out the structure to the south. I couldn't see a driveway or road on sat images, but I see a narrow track over there with grass tramped down. Looks like tire tracks. Maybe Dixon or his mercs stopped here before continuing on. If I kidnapped someone, I wouldn't keep them at my house, but I'd keep them nearby."

Without waiting for our response, she set off, and we followed. Leon took second position, I followed third, and Jesse brought up the rear. The hike marked another torturous wait, and not finding her at the house fed the demons of doubt in my mind. Would Dixon have been able to take her if she was sober? Would she have been sober if she was happy in our relationship? What if I'd been home and available to pick them up—could I have prevented this from happening in the first place?

Jesse, situated behind me, jabbed his finger sharply against my ribs. "We'll find them."

Without looking back, I nodded.

I don't know how he knew the caliber of self-recrimination running through my head, but I appreciated that he'd pulled me out of it. I couldn't afford to let my mind wander from this mission.

A light in the distance peeked through the trees, and that gave me hope. Someone was home. It grew stronger as we approached, and then suddenly we were there. At one time the house had been in a clearing, but over the years the forest had started to reclaim the space. I crouched next to Leon, who already had binoculars in hand, and I studied the situation. The house was about twenty meters away from our position, and I could see figures through the front window.

As I was trying to ascertain numbers, a face peeked through the window, and I recognized Grayson Cuyler. "Jackpot."

Frankie and Jesse were keeping watch for other things while Leon and I looked through the window. Frankie held out a hand for my binoculars.

I handed them over. "Cuyler just looked outside."

Jesse messed with a gadget, and I recognized an infrared sensor. "I have two bodies inside. We know one is Cuyler. The other one is smaller and seated."

That wasn't right. At least two people were missing from this mess, and I'd expected a team of bodyguards. Where was Dixon?

"Cuyler is a wily son of a bitch, so watch out." Frankie handed back my binoculars and stood. "Leon and I will take the back, David and Jesse take the front. Ninety seconds."

Leon hesitated for a second, probably considering the merits of arguing with her order, but I shoved at his arm, and he got over it.

244

Jesse and I crept to the door, mentally counting the time as we went. We made it to there in less than twenty seconds, and even though this wasn't a long time, this was the worst wait yet. I jumped the gun, and Jesse jumped it with me. The door was locked, so we kicked it in—both of us working together to double the amount of force. It crashed open, and we rushed inside.

Jessica sat in a wing chair, her wrists and ankles bound with rope. Cuyler stood behind her, the barrel of his gun against her temple. He smiled pleasantly. "More prisoners. How fun." He motioned to the handcuffs on the table next to the front door. "Go ahead and cuff yourselves to the radiator under the window."

I scowled. "No fucking way. Where's Autumn?"

Jessica frowned and launched into a very loud diatribe. "You mean Brea. She changed her name and broke up with you because—"

Cuyler placed his hand over her mouth and eyed me with cool detachment. "You came all this way for a woman who dumped you? That's pathetic. I'd have left her to her fate."

A glance around the room confirmed the information from Jesse's infrared sensor. "Where is she?"

Cuyler's grin didn't diminish. "Cuff yourselves, be good prisoners, and if she gives Dixon what he wants, then you'll see her in a few hours."

At the idea Brea would have to 'give Dixon what he wants,' rage clouded my vision. Jesse clamped a hand on my arm before I could lunge at Cuyler, and he shoved himself in front of me. "What does he want from our former receptionist? Does he have a lot of papers that need filing?"

Behind Cuyler's hand, Jessica broke into peals of laughter. I wondered if she wasn't afraid or if she'd lost her mind. Before Cuyler could tell us to cuff ourselves again, Frankie's roundhouse kick knocked his gun hand away from Jessica's head. It went off—Cuyler didn't care who he shot—and he whirled to face his attacker.

Leon, ready on the other side, smashed the butt of his gun into Cuyler's temple. The mighty mercenary crumpled to the floor. Leon stood over him, a severe frown darkening his features. "Nobody points a gun at my sister." He reached over and squeezed Jessica's shoulder.

A small, bittersweet smile twitched on Jessica's lips. "Thanks for the save, little brother. I appreciate it."

Knowing Frankie and Leon would take care of securing our unconscious prisoner, I rushed to Jessica. "Where are Brea and Dixon? What does he want her for?" I attacked the ropes binding Jessica's arms, and Jesse saw to her legs.

"They went to the tunnel to find the treasure. Dixon knows where it is, but he needs Brea to open the vault. He marked it on the map. It's built into the rocks, and it might be rigged so that it'll blow up if the door is damaged."

It made sense to take Brea. She was gifted in that area. At least I knew he wasn't otherwise assaulting her. "Where is it?"

Her eyes darted around, anxiety and helplessness battling with anxious resolve. "They took the map, and I don't know the area. I know it's by Murder Rocks, but I don't know where those are. She'll do it, you know—she'll get it open, and then he'll bring her back here and let us go."

Men like Dixon didn't release people who could sully his reputation or level legal accusations at him. Men like

Dixon tie up loose ends by ending lives, and he knew how to hide the bodies. I exchanged a glance with Jesse.

He clasped Jessica's hands between his own, holding her like she was breakable, and he locked his gaze with hers. "Are you hurt?"

She withdrew one hand from his hold and touched his cheek briefly. "No. I'm sore from being tied up for so long, but Gray gave me something for the hangover, so my head feels much better."

Things clicked in my head. Jesse hadn't wanted to look good to Brea because he liked her—he had a soft spot for Jessica, and Brea told Jessica everything. Knowing Jesse, it wouldn't amount to anything, but it was great that he had any kind of mushy feelings for another person. I'd never seen it happen before. Still it wasn't the time for a tender moment. "Tell us everything that happened, okay—every detail is important."

Jessica launched into a recap, not stopping even when Leon lifted her for a tight hug. When she finished, we all looked to Cuyler. If anyone knew where they'd gone, it would be him.

Sighing Jessica said, "It's too bad Brea lost her phone. It had a picture of the map. She showed it to me last night, but I can't really remember it."

Jesse, who'd settled on the sofa, fumbled in his pocket. "It was by Dixon's house. That's how we found you." He threw it to me.

I unlocked it and swiped through the photos until I found the map. "Here it is, but it doesn't make sense. It's symbols and X's, and there's no legend."

Frankie called up satellite images of the area and held her phone next to Brea's. She navigated the images, stopping on one that illuminated the map. She pointed to a landmark. "Murder Rocks." Then she pointed out the same place on her map. "This is where we need to start."

"Are we bringing everybody with us?" I sure as hell wasn't staying behind to babysit Cuyler, but he needed a guard, and Jessica didn't look like she was up for a strenuous hike.

"Yes." Frankie motioned to Jesse. "There's a van out front. Find the keys."

Taking Cuyler's vehicle was a great idea. If Dixon saw it coming, he might be annoyed that his instructions weren't followed, but he'd be less likely to shoot at it.

Jessica pulled the keys from under her left thigh. "I took them when he was tying me up." Using the arm of the chair, she struggled to her feet, and Leon slipped his arm around her waist. "I think my leg is asleep."

Jesse scooped her up, effectively taking her from Leon. "I've got you. Give the keys to Frankie, and let's go."

Leon narrowed his eyes at Jesse, but he didn't pursue the matter. Brea was still in danger, and I know he was focused on the next phase of the mission. He and I lifted Cuyler by the arms just as he started to come around. He moaned softly and tried to lift his head that had flopped forward.

"Don't try anything," Leon warned, his eyes, so like Brea's, flashing emerald fire. "I don't mind hitting you again."

Cuyler let his head drop back down, but I wasn't fooled by his acquiescence and neither was Leon. Though they were bound, we kept an eye on his hands to make sure he didn't filch a weapon from our belts or pockets. We loaded him into the back of the van, and Jesse placed Jessica there as well. Except for the driver and one passenger, this van lacked seats. Frankie drove, and Leon rode shotgun, so Jesse and I piled into the back.

Jessica grabbed a bag from under the driver's seat. "There's my purse." She dug through it, and then she leveled a severe frown at Cuyler. "My cell phone is missing. Gray?"

Cuyler shrugged. "I destroyed both your cell phones at the restaurant."

He hadn't. We'd found him because we'd tracked Brea's phone to Dixon's house. Jesse tilted his head and scrunched up half his face. "Thankfully you missed one."

His frown merging with a wince, Cuyler disagreed. "I smashed them both and threw them in the trash. I'm not an idiot."

At this Jessica giggled. "I might be inclined to pick pockets when I'm drunk. This worked out well."

With a pained expression, Jesse regarded Jessica. "You're going to need to break that habit."

"Probably." Jessica followed up with the same sweet smile Brea gave me when she disagreed with me, but she was finished discussing the issue.

I wasn't going to bust her chops. While morally wrong, it had saved her life, and now it was going to save her sister. "Brea will appreciate the irony when you tell her."

Cuyler's lip curled. "It's sad to see what you've become—a pathetic excuse of a man doggedly pursuing a woman who has rejected you."

His jab didn't hit home. Not only had he strayed far from the path of good, but my mind was occupied with finding Brea. "Don't feel bad on my account." Any man who throws away the greatest treasure of all just because the path is rocky is not deserving of that woman's love or devotion.

Cuyler stared at nothing, his mouth twisted bitterly, and he remained silent.

"We're here." Frankie pulled up behind Dixon's Jeep. "But they're not." She cut the engine, but she kept the headlights on to make it difficult for anybody who might be hidden to see inside the van. "Jesse and Leon will stay here with Jessica and Cuyler. David and I will search out the locations marked on the map."

Frankie killed the lights so that she and I wouldn't be at a disadvantage once we exited the vehicle. We set off in the direction of the closest X, which was at Murder Rocks. The road had been moved decades before, and so we hiked quite a distance before we found the infamous landmark. It rose from the earth like a series of spiky monoliths, and I could see where a gang of outlaws could hide and prey upon travelers. It provided perfect cover, which meant Frankie and I approached with caution.

We climbed behind the cluster of boulders, searching for any scrap of evidence that Brea had been here. My flashlight illuminated scuff marks in the dirt that appeared fairly fresh. Jessica was wearing flats because she was still practicing basic walking techniques, but heels had been missing from Brea's closet. Unfortunately the surrounding landscape was rocky, so their direction of travel was not discernible.

Firearm at the ready, Frankie panned her beam of light around the area. We seemed to be utterly alone. "They have to be nearby." She kept her voice low in case our quarry was listening from a hiding spot.

"Let's find the first X."

"It's that way." She pointed to the southwest, and I followed her the forty feet indicated on the map.

We found another cluster of rocks, though these were smaller. The earth had been disturbed, but whoever had done it had cleaned up the mess. This was not the correct location, so we journeyed to the next one. The map contained six X's, and we struck out six times when a terrific rumbling shook the ground under our feet.

I'd experienced earthquakes before, and this wasn't one. "That was an explosion." I pointed the beam of my flashlight to the ground in hope of finding where the blast had originated.

"They're underground." Frankie scrambled up an outcropping of limestone that overlooked Murder rocks. "There has to be an entrance somewhere."

I pictured Brea—terrified and trapped underground with Dixon—her green eyes frantic and brimming with tears, and I circled the outcropping, my eyes wildly searching for an opening. I made it back behind the cluster of rocks without finding anything promising.

Frankie was still on top of the plateau that overlooked Murder Rocks from about thirty meters away. She peeked over the cliff's edge and whisper-shouted to me. "Find anything?"

Part of her light cascaded down the rocks and glinted from something halfway up, and that's when I saw it—a narrow opening just above my head that was large enough for a man to fit through. The rocky cliff, weathered by water and wind, proved fairly easy to climb. I shined my light inside. The rock dropped away on the other side, but it didn't fall as far as it did on this side. Two broken heels lay at the base of the rock. It was all the proof I needed that Brea was inside, but I also caught the barest trace of a man's voice. He sounded angry or irritated. Brea was definitely with him. There was no way she'd make it too long without talking back or taking him to task for a long list of grievances.

I jumped back to the ground to find Frankie waiting at the bottom. She glanced up the face of the rock. "Well?"

"She broke off the heels to her shoes, and they're down there. I also heard what I think is Dixon's voice."

"Jessica said that it was just the two of them." Frankie's brow furrowed. "I wonder if they brought a ladder. You didn't notice one inside, did you?"

"Nope."

She tucked her gun into her holster. "I haven't been rock climbing in a while. It was thoughtful of Dixon to think of this."

I laced my fingers together to give her a boost. In one graceful move, she hoisted herself the rest of the way and disappeared through the opening. I climbed the rock and followed her into the cave.

She shined her flashlight around the inside, noting the blast and chisel marks. "Someone widened this opening." She half-mumbled and half-whispered.

I followed suit. No sense in letting them hear us approach. "Or a group of people." If Bolin's gang had spent a ton of time at Murder Rocks, it was conceivable that they'd have time to do this kind of work. Taking the lead, I started down the incredibly narrow and uneven passageway. At times like this, a helmet with a light and some backup flashlights would have been useful.

It didn't take long for the sounds of Dixon's voice to become louder, though I couldn't make out what he was saying. I did, however, hear the impatient *shush* that Brea yelled. It seemed to be just around a sharp turn ahead of us where a stream of light spilled into the passageway. I motioned for Frankie to stay back while I checked it out. Sometimes it was better to let the fact that I wasn't alone be a surprise.

Turning the corner, I found a large room carved from the limestone. Dixon had set up a bright work light on the floor, so I stowed my flashlight. This wasn't a natural cave. Someone had painstakingly hollowed it out. On the far side of the room, a magnificent clockwork—at least twelve feet tall—stood guard, dwarfing the two inhabitants of the room. Dixon, his back to me, had his gun pointed at Brea's head. Brea knelt on the ground, her dress long enough to cover her bare knees, but too thin to matter. She held the bell end of a stethoscope to a vault door, and she slowly turned the dial on the lock. The door was small for a vault, perhaps three feet wide and four feet tall. It was set into the rock wall, which meant the pins extended into the limestone.

Neither of them had heard me. Right now I had a choice to make—I could borrow Frankie's move and kick the gun from his hand, or I could point my gun at him and order him to drop his. If I was an actual mercenary, I'd skip straight to the option where I shot him in the head and he died immediately. But I wasn't a cold-blooded killer. Both acceptable options presented a danger for Brea, though the first option used the element of surprise, so that's the one I selected.

On silent feet, I advanced, but in this impermeable place, all sound ricocheted from the walls. Dixon turned as I delivered a bone-breaking kick to his wrist, and I hit his upper arm instead. He came back with a solid punch, but I danced aside. Just then, an explosion jolted the place.

Rock and dust rained down behind us, blocking the entrance to the room. "Frankie? Status."

"On it." Her voice, strong and sure, came through the cracks and crevices, and I heard the telltale sounds of rocks moving. She was digging us out.

"No guns." Brea's warning was laced with impatience. "This place is full of hidden nitro."

Dixon lunged at me. The room wasn't large enough for me to really go anywhere, so I met him halfway. We grappled, and I landed a solid blow to his ear as he knocked the wind from my midsection. Brick Dixon was pure muscle, and he was stronger than I. He rammed me against the wall, pinning me there as he pummeled my midsection.

Brea, for her part, ignored us. Her eyes were closed as she concentrated on her task. I wanted to yell at her—*For fuck's sake, help Frankie* or *Get the gun he dropped and take a shot, Sugar*—but I couldn't get enough breath to speak. Another explosion rocked the room, reminding me of her warning about the nitro and further barricading the entrance. I couldn't see where the nitro was hidden, but I knew that I had to end this fight and get us out of there before the entire thing came down on our heads.

Dixon pulled back for a harder hit, and I chopped his arm away from my shoulders, whirled, punched his nose, and drove my elbow into the place just below his solar plexus. His nose crunched, the noise louder because it echoed, and blood spurted everywhere. While he was stunned, I moved in to take him down. One swift, upward blow, and I flattened his nasal cartilage. His eyes rolled back, and he crumpled like a demolished brick building. He wasn't dead, but he wasn't going to present a problem anytime soon.

I dropped to my knees next to Brea, ready to take her into my arms. No matter what had happened between us, she had to be relieved I was there. One of the last things she'd said to me was that she'd never stop loving me.

But she pushed my hands away and wrote something on a piece of paper near her right knee. Her hand trembled.

I stared at her hand and beat back the rising tide of agony that had nothing to do with my possible broken rib or internal bruising. After all this, I'd come to view a jubilant reception from her as validation that I was right— she didn't want to end our relationship; she just wanted things to change. If she was indifferent, then that confirmed my worst fear—that she'd already locked me out of her heart.

Treasures

I heard David whispering in the tunnel, but Brick had not because he breathed loudly through his mouth. The dust kicked up by the first explosion had set off his allergies. I had to consciously stop my shoulders from sagging with relief. From Brick's behavior, I realized that he had no intention of letting Jessica or me live to tell this tale. As I scrambled against a clock to get this vault open, half of my brain concentrated on figuring out ways to survive.

But now the cavalry was here, and my ex-Sir was leading the charge. I listened for the almost imperceptible clicks that would tell me everything I needed to know to figure out the combination to this lock, and I ignored everything else.

David came in, and he fought with Brick. I didn't see much because they were mostly behind me, but they did bump into me twice. I couldn't tell who'd knocked into me, and it didn't matter anyway. Another explosion went off not more than ten seconds after the fight started. This one had a massive rumble that set off the crash of rocks and other debris, and I heard David call out to Frankie.

Thankfully he hadn't come alone, though she didn't make an appearance. In the back of my mind, I noted that oddity, but I couldn't think about it now.

When the fight was over, David knelt next to me and held out his arms. One hand got too close to the dial, and bumping it would set back my progress, so I pushed it away. He sat back, and I felt the heat of his gaze burning the side of my cheek.

A glance over showed shock on his ashen face, and I realized he'd taken my actions the wrong way. Well, maybe not the wrong way. While I was grateful that he'd rescued me, that didn't mean we were back together. Still I hadn't meant to hurt him, and so I explained my actions. "If I don't get the door open, the whole tunnel system will blow up, and we'll be crushed to death."

Some color came back to his face. He glanced at the giant jumble of gears and levers. "That's a timer?"

I nodded as I listened to the internal mechanism in the vault door.

With a grunt of pain, he got to his feet and went over to the clockwork. I knew he was studying it, looking for a way to stop it. As he did, another explosion sounded. I'd seen evidence of those fun treats when we'd come into the chamber. While Brick had been fixated on the vault and the clockwork, I'd looked into the ceiling to see hundreds of small holes drilled in the rock near the entrance. I wasn't sure of how the whole thing worked, but I knew enough from Jessica's stories to figure out that this was one of the dangerous traps Bolin had set. The first six explosions hadn't done much additional damage, and so I concentrated on my task and tried to block out the ground-shaking bursts.

David muttered to himself as he studied the clockwork, and I closed in on the third number. Spinning it quickly to line up the tumblers, I entered the combination. Then I got to my feet and put all my effort into twisting the wheel that would draw back the pins, but nothing happened. "Sir—I need your help."

David sprinted over, and I stepped back so that he could give it a try. He groaned as he pushed and pulled the wheel, but it didn't move. "It's rusted."

I moved in to help, and he scooted over. Together we used all our strength, and after another explosion, we were rewarded with the creaking of an old wheel turning a quarter inch. This gave me hope, and I doubled my effort, not that I'd been holding back before. I'm not sure how long it took, but we moved that thing by slow inches until the ticking of the clockwork ceased.

Sagging against the door, I finally let the stress and pressure of this ordeal melt away. Only it let in a flood of other feelings, ones I didn't want to face. David pulled me into his arms, and he held me against his chest. I soaked up the strength and reassurance he offered.

He stroked my tangled, matted, dirt-streaked hair and pressed his cheek to the top of my head. "It's okay to cry."

I slipped my arms around his body because I had no shame. I intended to hold him one last time, but his grunt of pain had me rethinking my intent. "Are you hurt?"

"Ribs bruised or fractured. No big deal."

I dropped my hold to his waist. "We should get out of here."

"We can't. One of the explosions knocked loose a bunch of rocks and dirt, and the entrance to the tunnel caved in."

Frankie had been out there. I drew back to look up at him. "Where's Frankie? I heard you call for her."

His rich brown eyes were heavy with the weight of the world, and his gaze traveled over my face. "She got trapped on the other side. She's okay, and she went to get help. Jesse and Leon are outside the tunnel with Jessica and Cuyler."

"Cuyler?"

"Grayson Cuyler. He's the man who kidnapped you." A shadow passed over David's face, but I was glad to see he was getting back some color. "Sugar, I don't want to break up."

Slowly, because I didn't want to jostle his injury, I withdrew from his arms. After a time, an offer of solace could become an intimate action, and if I let him keep holding me, then I was telling him with my body language that there was a chance for us. Since I couldn't meet his gaze, I stared at the ground. "I know I wasn't sober when I called, but I meant what I said."

"I know you did." He took a step closer to me, but I scooted back, and he stopped. "Relationships aren't easy. I know I'm not perfect, but please understand that I never meant to hurt you."

I knew he hadn't. If he had, I might have positioned him under one of the explosives and let Alf Bolin take out a horrible beast. As it was, Dixon was in prime range if we didn't move his unconscious body. Well, also if I hadn't stopped the timer from dropping bombs at random intervals.

Part of me—the submissive part who very much wanted to serve this man—yearned to comfort him. However I had to be strong because I'd meant what I'd said about not letting him walk over me again. I forced my gaze up to meet his and accept the pain I saw so clearly. "I know. I couldn't have fallen in love with you if you ever intentionally set out to hurt me."

"Sugar—"

"David, please stop calling me that."

He pressed his lips together, and I took that opportunity to plow ahead.

"While you were away, some things hit me—painful things that I'd buried—and I realized that you have a lot of things in common with Brian Sullivan, and I can't have that in my life, not if I'm ever going to come to terms with exactly what he did to me."

David's head jerked as if I'd slapped him with a two-by-four. "Brea, I know that I pushed too hard. I know I crossed boundaries. I didn't know it then, but I get it now. I see that I took things from you that I had no right to take, and I'm sorry. I'm so fucking, miserably sorry."

Okay, so now my eyes heated up and some tears spilled out. I wasn't ready for his heartfelt apology. David almost never admitted he was wrong without turning things around to make me somehow equally at fault.

"I dug into your past when you told me it was none of my business. Even when I knew you had nothing to do with the embezzlement at CalderCo, I didn't respect your right to keep your secrets. Instead of earning your trust and your confidence so that you would tell me everything in your own time, I went behind your back. I violated your trust, and then I convinced you to give me another chance. I was selfish because I loved you, and I refused to imagine my life without you beside me."

I didn't think he'd been selfish. I'd wanted to be with him just as much. I still wanted to be with him, but in realizing how my kidnapper had controlled and manipulated me, how he'd stolen my life from me, I saw that David did some of the same things to me. Part of it was my fault. I didn't know how to play on a playground with real friends, and so I'd let him keep demanding things I wasn't ready to give. Because I was afraid of being rejected, I'd done anything I could to keep his love.

But David wasn't finished. "You kept telling me that you weren't ready to accept your parents and brother into your life, but instead of helping you work through it, I pushed you into associating with them. I have no excuse except that I wanted to take away your pain. I had good intentions, but that's not enough. I see that now."

Lord, but he had a silver tongue. If I didn't watch, he was going to barrel past my defenses again, and we would both end up miserable. "I know you meant well. It's one reason I tried so hard to please you. But this isn't all about you. There are things you can't fix, and you shouldn't have to. Just like you pushed your way into my life, I pushed my way into yours. You didn't want me at SAFE Security, but for some reason I thought that if I couldn't show you that I was useful and valuable and...and necessary, that you'd forget about me. That I'd become part of the furniture in your life. I did the same thing to Dean, Jesse, and Frankie. I'm sorry for that, David. You were all so good to me even though I didn't deserve it. Please tell them I'm sorry."

He stared at me for the longest time, his eyebrows drawn together in two severe slashes and his teeth teasing his bottom lip. I remembered the first time I'd seen him concentrate that deeply. I'd told him that he was cute, and a smile had transformed his face from handsome to beautiful. Right about now, I was wishing for someone to break through the rubble to rescue us from this conversation.

I gestured to the pile of rocks blocking the exit. On the other side, I could hear the sounds of people digging us out. "We should probably start digging out from this side." I turned away, but he grabbed my arm and pulled me back to face him.

Inches from my face, his intense, rich brown eyes locked onto my soul. I couldn't break his hold if I wanted, and he wasn't holding me very tightly. "Brea, you've gone through your life segregated from a world you've desperately wanted to be part of. In walking away from me and everybody here who loves you, you're giving up your chance to belong. I'm not perfect. Nobody is. But I love you. I love you so much that sometimes when you look at me, I can't breathe. I can't move. All I can think about is how fucking lucky I am to have you in my life. I want this to work. I'm willing to own up to my mistakes and take steps to keep from repeating them, but I can't do that if you're not there to keep me in line."

I needed space. I needed to get away from him and all the mistakes I'd made that couldn't be undone. But the surety in his voice when he told me that he loved me shook me to the core, breaking loose all the love I had for him that I'd shoved to into a tiny lockbox in the far reaches of my heart. Okay, it was a huge box, and it took up most of the space. I tried to wrestle it back into that safe space, but it threatened to overwhelm me. "I can't go back to the way things were." I meant that I couldn't go back to him, but he chose to take it literally.

"I'm not proposing that, Sugar. We never sat down and wrote out our hard limits, and that was a mistake."

Only a man would take this conversation and connect it to sex. Though I'd expected him to eventually lead this back to sex, I frowned. "We had clear hard limits. Sex and kink were never part of our problems."

A hint of a smile chased away the worst of his frown lines. "I meant hard limits with regard to the D/s aspect, where you tell me when I'm close to crossing a line that can't be uncrossed. Where I listen to you and respect that line. Sugar, I assure you that I am willing and eager to learn from my mistakes."

His solution sounded so sensible. It wouldn't be easy, but we could do it. Only there was one huge obstacle he was overlooking. "I'm not the same person you fell in love with."

He stepped back, his hands on my shoulders holding me at arm's length, and he looked me up and down. My dress was soiled and torn, my shoes were irreparably damaged, my hair hadn't seen a brush for far too long, and I was dirty from feeling my way through a dimly lit tunnel. Then he released his hold. "You sure look like her—a little grimy and bedraggled—but otherwise the same."

"That's not what I meant."

"You mean on the inside. I have news for you, Sugar. Your insides are the same too."

David wasn't obtuse, so I knew he was purposely pretending not to get my point. With a huff, I started moving the smaller rocks away from the entrance. "I asked you not to call me that."

He wrapped a hand around my wrist to halt my actions. "Is that a hard limit?"

I'd reached my limit, and my temper exploded. Using the move Frankie had taught me, I severed his hold. "We're not together, David. There are no soft or hard limits because there's nothing between us. I'm not Autumn. I'm not the woman who would do or be anything you wanted just to please you."

David didn't back down. He grew before my eyes, crowding my personal space as he transformed from being his regular dominating self to being my Dominant. He didn't need to touch me to hold me in place. "You *are*

Autumn, Brea. You're an amalgam of every persona you've ever adopted. They were all *you*, Sugar. Maybe they were pieces or fragments, but they were you. Right now you're struggling with how to put it all together, and you think I'm going to reject you when I get to know the real you, but I have news, *Sugar*. Autumn never changed who she was to please me. She argued and misbehaved. She was naughty and bratty, and I loved her for it. I love *you* for it. I'm glad that you've decided to stop holding back because I want to know everything you've kept hidden—only I'm not going to pry. I'll wait as long as it takes."

I didn't understand why he was so sure about me when I wasn't sure about myself. I didn't even know what kind of crap I'd kept hidden. Unable to shrink from his visual manacles, I whispered one last, desperate plea. "Why?"

He touched my temple, a gentle brush of his fingertips against my skin. "I told you why. I love you, and I know you love me. What we have is rare and precious. I'm not willing to throw in the towel just because it's hard." That gentle caress worked its way down my cheek. "You and I both have strong personalities, and we're both stubborn. Sometimes we're going to fight, and those fights might get heated because we're both passionate people, but that's not a reason to give up the most precious treasure in the world. We're worth it, Brea, so think long and hard before you decide to throw it away."

I didn't want to throw it away, but I had no idea who I was or how I wanted to live my life. "What if I decide that I don't want to be a submissive anymore?"

He thought about that for a few seconds, and his caress moved back up my face. "That would suck, but I'd adjust. My love for you isn't tied to D/s. It's inextricably linked with who you are in your heart and soul. Also, I love your sense of humor and your flair for drama. This outlaw lair is a bit over the top, but it's so *you*."

I blinked. He'd made a joke. In the midst of a heart-wrenching breakup, he'd poked fun at me for being a drama queen. Or maybe for my penchant for getting into sticky situations. Or my past as a thief.

"Also it's unlikely that I'll stop being dominant. It's who I am, and since I know you love who I am..." He ended with a shrug that urged me to agree with him.

"You're impossible to break up with."

He grinned, a cocky salute to his true nature. "You're impossible to let go."

Damn, but he could be so sweet. "That sounded a little stalkerish."

His grin didn't waver. "I refuse to apologize for that."

I thought about the compelling argument he'd made—about the deep love we had for each other and the fact that he wasn't afraid of my emotional instability—and I wanted the life he described. I wanted to heal and grow with him always next to me.

"I need to know, Brea. Are you willing to treasure, honor, and protect what we have?"

"Yeah. I think I might need to see a therapist, though. Jessica said she has a good one."

He kissed me, a deep, dominant kiss that renewed the bond of love we shared. I scratched the stubble on his face and ran my fingers through his hair. I wanted to rub my body lasciviously against his, but I wasn't sure about the extent of his injuries. He solved that problem by pulling me closer, plastering my body against his and engulfing every one of my senses.

After the intense need to devour each other faded, he held me tightly in his arms even though it probably hurt his ribs. "Absolutely you can talk to someone, Sugar. I'd offer to go with you, but Dean made it clear that I can't fix your problems for you. He said I can only hold your hand while you work through them."

I'd forgotten that Dean had heard my entire phone call. "Sorry about that. I don't know why you kept me on speaker phone, though."

"I needed both hands for other things." He jerked his head toward the vault. "Aren't you the least bit interested in what's behind that door? I mean, you almost lost your life over it."

While I admit to curiosity, I mostly wanted to get out of there. The crew on the other side was getting closer. Shouts came through the debris. "We're on Dixon's land, so it's his treasure." I glanced at his still form, and I wasn't sure he was alive. "Or rather, it belongs to his estate. I don't want to be tempted to pocket something and it come back to haunt me later."

David steered me to the vault. "Sugar, we're on public land. Whatever's behind that door is yours. Finders, keepers."

After all I'd been through, that fact took a moment to penetrate my brain. But when it did, I plowed forward. "Well, then let's see what kind of rusty, moldy old stolen treasure I've found."

Together we wrested the old metal door open. David pointed his flashlight inside, but I redirected the beam of the industrial light Brick had brought down there. At first it was difficult to figure out what we were looking at, but after a few minutes, it became clear. The vault door, set into the rock and not a metal casing, hid a shallow closet that was perhaps two feet deep. The wooden shelves had rotted through, and the contents had fallen into a heap at the bottom. It seemed to be a lot of odds and ends—

266

buttons, belt buckles, cameos, and unfamiliar tools—in a bed of musty, rotting fabric. I spied a hat, and I reached down to grab it.

David set his hand on my shoulder. "There's broken glass, so be careful."

I picked it up and shook remnants of glass from it. "Looks military, though I doubt it's from the Civil War. Maybe World War I."

David peered closer. "I'm not an expert. What makes you think World War I? Alf Bolin was terrorizing this area during the Civil War."

"Yeah, but combination locks weren't invented until 1878, and those only had two tumblers. This one had three, so it had to be put there after the turn of the century." Even if these things were from a different era, they were still part of history. "I wonder who put all this here?"

David picked up a cameo and looked on the back. "1862. Are you sure about the combination lock thing?"

I was sure. "It looks like we have another mystery on our hands. I'm going to be busy."

Just then a voice called. "David? Brea?"

"We're here," David shouted. He strode to the rock pile and began removing larger rocks. "We're okay. Dixon needs an ambulance."

I closed the vault door. The next person to see this would be Jessica. It was hers just as much as mine. Then I went over to help Sir.

Stress and exhaustion caught up with me, and the rest of the night passed like I was looking through a Viewmaster that kept getting stuck between slides. It stuttered into focus every now and then. I remember...

...Frankie climbing through a small hole at the top of the opening. Like a superhero, she pivoted her body in a liquid motion that had me wondering if she was part cartoon, and she jumped to the ground in front of me. She threw her arms around me and held me tightly. "Workouts start Monday. The next time someone tries this shit, you will be skilled at kicking ass."

...Jesse's lips pressed together tightly as if keeping a diatribe of ill-advised comments to himself. In the reflection of the bright work light from the dark limestone walls, his pale blue eyes studied David's injuries while he ignored David's protests that he was okay.

...The first rush of fresh night air and the twinkle of stars in the sky when I poked my head through the high opening that served as an entrance to the cave. Never had the sky looked so beautiful as when I didn't think I'd see it again.

...The bright glare of headlights from the unmarked FBI cars illuminating Leon and Jessica hugging me so tightly that I couldn't breathe. I wasn't cut out to be the middle child, but I hugged them back just as hard. "I didn't think anyone would know we were gone.

Leon leaned back, a promise in his emerald eyes, and looked at me. "I've spent my whole life thinking you two were dead. I'm not going to let that happen again."

...The tight expression of pain on David's face as the EMT wrapped a stiff bandage around the middle of his chest. I wanted to go to him, but all I had to offer was a hug, and that would only hurt him more.

Jesse appeared at my side with an offer of a juice box with the bendy straw already pushed through the foil barrier. "It's apple-cherry. Drink it, and you'll feel better."

As I took it from him, I saw that my hands were still shaking. "Did you like your cake?"

"Not particularly."

That jolted me into the moment. Had I forgotten something important—like sugar? Shocked I gazed at him, but he seemed intent on keeping an eye on David's medical treatment. "It tasted bad?"

"Guilt isn't a flavor I enjoy. Come back to SAFE Security. We shouldn't have let you quit. We need our favorite office manager back. And maybe if you're there, you won't be almost getting yourself killed every six months."

"Jessica was with me." I'd meant that being with someone didn't guarantee safety.

"I'm sure we can use a part-time receptionist, and if she's as prone to danger as you, then it might be best if we keep a close eye on her as well." He glanced down at me, and for the first time in far too long, a small smile softened his expression.

I wasn't sure whether I ever responded to his offer of a job.

Two weeks later I found myself in my apartment serving blueberry pound cake and coffee to my parents. David lounged on the sofa. He had firm instructions to restrict his movement for the next six-to-eight weeks. Brick Dixon had fractured three of David's ribs, and David had broken the pinkie finger of his left hand. He brushed off that injury because this was the third time he'd broken it, but I didn't let him get away with doing anything against the doctor's instructions.

Brick Dixon was not dead, but he was still in the hospital. When he woke up, he'd been charged with kidnapping and assault, and the kidnapping had given the FBI cause to search all of Dixon's properties. Other charges were pending.

269

Warren carried the tray of coffee mugs into the living room while I brought up the rear with the pound cake I'd baked that morning.

"Leon has been working almost nonstop." Sylvia moved David's laptop and phone from the coffee table to make room for the tray. "The FBI gave him credit for this bust, and he's heading the investigation into this Dixon man. He can't tell us anything specific, but I think this man is involved in some pretty shady deals."

I presented plates of cake, which were eagerly received. David winced as he reached for his plate. "Thanks, Sugar. You didn't have to do this." He was, I had noticed these last fourteen days, very careful not to take my baking for granted.

Sinking down next to him on the sofa, I smiled. Now that he wasn't pushing me to change careers and devote myself to the kitchen, I'd rediscovered my love for baking. Maybe I'd rejected it because I hadn't planned for it to be part of my new identity, not because I was finished making sweet confections. "I wanted to."

Warren took a bite and closed his eyes. "Oh my God, Brea. This is amazing."

Sylvia echoed the sentiment, and things quieted down as people devoured their cake. This was the downside of being a good baker—people stopped conversing and an awkward silence settled over the room as people chowed down.

"Brick Dixon ran an organized crime ring in Kansas City. Leon's going to be busy for years. Make him take time off." My brother might not be able to reveal sensitive case details, but I hadn't taken an oath of secrecy. Besides, all the locals knew the real story behind the man. I couldn't let my parents run around in a new city not knowing what the hell was going on.

270

Some color drained from Sylvia's face. "Is this a man you knew...from before?" She still didn't like talking about the part of my life I'd spent engaged in criminal activities.

"No. I mostly knew small time criminals and some arms dealers. BS liked to steer clear of cartels and mobsters." I'd stopped thinking of and referring to Brian Sullivan as my father. Nikki Eliachevsky, my new therapist who was also Jessica's therapist, said it was progress. I liked her, and I found myself sharing thoughts and reactions with her that I'd never shared with anyone, not even Jessica. It felt good to get it out, and I was giving serious thought to the kind of life I wanted to have.

"That should make me feel better." Warren set his empty plate on the table and picked up his coffee mug. "But somehow I think that neither you nor Leon are ever going to settle down to a quiet, safe career."

David tried to come to my rescue. "She and Jessica are spending most of their time sorting through their treasure. They've rented a storefront on the first floor of the SAFE Security building, and they're turning it into a museum and gift shop. They've removed the clockwork from the cave to set up in the museum, and now they're working on getting the vault door out."

I jumped in to assure them I had no dangerous activities planned. "We're researching the stuff we found. It's in excellent condition. I never knew that buttons and cameos from the 1800's were worth so much money. And the tools—wow. I wouldn't pay that much for obsolescent tools, but lots of people don't share my opinion on that."

Jessica and I had a theory that most of the treasure had belonged to Alf Bolin, as had the hiding spot. We postulated that the vault door and clockwork were added fifty years later, possibly by someone who had stumbled upon the treasure and wanted to keep the cache secret.

Warren shook his head. "Watch her, David. I think she has a nose for trouble."

"That's just one of the things I love about her." David kissed the tip of my nose. Three days after he'd rescued me from Dixon, we'd sat down and hashed out the major boundaries I needed to have in place. When I refused to let him microchip me—in case I was kidnapped a third time—David had extracted from me a promise to inform him of any potentially volatile situations before they happened. If he wasn't around, I was to tell Frankie, Jesse, or Dean. "And that's why her shop is two floors below SAFE Security."

Dean was leasing us the space for a dollar—that's why we were two floors below them. That rent price was unbeatable. "It also makes it easy for me to work part time as your office manager."

Jesse had offered a receptionist position to Jessica, but she'd turned it down, citing the fact that she wasn't temperamentally suited to being sunshine and roses all the time.

Sylvia sipped her coffee, and then she set the mug down rather hard. "Sorry. I'm ready to see pictures now."

I'd invited them over to see my prized pictures, one of the only things I had to commemorate the life I'd spent living on the fringes. Even though I was part of something now—I had parents, siblings, friends, and a fabulous boyfriend who loved me despite everything—it was difficult to accept that I had a real place in this world.

But I was trying, and every day it got a little easier.

Treasure Me

Music blasted through my headphones, drowning out the sounds made by the waves lapping the shore. I would have preferred to listen to that tranquil noise, but Sir had commanded me to listen to this playlist until he came to get me. And so I lounged in a comfortable chair on the private beach of the house he'd rented in Costa Rica. The sun soaked into my skin, warming me pleasantly, and a gentle breeze teased the ends of my hair. I could get used to this kind of life.

I knew what he was doing, but I didn't let him in on that fact. He wanted this to be a surprise, so I was going to let him think I was ignorant of the ring he'd kept hidden in his pocket on the trip down here.

My answer would be a resounding yes.

In the last three months, I'd come to the realization that my journey through life was destined to be difficult, and David was the man I wanted at my side to help me face the demons of doubt that still plagued my nightmares. Not only was he sweet, strong, fearlessly dedicated to making me happy, and equipped with a great sense of humor, but he was easy on the eyes. I chuckled aloud at my dumb joke.

My headphones slid off, and I looked up so see David standing behind my lounge chair. His eyebrows lifted. "What's funny?"

"I was just thinking about how handsome you are."

"And that makes you laugh?"

"It was a gloating kind of laugh."

Accepting my explanation, he pulled me to my feet and kissed me hard. "We're going to have a light lunch before our scene. It's going to be strenuous, especially for you, and I can't have you passing out until I've had my fun." He sat where I'd been, and he patted his lap.

"Would you like me to undress, Sir?" I wasn't wearing much, but the bikini covered some key parts of my anatomy that he liked to see.

"Not yet."

I sat across his lap, and his arms came around me. I snuggled closer, drowning in the love and security he offered. We sat that way, with him holding me, for a little while. Then I noticed the tray of finger foods he'd set next to the lounge chair before removing my headphones. "Would you like me to feed you, Sir?"

"Sure."

I selected a cracker-sized sandwich and put it into his mouth. He closed his lips around my fingers and sucked as I pulled them out. Fascinated by his lips, I stared at them as he held another tiny sandwich to my mouth. We fed each other fresh fruit and miniature sandwiches while our gazes roamed each other's faces and bodies.

"I'm going to make you perform some lewd and lascivious acts, during which I may engage in light impact play and nipple torture."

I trailed my palm down his sun-warmed chest. "Will I be performing these acts on you?"

"Perhaps, if you're very, very good."

"Oh, Sir. I am very good. Before we left to catch the plane, you told me that I was gifted at giving head." Sliding my hand down further, I rubbed my hand over his soft cock, urging it to get ready to play.

He thrust against my hand. "Yes, your mouth is both talented and smart."

"It's an enviable combination."

"Agreed. But our scene doesn't start out this way, Sugar. I don't recall giving you permission to touch my dick."

Reluctantly I gave it one last light squeeze before I abandoned my pursuit. "Sorry, Sir. I was hoping for dessert."

"Stand up, Sugar, and take off your bathing suit."

I stood next to the lounger and undressed. It didn't take long. Since he hadn't given another order, I assumed a submissive pose—legs spread, arms linked behind my back—and stayed still. He looked at me for a long time, his gaze moving over my body like a soft caress.

Finally he nodded. "Go inside and lay on the bed, face down presentation pose."

The house he'd rented was quite large and luxurious, and the bedroom was on the second level. He followed me inside, and so I wasted no time hurrying up the stairs even though he stopped off in the kitchen.

The bedroom had glass doors that spanned one whole wall and could be opened to include the balcony in the bedroom space. I noticed that one panel was open, and the soft tropical breeze whispered over my nipples, teasing them as effectively as David's fingertips. I arranged myself on the bed with my knees under me, spread wide so that my bottom was in the air and my pussy was bared to my Sir. I bent my arms and rested my hands on the back of my neck. My left shoulder twinged, and so I repositioned my arm into a secondary pose that Sir had approved for these situations.

"Beautiful." His warms hands splayed over my flesh, squeezing and scratching my ass, thighs, and lower back. "How is your shoulder?"

"It's okay now, Sir."

"I'm going to make you climax a lot today."

"Thank you, Sir."

His wicked laugh rolled through my psyche. "You may not be thanking me later."

But I wouldn't SAM. We'd agreed that I needed to clearly communicate when I needed or wanted to scene as a smart-assed masochist. He no longer delivered that kind of punishment without a clear delineation of intent. I swallowed at his warning. "As long as I can please you, Sir."

His lips brushed against my upper thigh. "You please me." Then I felt the distinct pressure of his teeth sinking into my flesh. I moaned against the pleasure-pain. It grew worse as he sucked harder, and I struggled to remain still. When the pressure eased, I knew he'd left his mark.

Next he grasped my vaginal lips and pulled them wider, baring all my pink parts to his view. He licked me from clit to hole, pausing to thrust his tongue into my pussy. Before long, he replaced his tongue with his fingers, feeling for my sweet spot. A soft moan escaped when he found it. He added another finger, and he fucked me with quick, smooth jabs. I couldn't keep from lifting my hips to meet his thrusts, and I felt the sharp smack of his open palm on my ass.

I stopped moving, but he didn't. He sped up, and a soft climax washed over me. I felt my pussy squeeze around his fingers, and he pressed harder on my sweet spot, intensifying my orgasm. Then his fingers withdrew. After a second, I felt them at my anus, spreading cold lube on that tight muscle.

"I'm going to fuck this sweet ass, Sugar."

"Yes, Sir. I was hoping you would."

"Get on your hands and knees and crawl to the head of the bed."

My current position was perfect for what he had planned, but I didn't question his directive. Obediently I got onto all fours and crawled forward. That's when I came face-to-face, or I should say, face-to-phallus with a large blue silicone dildo attached to the headboard.

The bed dipped between my legs, and Sir's thighs brushed mine. "While I'm fucking you, I want you to pretend that's my cock and you're giving me head with your gifted mouth."

It was significantly larger than his cock. Sir liked to use impossibly large dildos and vibrators on me. I'd expected to have something like this shoved into my pussy, not my mouth. He eased his cock past my sphincter and buried himself deep. That familiar tingle started at the base of my spine. My pussy, empty and abandoned, wept with envy. I took a deep breath and took the dildo into my mouth. Closing my eyes, I still couldn't mistake this for Sir's cock. This act was definitely lewd, and I gladly submitted to his wishes. My body was a vessel for his pleasure.

He gathered my hair with one hand and gripped my hip with his other one, and he fucked me harder. "Suck it, Sugar. That mouth is mine. This ass is mine." He smacked my ass as he increased his pace, and I moaned as I sucked that fake cock. Pleasure wended through my body, not just the pleasure of sex, but the pleasure of knowing that I belonged to him, that I was his to use as he pleased. Those noises he made, from the soft moans to the teeth-grinding grunts to the half-articulated syllables of my name, reinforced my submission. I loved being the one who could make him lose himself like this.

By the time he came, my pussy pulsed with need. Having my ass fucked was pleasurable for me, but unless he also stimulated my clit or had a vibrator in my pussy, I wasn't going to orgasm.

He withdrew slowly. "Keep sucking that dick, Sugar. Don't stop until I tell you to."

The room grew quiet, and I knew he'd left to go clean himself in the bathroom. I closed my eyes and sucked that dildo as if he was watching and getting off on the show. Even when I felt the warm cloth press to my backside as he cleaned away excess lube, I didn't stop. When the bed dipped, I opened my eyes to find him watching me, his eyes fever bright with desire.

"You're so fucking sexy, Sugar, and you're mine to use however I want."

I was—within the confines of our negotiated limits—and I wanted to echo his sentiment, but my mouth was occupied. I settled for slowly licking the ridge around the crown of the dildo, the heat of my gaze fastened to the crotch of his shorts.

That wicked, slanted grin stretched his lips into something infinitely kissable. "Turn around, Sugar. You're going to fuck that thing while I watch."

This was new. Well, having a dildo stuck to the headboard was new too, so I guess all the things he was going to have me do with it counted as new. Still on my hands and knees, I turned around so that the dildo pointed to my pussy. Sir drizzled lubricant onto the dildo, and he rubbed some into my pussy.

"Damn, you're wet. You like this, don't you? You get off on putting on a show for me."

"Yes, Sir. I live to serve you." For once I wasn't being sarcastic. Since I'd given myself permission to embrace everything I wanted, I'd come to realize that serving David was a vital part of who I was. There were other pieces, but this was the part in which I was currently indulging.

He lined the dildo up with my vaginal opening, and I pushed back. It was a large phallus, one that had barely fit into my mouth, and it filled my pussy. As I adjusted, I became aware that the lube he'd put on me was growing very warm. If my pussy had been hungry before, it was starving now.

Sir gathered my hair into a ponytail and bound it with a hair tie. "You are allowed to have as many orgasms as you can get, but you cannot stop fucking that thing until I tell you to."

Knowing Sir, I was in for more orgasms than I thought I could stand. "Yes, Sir."

"If you stop for any reason, I will deliver one stroke from my belt. If you stop more than four times, I'll tie you up and force you to orgasm until I've decided you've had enough."

He'd never used his belt on me before, so I didn't know what my tolerance for it would be. For that reason alone, there was a good chance I'd stop at least twice— once often wasn't enough to figure out if I liked something or not. "Yes, Sir."

"Begin, Sugar, and don't bother being quiet."

I started slowly, getting to know the limits of the new toy. It fell out a few times, but Sir was there to guide it back into place. When I found a good rhythm, he pulled a chair closer and sat down, his knowing eyes roaming my body from head to foot. Mostly he stared at the place where the dildo slid in and out of my pussy. The thing's wide girth meant I would orgasm faster because it didn't give my sweet spot any respite. Heat coiled in my core, and an orgasm washed over me. I cried out, calling my Sir's name over and over.

It was small enough so that I retained control of my legs. Though they trembled, I kept going. He stood over me, running his hands over my ass and across my back. "I'm going to do things to you, Sugar, and you are not to stop what you're doing."

"Yes, Sir." I gasped between thrusts.

Laying on his back perpendicular to me, he slid under my body so that my dangling breasts brushed his face. He palmed one and captured the other in his mouth. The heat and the sharp spike of pain traveled straight to my pussy. I moaned loudly, and then I felt the fingers of his free hand circle my clit. Deft and sure, they helped the dildo drive me to an orgasm that hit me hard. My elbows gave out, and I collapsed onto his head, but I'm sure he didn't mind being smothered by these pillows.

The dildo slipped out of my pussy. I reached back to try to get it in place, but my hands weren't cooperating. Sir wiggled out from under me. I thought he might help until I heard the sharp crack of leather against my flesh. The actual feeling—the streak of liquid hot pain lighting a fire on my left ass cheek—took longer to register. I cried out a protest, but he had no mercy.

"Get back up, Sugar. There's no rest for the wicked."

"I'm being good, Sir. You're the one who's being wicked." Another crack of the belt had me scrambling to

280

get back on my hands and knees. "Sorry, Sir. You're not wicked."

"Sure I am.

"I would say evil."

"That too." He squirted more lube on the dildo and set the head against my opening.

I pressed back, helping it sink into my body. The embodiment of his desire, it filled me. "Have I told you how much I love your evil, wicked ways?"

"No, Sugar. Tell me how much you love my evil, wicked ways."

"Almost as much as I love you."

He kissed me, his tongue teasing mine in a tender declaration at direct odds with the carnal nature of the scene he'd devised. When it ended, he gazed deep into my eyes, his love etched deep in his soul. "Sugar, you stopped again."

I'd been so swept away by his kiss that I hadn't been able to concentrate on anything else. "Sorry." I got back to work.

He grabbed the belt from the bedside table, and from the periphery of my vision I saw it sing through the air. It landed on my ass with a searing hot and sharp sting that nearly had me calling yellow. Tears pricked behind my eyes, and I blinked furiously to keep them from spilling. "That's three. One more, and I get to torture you." He dragged his finger over the marks the belt had left, and shivers ran from that point of contact to the center of my shoulders. "One more, Sugar. Give me one more orgasm."

Closing my eyes, I concentrated on giving him what he wanted. I twisted my hips as I rocked on that blue dildo. When I opened my eyes, I saw David stroking himself over his shorts as he watched my body move.

That pushed me over the edge. With a long, loud cry, I came. My body trembled and my knees threatened to give out, but I forced myself to keep going. My cry went on and on, not stopping until I ran out of breath and my feet lifted from the bed.

Sir pulled me off the dildo and into his arms. He held me on his lap, pressing kisses to my forehead and temples, until I stopped trembling. "That was gorgeous, Sugar. Let's give that pretty pussy a break. I'm going to flog you."

I sat still while he buckled thick leather cuffs onto my wrists and just above my knees. To the ones on my legs, he attached a spreader bar. Then he carried me to the St. Andrew's cross set up next to the fireplace. He attached my wrist cuffs to the cross, and then he did the same with the ones on my legs. It was an awkward position, but it was one he liked. I relaxed my body against the beams of smooth wood.

Something pressed into my anus, and I relaxed against the intrusion. It was large and ovoid, and so I guessed at a plug.

Sir was very skilled with the flogger. He started out with deerskin to warm up my backside, and when I was nice and relaxed, he switched to elk. The thuddy sting hurt at first, but he set a steady pace that made the sensation of each blow blend together. It melded into pure pleasure, and my mind floated free. I wasn't sure how long he kept it up—he'd been using the flogger as physical therapy after his ribs had healed—but after a time I found myself laying on the bed and staring at the ceiling.

Slurred words spilled from my mouth. "Love you, Sir. Whole heart."

He peppered kisses on my cheeks and nibbled on my jaw. "I love you too, heart and soul."

I wanted to hug him, but the cuffs on my wrists were attached to the spreader bar. Blinking the world into focus, I saw that he had a powerful vibrating wand in his hand. He pressed it to my clit, and my entire body jerked. I tried to fight it away, but he just pushed the spreader bar up toward my chest and pinned me down.

"You have an amazing body, Sugar. I love how responsive it is."

The haze of subspace was fading, but submissiveness had settled in my core. I relaxed and let him play with my pussy. The moment I did that, he eased his hold on the spreader bar. Moving at a blurry speed, he shed his shorts and positioned his cock at my entrance. He sank into me slowly, his eyes rolling back into his head. I was extra tight due to the plug in my ass and the way he had my legs hiked up and spread.

With a hoarse cry, I came almost instantly. Sir gritted his teeth, and sweat broke out on his chest, but he refrained from following me over that cliff. My body went stiff, and he turned off the vibrator. He set it aside, and then he undid the latches holding my cuffs to the spreader bar. Lastly he rolled me so that I was on top of him and eased the plug from my ass. That ended up on a towel on the floor where he'd also put the vibrator.

Then he reversed positions again so that he was on top. He touched my face and hair, and he caressed my body. Since I was no longer restrained, I gave into my need to feel his heated skin and hard muscles. I wrapped my legs around his thighs and let my hands roam free. My eyes met his, and his penetrating gaze held me spellbound. He made love to me, his cock moving in me with slow, determined strokes that drove me to a climax that stripped me bare and reaffirmed that I belonged to him.

Sometime later, when our bodies had cooled and we lay with our limbs tangled together, Sir stroked my hair while I traced lazy patterns on his chest. "Sugar, I have a surprise for you."

This was it—the ring I'd spied in his pocket had to be nearby. Emotions ran riot inside me. I wanted this very badly. I remembered our conversation the last time we'd been alone near a tropical beach, and I prepared myself for a romantic proposal.

"What's that, Sir?"

"It's on the kitchen counter. Why don't you go check it out? I'm going to take a nap." His eyelids closed, and his breathing slowed. David could fall asleep faster than anyone I knew. He'd attributed it to his stint in the military, when he'd learned to grab moments of sleep whenever he could.

Well, this wasn't the proposal for which I'd hoped, but I was always up for a surprise. I pulled on a robe and padded downstairs to the kitchen on unsteady legs. Perhaps when I got my groove back, I'd make cinnamon rolls. The scent of those seemed to wake him up better than coffee.

Sitting on the counter, I found a safe. Plain gray and kind of small, it had a dial on the front. I didn't bother to look around for a combination. If I wasn't going to get a romantic proposal today—I wasn't in hurry, as we planned to stay for six more days—then this was the next best thing. I inspected it closer to find it was a Vault— similar to what Dean had in his office. This was an older model, one that I'd cracked before. It wouldn't present too much of a challenge, but it was the thought that counted, right?

I mixed batter, rolled dough, and set it aside to rise while I worked on the safe. By the time David came downstairs, refreshed from his nap, I had rinsed off in the shower, the cinnamon rolls were almost done, and I had four of the five numbers worked out. He glanced at my graph. "I'm always amazed at how quickly you can do this."

I paused in my task and wrapped my arms around his neck. "I'm amazed at your thoughtfulness. I love a good puzzle. Thank you, Sir."

He kissed me briefly. "You're quite welcome. Go ahead and finish."

Part of me suspected that the ring was in the safe, but when I got it open, I realized that I was wrong. The black velvet box inside was too large to contain a ring. I opened it to find a beautiful white gold necklace held together with a jeweled lock. Diamonds and emeralds reflected from the bright evening sun streaming through the windows, casting a rainbow of refracted light all over the room. I stared at it, but I didn't dare touch it.

David studied me. "It's a collar."

My mouth opened, but no words came out. I'd expected a marriage proposal, but this was so much more.

"We haven't talked about this, Brea. I know it's maybe a little unexpected, but I want you to wear my collar."

My mind had gone blank with joy. He wanted this formal declaration of our relationship. I knew what this meant to him—it was a bond more sacred than marriage.

"Nothing will change, except that I'll microchip you."

Now my brain kicked back into gear. I knew he was kidding, and so I threw him something sweet in return. "No microchip. I've promised not to get kidnapped again."

By way of response, his mouth curved to form a smug smile. "And I want you to change your last name to Eastridge."

"What?" My new license sported the name Breanna Zinn. It was only ten weeks old.

"Sorry. Context is good here." He dropped to one knee and fumbled in his pocket.

I couldn't help it. I clasped my hands together in front of my chest and squealed. "You want to switch? Yes—you can be my sub sometimes. Oh, my God, do I have some wicked and evil plans for you."

He froze, his intention arrested. "Switch? I can't—I'm not—What?"

Giggling at his inability to speak, I held his face in my hands. "But I love that you want to try. My inner Domme misses asserting herself." Then I pressed his cheek to my abdomen and stroked his hair. "I'll call you my Precious."

He shook off my hold and got to his feet. "I should not have made you watch all twelve hours of the Lord of the Rings movies in one day."

I'd only done it as part of my effort to keep him quiet while his ribs had healed. I'd watched more movies and TV shows in those weeks than I had in my entire life. I touched his wrist. "We all make mistakes, Precious."

In response, he held up a ring. "I should probably have gagged you for this, but Brea Zinn, will you do me the honor of marrying me?"

Even though I'd been expecting this proposal, tears of happiness, the likes of which I'd never thought I'd experience, streamed down my cheeks. "Yes. I will."

He slid the ring onto my finger, put the necklace around my neck, and then he wrapped his arms around my trembling body. "Thank you, Sugar. I promise to honor you and always do right by you."

Pressing a kiss to his neck, I hugged him back. "I know you will, Sir. And I can't wait to tie you up and have my way with you."

If you enjoyed this title, please consider leaving a review at your point of purchase.

Michele Zurlo

I'm Michele Zurlo, author of the Doms of the FBI series. During the day, I teach English, and in the evenings, romantic tales flow from my fingertips.

I'm not half as interesting as my characters. My childhood dreams tended to stretch no further than the next book in my to-be-read pile, and I aspired to be a librarian so I could read all day. I'm pretty impulsive when it comes to big decisions, especially when it's something I've never done before. Writing is just one in a long line of impulsive decisions that turned out to showcase my great instincts. Find out more at:

www.michelezurloauthor.com or @MZurloAuthor

Lost Goddess Publishing

Visit www.michelezurloauthor.com for information about our other titles.

Lost Goddess Publishing Anthologies
BDSM Anthology/Club Alegria #1-3
New Adult Anthology/Lovin' U #1-4
Menage Anthology/Club Alegria #4-7

Lost Goddess Publishing Novels
Re/Bound (Doms of the FBI 1) by Michele Zurlo
Re/Paired (Doms of the FBI 2) by Michele Zurlo
Re/Claimed (Doms of the FBI 3) by Michele Zurlo
Re/Defined (Doms of the FBI 4) by Michele Zurlo
Re/Leased (Doms of the FBI 5) by Michele Zurlo
Blade's Ghost by Michele Zurlo
Nexus #1: Tristan's Lover by Nicoline Tiernan
Dragon Kisses 1 by Michele Zurlo
Dragon Kisses 2 by Michele Zurlo
Dragon Kisses 3 by Michele Zurlo
Treasure Me (SAFE Security 1) by Michele Zurlo

Coming Soon: Re/Viewed (Doms of the FBI 6)

Made in the USA
San Bernardino, CA
24 June 2017